KEPT IN THE DARK

Copyright © Robin Murphy 2025

All rights reserved.

No portion of this book may be reproduced in any form without written permission from the publisher or author, except as permitted by UK law.

This is a work of fiction. Names, characters, places, events, locales, and incidents are either the products of the author's imagination or used in a fictitious manner. Any resemblance to actual persons, living or dead, or actual events is purely coincidental.

ESBN: 9798313539331

KEPT IN THE DARK

ROBIN MURPHY

One

The youngest of the three men arrived at the house first. He stood at the broken gate and scanned the scraggy path of weeds. There was nothing to suggest they'd felt footsteps recently. They crunched as he fought through the neglected hedge for his marker and retrieved his key. It was wrapped in plastic that offered little protection against the many rains that had fallen since he'd buried it, and he kept an eye out for nosey neighbours as he scraped off the rust. Then he forced it into the lock and took his first step into the house for thirteen years. He'd vowed never to set foot in his hometown again, never mind the house, but when he heard the news he had to return. He had unfinished business. He closed the door and listened in the dark, even though it was clear nobody lived there.

Stale air slid over his tongue and up his nostrils as he felt his way down the hall to the living room, where he again stood in the dark, before opening the curtains to disturb a sheet of dust that fell on his shoes. The window was opaque with grime and took a shove to open it, but a welcome breeze followed the light in and startled the stagnant air as he took a fresh breath and looked around. It was as he remembered it. A couch and a television.

*

The bedrooms were also as he remembered them. A bed with a battered chest of drawers in the large one, and a mattress with a cardboard box for a table in the small one. He left the windows and doors closed: the beds wouldn't be needed tonight.

He expected the kitchen to be as dark and lifeless as the other rooms, but he had to wave through flies that played do-or-die between cobwebs that hung from all four corners like Halloween decorations. The venetian blind was down, but damaged, and light poured through the twisted slats to outline the cupboards. Everything was as he remembered it. Except his mother's body wasn't lying on the floor.

He pressed the light switch – nothing – so he yanked up the blind and saw the fitting had no bulb, and the memory he'd suppressed for the last thirteen years resurfaced: the old man who'd leapt to a height that betrayed his obvious physical limitations and sent shards of light bulb falling into his mother's wound. Not that it mattered to her by then.

He held his breath all the way back to the front door and walked into town, intending to stake out the public house, for that would surely be his target's first stop. Until he saw the eldest of the three men at the crossroads, preaching the Word of God with a bottle in his hand. The young man didn't expect him to still be alive, but since he was, he could be useful. He also didn't expect the preacher to recognise him, so when the preacher locked eyes with

KEPT IN THE DARK

him before turning tail, the young man knew that old times were about to be resurrected.

*

The eldest man had been preaching the same word, at the same time, in the same spot, every day since before the younger man
was born, but no one ever paid him any attention.

At noon, he paused to squint through his overhanging eyebrows at the town hall clock. His saviour would be here soon, then his life's mission could continue. Until he saw the young man staring at him from across the road. Leaving the Word of God in his mind, he stuffed the cash in his pockets, screwed the lid on his bottle and fled.

*

The young man kept his distance as the preacher crossed the park and disappeared into the bushes. Then he ran. He didn't know why, as he doubted the old man would bolt and might even be asleep if he walked, but his adrenaline rose and he ran.

The preacher hadn't bolted and wasn't asleep. He was ready with a raised bottle, but not ready enough, and the younger man was soon counting the money. Then he stuffed it back in the preacher's pockets and marched him across the park.

The preacher didn't struggle or protest and the young man was alert for any attempt at escape. It wouldn't be difficult to detain him: the old drunk couldn't run at speed and his punches would be laughable to the younger man. Two old ladies said 'Hello' as they passed, without giving the preacher so much as a glance. The young man returned the greeting and heard the ladies mutter about the smell as they walked on, but neither of the two men said a word between them during the ten-minute walk to the house.

The preacher smiled as he was shoved into the living room and onto the couch, where he quickly retrieved his bottle from his pocket. The young man stood at the window, listening to the irritating rustle of money and the smacking of the old man's lips.

He moved from the window to behind the door when a heavyset man entered the garden, then did a double-take at the preacher. The old man's eyes were open, but he looked dead. The skin on his face was translucent and he wore a distraught yet determined frown; his pockets were no longer filled with cash, and only two fifty-pound notes rested in his hand. He rolled one into a ball and grimaced as he swallowed it whole, washing it down with a glug of whisky.

*

The middle aged of the three men arrived in town one hour after the youngest. He was tired, and torn between a much-needed drink in the pub and a similarly necessary nap in his own bed. Each would be for the first time in thirteen long years.

After a moment's thought, he opted for the pub, but ten minutes and two drinks later, his weariness overwhelmed him
and he headed to the house to retrieve his own key from under the hedge. He wiped the rust with his sleeve and opened the front door. Then stopped. Fresh footprints were on the dusty floorboards. He prayed the intruder was his son, but knew there were some prayers God would not answer. He also knew it could be the preacher, which

would also be good – if he'd kept his word. Either way, his nap would have to wait. He kicked the living room door open as the preacher fed the last fifty-pound note into his mouth, then the young man emerged from behind the door and two minutes later all three of them were dead.

There were no bodies found and no sign of a struggle. Just a knife on the floor, next to a pile of soggy, screwed-up fifty-pound notes in a puddle of whisky.

The preacher went to Hell, the middle-aged man went to Heaven, but no one seemed to know where the young man was supposed to go. Least of all himself.

Two

The wait was unexpected; I would've imagined I'd be there in an instant. Where *there* was I did not know, but was sure this was not it. I had no need to move or concern that I couldn't, and wondered why I was alone.

There was nothing to look at. No walls, windows or furniture, but the calmness made any visual treats unnecessary, and the absence of feelings, conscience and my body cleared my mind of the headache that had plagued me since my first memory.

As I contemplated the success and subsequent failure of my last moments on Earth, I drifted off with the nothingness that surrounded me into a new dimension that gave me a sense of euphoria I couldn't have imagined. Waves of elation swept through me, and I know this sounds absurd, but I'd never felt so... well, so alive.

There was no sky, ground, wind or colour. Just space. There were, however, people. Tens of thousands, hundreds of thousands, millions, billions, yet I felt I could've counted them on one hand. I had no feelings, yet I felt everything. Intensely.

KEPT IN THE DARK

If I thought about eating, I tasted the most delicious foods imaginable. If I thought about music, my mind burst with the most captivating sounds one could hear. I could turn fits of laughter on and off like a tap, and if I thought about sex, my mind erupted with multiple orgasms. And apparently, this goes on forever and ever. If you're lucky enough to stay, that is.

But something was wrong. Lurking in the ecstasy was a hole. The hole of knowledge of good and evil. Knowledge from the comfort of Heaven that there was a Hell. Everyone had a hole, a piece missing, a loved one that never made it, a pinch of yearning and wonder that would remain for eternity. But these people hadn't seen Hell, so they could use their positive thoughts to fill their idea of it with something gentler than the cliché inferno raging downstairs. It wouldn't be hard to do. The elation of Heaven was powerful and constant, so to assume the complete annihilation for those deemed too wicked to share their eternal years with their loved ones who made it would be easy, or another Heaven. Good, but not as.

But I had no such advantage. I soon found out what lay in wait for those who hadn't made the cut, and I found out the hard way.

I didn't know I couldn't stop until I tried, and stared at the other souls but they didn't stare back. The wonderful feelings drifted out and floated above me, toying with me, teasing me. The calmness, the elation, the sensations. My mind returned to its life state, with all my insecurities, fears and phobias. Then the way ahead darkened. A thick, sinister dark that was clearly out of place there and I knew I was in big trouble.

I tried to veer off to avoid the horror that surely awaited me and was dragged back with a pain that ensured I wouldn't try it again. I couldn't change direction, slow down or speed up. I was on rails. A train programmed at one speed, bound for one destination. Why was this happening to me? Why had I been brought to that wonderful place first? Teased with the joys of Heaven, then dragged off without explanation? On and on I went into the dark, bracing myself for the very opposite of the place I'd left behind.

Then I dropped. Not to the ground, there was no ground: I just fell. But instead of air rushing past there were thoughts and feelings. Every bad desire I ever had. Every wrong action I ever performed. Every sin I ever committed. They stabbed and stung like vicious wasps: the blasphemy, the cheating, the lying, the stealing, the killing. I spun around in a frenzied attempt to defend myself, but they kept coming faster and harder, and after being assaulted by every bad memory from every day of my life, the attacks subsided, my velocity slowed, my mind faded, then... nothing.

I couldn't open my eyes, but I was aware I had my body back. I was naked, with blistered skin from the crackling fire nearby. Jagged rock cut into my back as I tried to shuffle onto my side, but my muscles wouldn't respond and my head felt like a cannonball. I listened for a sign of life – nothing. I forced open a slit in one eye. My vision was blurred, but I was aware of something emerging from the fire.

Three

My eyesight sharpened as I was dragged towards the fire and saw what awaited me. The inferno stretched into eternity with flames an evil black that knew where they were and what their job was. They lunged, hungry to attack, but were yanked back as though on a leash. I dared not look at my captor, for I knew he wouldn't be pretty – nothing could be anything other than hideous in this place. The stench of pain and misery was way beyond anything on Earth.

I closed my eyes, and for the first time ever, I prayed. And as I waited for the unspeakable pain to engulf me, I thought back to that day. Was that what this was about? No judgment. No explanation. Just straight into the fire. The flames opened to welcome me in like an old friend, but the instant they touched me, everything vanished – the fire, the heat, the pain, and my body. I felt myself rising from the darkness into a soft light.

Relieved but bewildered, I tried to focus. The vastness was blinding, only this time without a soul in sight, and I couldn't see or sense anything except the questions swirling inside me. Why was I alone again? Was I in Heaven or Hell? It wasn't torture, but not the joyful place I'd been to before either. I wished that someone would make up their mind.

As it happened, that someone was already with me, and was going to be for as long as he decided to be. Fair enough, it was his house, but there were only two doors leading out and I needed to be on form to make it through the right one.

There wasn't much about him to describe, to be honest. He was devoid of any shape or features, or dare I say it, personality. A bit disappointing really, but I wasn't going to let him know that. He did nothing at first except reveal he was there and I got the impression he wasn't happy – that made two of us – but I stayed silent. Something told me he was to speak first.

'Do you know why you are here?' God said, as though he didn't know either.

'I think so,' I replied. 'You want to apologise and explain what the fuck just happened.'

Not a good attitude to start with, I guess. But I wasn't in the mood for exchanging pleasantries.

'You are with a dark soul,' he said. 'Yet you died not knowing me.'

'I died not knowing a lot of things,' I replied. 'If you show me your face it might ring a bell, but I'm getting nothing at the moment.'

He seemed a bit taken by my tone. He obviously expected me to be shitting myself.

'You will reveal how the Dark entered you,' he said.

How the Dark entered me? Did this guy seriously expect me to explain myself in perverted riddles?

'Look, pal,' I said, 'I'm really not in the mood for this, so either talk properly or fuck off. I never even knew you existed until five minutes ago.'

'You will answer my questions,' he said.

'You want me to answer *your* questions? That's funny, because I have a few of my own.'

I wasn't going to let him dictate the pace here. He was going to do to me whatever he was going to do, or so I thought, but he needed to hear a few home truths first.

'You committed many grave sins,' he said.

I couldn't deny that, at least not by his definition of a sin, but I was ready to defend myself against any wrongdoing, given the context of my life. I let him line them up.

'Such as?' I said.

'Thou shalt not kill.'

I knew he'd jump straight in the deep end. Why wouldn't he? No point in starting with *Thou shalt not work on the Sabbath* then work through the list to the bad ones.

'That's a bit rich, coming from you,' I said. 'Besides, it was justified whether you think so or not.'

'It is not for man to judge man,' he said. 'You shall explain your reasons for killing, and I shall judge whether you have failed me.'

Failed *him*? Was it possible to fail anyone other than yourself? If it was, then I had indeed failed, because the only person who needed me not to fail them was my mother, but hell, I tried. Plus, he was supposed to be God – he should've known why I did it.

'They weren't proper people,' I said. 'One was a homeless man who was as good as dead anyway, and the other was a fat bastard who had it coming.'

'Did you kill a man because he was fat?'

I had a chuckle at his choice of words. Then I noticed that he seemed a little confused again.

No, that actually made it harder to kill him,' I said. 'And he wasn't just any man...' I stopped short. That he referred to Fatty as a 'man' instead of my father made me wonder if he wasn't sure whom I'd killed, and I didn't want to volunteer that information. I knew that *Honour thy father and thy mother* was one of the ten. Fatty was well-versed in the Bible and would quote passages and commandments from it daily. Although I don't recall him ever mentioning *Thou shalt not kill.*

He held his silence while his wheels turned. I had indeed committed the gravest of sins and had every right to defend my actions. But I was reluctant to let on that I'd killed my father because he'd killed my mother, for Fatty was a believer and Mum was a non-believer, and I feared old Nobby would send me to back to Hell for killing a believer in revenge for a non-believer.

But it had become apparent that he couldn't read minds like they would have you believe, hence the questions, which was handy, so at this stage I wasn't too worried. I was more interested in how he was going to answer *my* questions.

'So, what now?' I said.

KEPT IN THE DARK

'The Dark will come for you again.'

He sounded serious, so I wasn't going to rock the boat. Although it didn't say much for his alleged omnipotence if the Dark could sneak into his office and steal dead people.

'Why?' I asked.

'Thou shall honour thy father and thy mother,' he said.

I had an eerie feeling there was a question mark at the end of that sentence. I really didn't think he knew I'd killed my father, which told me he didn't know that my father had killed my mother, which told me he didn't know his arse from his earhole. He also didn't seem to care that I'd killed the old man. Perhaps because it was in self-defence or for some sick reason he cared more about Fatty. But Fatty was only my father by blood: nothing he ever did reflected what fatherhood should be, so there was no honour to be had.

And I wasn't going to have him tell me that I didn't honour my mother. Hers was the only life I cared about. It got cut short, but I was there till the end. Never before had there been a son who helped his mother as much as I did, or willingly took beatings from Fatty so she could get some rest, or who would hide his own wounds so he could nurse hers first. Maybe Nobby should've included something like *Thou shalt not beat thy wife and child*. Besides, I had honoured my mother when I killed my father.

But I had to tread carefully. He was fishing for an answer he didn't know but pretended he did, and I thought the real question was: *Who* did you kill?

'Look, this is all very interesting,' I said, 'but I don't know what you want me to say. You already know what sins I committed, and you obviously don't think I'm evil or you would've left me in Hell.'

'Why did you kill?' he asked.

I stayed calm but said nothing. I had tried to steer the conversation away from my life, because even though he didn't know the details of my sins, he sure knew I'd committed them and I was waiting for him to mention that I'd also coveted my neighbour's wife.

But he was more interested in the murder. Understandable. But murder is murder. Why would the details worry him? I felt that underneath this was a petty squabble between him and the Dark with me as a messenger to shoot.

'My father beat me and my mother for years, so I killed him,' I said.

There was a brief silence and I tried to read his expression, which wasn't easy seeing as the miserable cunt didn't even have a face.

'You killed your father?' he said, almost with a wobble, as though I'd just admitted to killing *his* father.

'Yep. He deserved it and I don't regret it. End of.'

Again, he paused. Awkward. But I wasn't sure which one of us was supposed to feel the most awkward. Then I found out.

He faded away as my surroundings began to warp with a turbulent energy and a rising heat. Then I fell, and this time there were no nice thoughts and feelings to be sucked from my mind, and no wasps to remind me of why I was there. Just the drop into the Dark

.

Four

I couldn't work out whether it had been a push or a pull, but there was no last-second reprieve this time, and I landed on a bed of bubbling liquid rock that kept me afloat as the flames tore at my skin. My only defence was to quiver as my face shrunk and my eyelids peeled, and I wondered what had possessed God to create such a place. Not to mention the nutjob running it.

I was desperate to pass out, but that doesn't happen there. I felt every flame licking my face and body, and every wave of lava that dissolved my skin and scorched my bones. My heart pumped boiling blood through my veins and my lungs collapsed and inflated with hot gas that ripped through my chest.

Something clamped my head and yanked me out, but it was no relief for I knew what it was. My screams were silenced by the foul liquid that spewed from my mouth as my spine slammed against the ground and my limp bones were dragged around like an animal carcass, encouraging the splintered rock to scrape away the last of my skin until I was hoisted up and given a shake. My bones rattled, sending a wave of pain through the little I had left. I was too scared to look down but knew I was more skeleton than body. I threw up trying to reach the monster in front of me. And then I saw him.

I didn't exactly expect the red dude with horns and a pitchfork, but he could've done a better job to look menacing. His demeanour was scary for sure and I knew I had my hands full, but I'd seen worse in the eye of my father many times before. Like Nobby, he was as bland as his surroundings with no real features and only discernible by an outline of energy. Also like Nobby, he had an attitude.

The last strands of flesh holding my legs in place made no sound as he cut them one by one and they crumbled into powder as he worked his way up. The strange relief was that every bone he severed became one less to feel pain in. Then as my guts splattered on the ground, he let me go. All I had left was my head on a pile of dust. The pain had gone, though, except for a thumping headache. My host then picked up my skull and crushed it and I again became nothing more than a train of thought. He moved away from the flames, but it was clear I was to follow, and I had no desire to disobey him. Yet.

We entered what I guessed was his office. There was no fire or molten rock, just empty space. He turned and enveloped me so all I could see was him. Was this guy for real? Did he not know whom he was dealing with here? Using similar scare tactics to that other idiot. I'd had a whole childhood to learn the difference between a threat and a promise, and a promise and an action. Fatty had never threatened or promised anything; he'd just acted, usually with his fists. That's who you needed to be scared of. The people who didn't give you a chance. And I don't mean a chance to do what they want or to explain yourself. I mean the chance to gain the upper hand, to turn the tables, to win. Where did this Lucifer character think I'd run to? He could've separated us by a universe and I'd still have nowhere to hide. No, Jimmy Linton doesn't fall for these kinds of tricks.

Within his blanket of rage was a sense of curiosity. Like he wasn't sure what to make of me. This only gave me confidence. *If he's not sure who or what I am, then he's susceptible to bullshit.*

'You are of a dark soul,' he said in a tone of intrigue.

His voice wasn't as devilish as you might think. To be honest, he sounded a bit camp, but I wasn't going to let him know that.

'So what?' I said.

Not a good attitude after what he'd just done to me, but I figured it couldn't get much worse and I wasn't in the mood for exchanging pleasantries.

'You belong to me, for you did not know Lord,' he said.

'I died not knowing either of you,' I replied. 'And it appears you and Lord don't know each other either. Why is that my fault?'

'You have spoken with Lord?' he said, as though he thought I'd gone straight from Earth to Hell.

'Yeah, and he didn't speak too highly of you.'

'You will reveal Lord's intentions.'

'Well, his intentions weren't really clear, to be honest,' I said. 'He asked me a load of questions that were none of his business and got upset at the answers. Unless, of course, his intention was for you to do what you just did.

'Either way, if you hadn't just destroyed my body I might have been a little more cooperative. But now you can get fucked.'

I should've braced myself for more torture, but by this stage I didn't really care what happened to me.

'What's your beef with this guy, anyway?' I said. 'You both seem as mad as each other. I thought you'd get along like a house on fire.'

'He is a coward.' I couldn't disagree with that. 'But you are his failure, and my success. I shall soon defeat him and destroy life.'

'What problem do you have with life?' I said.

'Life is a mistake, and I shall not rest until it ceases. That is my only concern.'

'Well, maybe you might wanna think about adding to your list of concerns. For starters, how do you expect to defeat Lord if you can't even find him? I only got here half an hour ago and I've already had a chat with the pair of you. You've been here since the dawn of time and you don't even know where the idiot lives.'

'I do not deny Lord's power, but he has become weaker,' he said.

'So what do you plan to do with me?' I asked, wondering why he was even talking to me.

'I shall remove your soul and send you to eternal torment.'

I didn't want to hear that, to be honest. But I gathered that if he wanted me in eternal torment, I would've been there by now. I wasn't sure everyone got this treatment when they died, so he was keeping me here because he thought I had info on Nobby, which was good, as it bought me time. But I didn't know what he already knew about Nobby, so I was careful not to make up anything and tried to keep the focus on myself.

'I killed two people. That's why I'm here. Does that earn me a few points?'

I swear I saw him shiver. I wasn't sure if he was glad I'd killed two people or insulted that I'd tried bargaining for mercy.

'Lord sent you here for killing two people?' he said.

Yet another one that didn't know his arse from his earhole.

'Well, only one counted,' I said. 'He didn't care about some old man I killed, maybe because it was in self-defence. But he didn't seem happy that I broke two commandments with one sin when I killed my father.'

'You killed your father?' he said.

'Yep. He deserved it and I don't regret it. End of.'

Then he too disappeared as the warping began and the heat subsided, and I rose to find myself back in Nobby's office, which was a pleasant surprise, but it didn't mean I was happy. I also didn't expect to be kept waiting.

Five

'You have spoken with the Dark,' Nobby said when he decided to turn up. I wasn't sure if it was a question or a statement.

'That is one nasty piece of work,' I said. 'Look what he's done to me?'

'You shall reveal the Dark's intentions.'

'Oh, don't you start,' I said. 'What the fuck do you two want from me? He annihilated my body then talked bollocks until he sent me back here. That's it.'

This wasn't the death I had planned: running back and forth between Nobby and old Lucy downstairs with little love messages. There had to be a way out.

Nobby lowered his voice to a cold hiss. 'You will be truthful or you shall return to the Dark.'

Now you might think that being threatened by God with Hell would make anyone crack and beg for mercy, especially if they'd already had a taste of the place, but I wasn't so easily fooled. When someone lowers their voice when making a threat, it usually means they don't want to carry it out, they just want to scare you, and although I was scared, I also thought I'd spotted a chink in his armour. Besides – and just like with Lucy – if he wanted me in Hell I would've been there.

'Really,' I said, aping his hiss. 'And then what? Will you come and save me again? Or will you accept that he's more powerful than you?'

I could feel his anger and frustration building up. If he'd had a head with veins I'm sure they would've burst.

'You will answer my question,' he said.

'He intends to defeat you and destroy life,' I said, wishing we both had faces, just so I could see the look on his when he saw the smile on mine.

'What are his intentions with you?' he asked, and I felt rather disappointed that there was so much he didn't know.

'He said he's gonna remove my soul and send me to eternal torment.'

He recoiled, as though I'd just told him he had a terminal illness.

'Are you seriously going to let that happen?' I said. 'I did what I did because of what my father made me. You're the one with all the hindsight. If you had a problem, then why didn't you tell me or stop me?'

My argument sounded valid to me, but I felt that me being right might not necessarily encourage him to do right. I paused for his response. It didn't come so I carried on.

'If you don't want to know the truth then send me to Hell. If you do, then shut up and let me ask you a few questions. You seem a bit mixed up about what's going on here.'

'Very well,' he said.

'Very well what?'

'You may ask questions.'

It was as though he'd taken a passive step back and revealed another chink. But I now know he was just humouring me while he decided what to do with me.

'Thank you,' I said. 'Now, let's start with the bleeding obvious. Why don't you destroy the Dark?'

'I cannot destroy that which I have created.'

'Then why did you create it?'

'To show man the contrast between good and evil.'

'I see. And that was the only way you could do it, was it? By creating a monster just as invisible and improbable as you, then expecting your sinful lifeform to know about the pair of you and take their pick?'

'Man has the knowledge of good and evil written on his heart,' he said. 'He who does not believe, his deeds are evil and he can do no good. He shall not be worthy.'

'So is that my fault or the Dark's? I'm confused.'

'The fault lay with your actions, which you chose with your freewill.'

'Then why did you give me freewill if you wanted me to be sinless?'

Again, he took his time. He really wasn't expecting me.

'You shall not question the methods of my creation,' he said.

'You just said I could ask questions, so don't go back on your word now.'

Silence. I had him ruffled.

'So come on then,' I said. 'Don't just stand there like a muppet, spit out the answer.'

'Man was created free of sin,' he tried to explain, 'and was given freewill to choose his path. Those without belief create their own sin.'

'So who decided we should have your so-called "gift of freewill"?'

'I did.'

'Well, if sins come from people abusing their freewill, and freewill is part of your creation, then sins come from your creation, right?'

'You were given commandments to abide by.'

'Don't change the subject. Sins come from you, right?'

He said nothing, probably cursing the day I died. I decided to turn the screw.

'So how come it's okay for you to sin?' I said.

'I am omnibenevolent. I am without sin.'

'Don't give me all that omni-bollocks. There are good people on Earth living insufferable lives, and some of them don't believe in you. And it's not because they're evil and their deeds are no good, it's because you're too much of a coward to show yourself. The life you created is morally superior to you.'

I waited, either for him to come clean or send me to Lucy for good. He stayed silent.

'Well I guess we'll just have to wait here until the Dark comes to get me again,' I said. 'Then you can follow me and have it out with him.'

I knew he'd never play that game, otherwise he'd have followed when Lucy went to town on my body. He was stuck there whether he liked it or not. I, on the other hand, at least had the ability to go between the two, albeit by force. But whose force I wasn't quite sure of yet.

Then he laid his first card on the table.

'You shall absolve yourself of your sins by defeating the Dark,' he said.

'Or you could just forgive me and defeat the Dark yourself,' I replied.

'There is no forgiveness without cost. You shall earn your salvation.'

I could never have known what he had in store for me at this stage. Not even a halfwit like Nobby could've expected me to go back to Hell and defeat Lucy, which meant he had another plan tucked away, and I could've guessed until the end of time and not even come close.

'You shall return to Earth and stop the seed of sin being sowed,' he said. 'Only then shall you be redeemed.'

'Or you could go and stop it yourself. I've already proved myself unworthy, remember.'

'Man can only redeem himself.'

'But the Dark destroyed my body,' I said.

'You shall be granted a new body. Be sure to use it wisely.'

There was no way he was going to take the slightest bit of responsibility for his failure to defeat the Dark when he created his land of man. He probably should've called it quits there and then, but as he couldn't admit he wasn't the perfect being – far from it, in fact – he had to pass the buck onto man, whom he'd also created, to take the rap. But I was going whether I liked it or not and had no desire to see Lucy again anytime soon. Plus, if it brought me a bit more time, there was no telling what I could manipulate Nobby into letting me do.

KEPT IN THE DARK

'Should you fail, you shall be at the mercy of the Dark,' he said. 'Should you succeed, you shall be redeemed.'

Sounded fair. I'd already been at the mercy of the Dark and couldn't think what else he could do to me; as he'd destroyed my body, I had nothing left to feel pain from. I supposed he could've still made me miserable, but I didn't have a choice.

'Okay, let's do this,' I said.

And as he waffled on about what I needed to do to stop sin and save the world, I thought back to my conversation with Lucy. There was something a bit fishy about him, and I don't mean the stench of his house. Why did he send me back to Nobby when he found out I'd killed my father? And why couldn't Nobby stop him from coming for me again.

Six

Crimson gas floated below a swirling storm of dragonesque clouds that spat lightning bolts to the ground as if searching for prey. The red ball that dominated the sky by day was now a shimmer over a mountainous horizon, peppered with volcanoes that growled as they spewed green lava that looked disappointed it had nothing to kill as it cascaded down to carpet the lifeless ground. Winds that would embarrass the strongest hurricanes on Earth tossed rocks the size of houses into the air before letting them drop to tear up the ever-changing landscape.

I stayed perfectly still, though. The steaming lava didn't affect my eyes, and the acid rain was just an obstacle to seeing into space. The truth was, of course, I was dead. No living human could have survived that atmosphere. I had no new body yet. I was just a mind resting on the rocky ground.

I stared in wonder at this pointless display of power, which soon changed to wonder at how Nobby could have been so stupid as to send me to a place that was overcast. I couldn't have seen the Earth if it was break-dancing ten feet above the clouds. My anger increased as I pondered the irony of getting there from Nobby's office instantaneously, then having to wait in that godforsaken place for a gap in the sky. I hadn't been given a weather forecast and couldn't move around. I thought about a plan: find Adam and Eve and keep them away from the young Lucy? Or find the young Lucy and keep him away from Adam and Eve?

I didn't know how I would do either. Finding Earth was one thing, but to then spot the only two people there would take some doing, never mind find a snake. I was six thousand light years away. Another thing bothering me was what the clown upstairs had said when detailing the mission. Something about how only two humans can be on Earth at this time. So if I was there alive and kicking, that made three people. Perhaps Adam wasn't there? But he had to be. Eve was made from his rib. Wasn't she?

Nobby's instructions weren't clear, but I recalled: *the seed of sin shall not perish, until a seed without sin has been sowed... love can only live without sin, when sin hath not been born* ...What the fuck did that mean? And why didn't he talk properly? What was with all this *hath* business?

The biblical poetry was irritating, but after some painful thought I concluded that sin hadn't been born yet, at least not where I was going, and eating from this one tree would be the birth of sin. Really? That was a sin? And the only one, apparently. Nevertheless, at that moment love existed and sin didn't, and I needed to keep it that way.

The sun dragged the clouds with it as it sank out of sight, and a constellation of multi-coloured stars twinkled like an acid trip, making me wonder if I was on acid. It would've explained a lot. I'd been assured that finding the Earth wouldn't be a problem as the Good Lord had blessed me with superpower sight. But I needed to find it tonight. There would be no tomorrow.

The ground creaked and opened to swallow a lake of lava, which meant I had to get to work. I was still bound by the laws of gravity and didn't fancy stargazing submerged. Scanning the night sky amidst the boulders and fire, I zoned in on one star, and if I'd had any breath it would've been taken away. It was as though me and the star came towards each other and met halfway, and I could see every detail I wished. I located the solar system with the blue ball and admired the clockwork of the planets as they obeyed the sun's gravity, and thought how insignificant Earth looked: a speck of dust in the middle of a storm. God's legacy: a pathetic, minuscule point of life, filled with creatures that have to kill each other to survive. And that's what I was there to sort out. It was time to stand up and be counted, to rid the world of sin and become the hero I always should've been.

The monotony of the place I once called home was only broken by the glistening of the polar caps as the auroras flickered across them with their trademark flashes. Where there was no cloud cover, I could see the outlines of the continents and zoom in on the oceans.

So this is what a world without sin looks like, I thought. Except that it wasn't. There was a bastard tree there somewhere. And not just any tree, it was the tree of the knowledge of good and evil, and I wondered why Nobby couldn't have destroyed it with a bolt of lightning or created an animal with a taste for its fruit. I mean, who gave a shit if an animal committed original sin? It also seemed the tree had been planted after Adam was created, otherwise it wouldn't have been a good strategy to put him and Eve only a stone's throw from it.

I scoured the landmasses and thought of the history yet to happen. The flourishing of mankind, the dominance of man over beast, the dominance of man over man, the pain, the suffering, the destruction, the wars, the genocide, the confusion about where it all came from. And now I had the chance – and the responsibility – to restart the clock.

But what would that mean? No pain? Not necessarily. Simple gravity is a sure-fire way to hurt yourself, regardless of whether you behave, and suffering is just prolonged pain. No Hell would be good from Nobby's point of view, as everyone would go to Heaven and Lucy would be fucked. But for mankind, it would be the death of humanity. Yeah, there would be no reason to question right from wrong, for there would be no wrong. No disputes over who sent the rains, for it was Nobby. No need to wonder what the stars were, for Nobby made them all. No destruction, except for natural disasters courtesy of Nobby's creative weather patterns. No wars, unless Nobby ordered one. No genocide, unless Nobby gave it the go-ahead. And, of course, the icing on the cake – no sin, unless you repented. Just people full of peace. But where was the fun in that?

I told myself to stop being a sissy and focus on the mission. Somewhere on that rock was a tree that wasn't what it seemed. A razor blade dressed in honey that was about to cut the ice from under the feet of mankind. Unless I could convince Adam and Eve to keep their grubby mitts off the fruit.

The garden was Paradise, supposedly, so you wouldn't have to be smarter than God to put it somewhere warm and near water. So although I was no environmental geography buff, I kept close to the equator as I followed rivers, scoured beaches, and circled lakes for any sign of human life. Even footprints wouldn't have been a problem for me and my bionic fucking eyes.

Night changed to day, day changed to night, acre by acre, second by second, and I thought about my opponent. The snake. The Devil. Young Lucy. As fresh off the boat as me. If I failed, what would it mean? Hell? Well, that was the deal, wasn't it?

As these thoughts rallied around in my mind, I glimpsed a colourful area by a river and zoomed in to see a true wonder. Meadows with grass greener than green, plants boasting flowers of every shade of every colour, and a host of peaceful animals drinking from crystal-clear streams that twisted between trees offering a hundred different fruits. My mind wandered to Eve. The first woman. Surely not even a miserable bastard like Nobby could screw this one up. She had to be a good sort.

Then I clocked her. Stark bollock naked. Her long blonde hair waving with the wind as she stroked the long grass with her fingers. I took a minute to admire my target. The perfect virgin. She must be easy meat. It wasn't like her mother told
her to be wary of boys. I looked around for Adam — nothing. I didn't know if that was good or bad, and

recalled the magic words that only Nobby could hear, through some Heaven-to-Universe landline wired up to my mind. I didn't care to know how light-speed vision turned into instant reality, so I didn't ask Nobby how he manipulated his own laws of physics to bounce me around the cosmos like Zebedee. But as the magic words were the last thing he said – after saying it was the last thing he was going to say – I caught them, thank God, so I repeated them and waited, again, for Nobby to remember he had a chosen one stuck in the middle of nowhere who was trying to contact him to save his skin.

While I waited, I tried again to piece together his irritating riddle: *the seed of sin shall not starve, until a seed without sin has been sowed... love can only exist without sin, when sin hath not been born...* So Eve eating the fruit would be the birth of sin, unless another seed was sown first. This sinless seed would have to come from Adam as he was without sin at this stage. He needed to get Eve up the spout *before* she ate the fruit, then the child would be born free of sin to restart humanity. So the mission wasn't to stop Eve eating the fruit, but to make sure she was knocked up first, and as Adam was nowhere in sight, I wondered if *I* was going in as Adam.

Maybe I didn't end up in sin – I was a chosen one, after all – maybe that little trip to see Lucy was my 'crucifixion'. It had to happen for me to be able to save mankind, and all that rib crap was just a fairy story. I mean, seriously, Eve was made from Adam's rib? No, she was made by God for me. Jimmy Linton had been called upon to outwit the Devil, seduce the perfect woman, and save the world. I only hoped Nobby would let future generations know it was me who should be worshiped forever.

How wrong I was.

Seven

There was a snap, followed by a vague sense of falling. I kept my eyes shut, not too keen on heights. I landed surrounded by trees that had no bark, branches or leaves. They were about ten feet tall and the same shade of green all the way up. I took a moment to gather my thoughts and wondered where I was. I'd chosen a meadow to land in.

I was lying on my front and couldn't feel my arms or legs. *What the fuck? Has he seriously sent me back with no limbs?* My sight was blurred, an extreme contrast to the super-vision I'd had just a few moments ago, but at least it was calm and quiet. I only hoped my arms and legs were on their way, or I was in for a long day at the office.

The sky was clear and blue and the air was warm, but the weather wasn't my main concern. I waited until my vision cleared, then turned my head and froze. There was too much body movement for my liking. I took a moment, then moved my head again and shot forward like I was on wheels. *What the fuck has he done to me?* I wanted to look at my body, but I wasn't sure I was ready, so I took a breath and poked my tongue out. It was forked. *Bastard! I'd thought I was going back as Adam.* So that explained the trees. They weren't trees, they were blades of grass and I was in the middle of the field I'd intended.

I plucked up the courage to look at my body, which was a good six feet long and a gorgeous blend of green and brown with jet-black lines down my sides. I didn't know what type of snake I was and didn't care. I was one handsome dude.

Powering along with more confidence, I thought I might not even need arms or legs. It wasn't like I planned on squaring up to young Lucy. He would've beaten the shit out of me. This battle would be about street smarts, gift of the gab, and James Linton was the man for the job. I wanted to seek out Eve straight away, but I needed to become familiar with my surroundings first. There was a certain landmark I had to locate.

Having no arms to sway drove me crazy and I still had the instinct to get up and walk, and as I zigzagged through the grass and into the woods with my tongue out on sniff alert for another snake, my mind raced with questions. *Where is he? Does he know I'm here? Is he even here yet? Will Eve still be where I saw her? Why am I a fucking snake?*

The early nature of Planet Earth in its untouched glory was eerie for its tidiness, and the absence of life – other than grass, plants, trees, a few birds, and the distant honking from I didn't know what – made me feel I was in a fairytale, where a wicked witch was waiting to lure a beautiful princess to her death. It would've been nice to think I was the knight in shining armour, but as I wouldn't be leaving with her, or even be getting a bit of slap-and-tickle, I guessed I was there to play the wise old owl. Or the wizard. The wise old wizard.

But as nice as this happy land was, with no sign of predator or prey, death or new life, and, of course, no human destruction, it was far too boring. The soil was untouched. There wasn't so much as a fallen leaf or a snapped twig in sight, and I got the impression the sun shone every day. There were no worms, bugs, mosquitoes, flies, spiders, rats or cats. In fact, the only creatures the other creatures could mistakenly be wary of were the two snakes prowling around. But they each had their own agenda.

The tree wasn't hard to find, even though I couldn't see much higher than a stick. It stood alone and proud in the middle of a large clearing near the river, and I felt it was by itself because the other trees were shit-scared of it. I coiled up at a distance and waited for something to happen that had already happened. Thousands of years ago. Yet I didn't know what, exactly. But something was going to happen. Soon. Today. Before the sun went down. Enough time for something like me to emerge and seek out Eve.

The air was still, eerily so, and then something happened that will stay with me until I've died a thousand times. The grass around the tree stayed rigid as the tree itself began to shake and sway as though in the middle of a tornado. No leaves fell and no fruit dropped, and every other tree stayed still as if watching with the same awe as me. It slowed to a stop after maybe a minute; fucked if I knew, I wasn't wearing a watch, then the lowest branch shed its leaves and twigs and I knew what was coming next.

I curled up and watched my fellow snake sever himself from the trunk and slither down into the grass. He looked a tad longer than me but had retained the texture and colour of bark. No imagination. Purely functional. I wondered why Lucy had come down dressed up as a snake. I didn't have a choice, but he could've surely made himself a man just as easily, and it would've stuck one up Nobby and his creation if he'd left his seed in the first woman. And I don't mean consensually either – he was the Devil. But that was irrelevant. Nobby had screwed up and passed the buck on to me to make sure Lucy did too.

I didn't want to go and introduce myself just yet; he looked a tad cranky, to say the least, best let him wake up a bit first. His head rose and he had a good sniff, then it disappeared and I saw the disturbance in the grass as he slithered in the opposite direction from where I'd seen Eve. Which meant his sense of smell was no better than mine.

Confident I'd find her first, I headed back the way I came, which was easy with my new senses – I felt the slightest movement on the ground, heard the most insignificant sound and smelt the smallest bird in the trees. I only hoped Eve had taken a shower or she might be a bit on the nose.

It wasn't long before I felt the vibration of something much larger than me and I had a good sniff. It was sweet and sour. The sour was BO, the sweet was a woman. Bingo. I followed her scent on top alert for an ambush by another snake. More vibration. Stronger BO. So close.

KEPT IN THE DARK

Her shape emerged through the thinning grass and I stopped, not sure if she should see me just yet. She was nibbling on small berries she'd evidently picked from the tree she sat under, blissfully unaware of what she was about to do should I fail to interrupt time. I needed a better look, not only at her but at her surroundings.

Being quiet on the move was easy with no leaves on the ground to disturb, and I was in the nearest bush with my head poking out without a squeak. Everything was still and quiet except for the sound of Eve chewing with her mouth open. A wave of anger washed over me; at that moment I wanted her to close her mouth more than I wanted her to mate with Adam. I couldn't even cover my ears. There was no sign of Adam or another snake, but I knew it wouldn't be long, for today was the day.

I looked at the beautiful creature under the tree and had to give Nobby credit. He clearly knew what a woman should look like. But any hope of banging her went out the window when I realised my pecker was the size of a toothbrush bristle. *Maybe that's why Nobby made me a snake. He knew I'd have a crack at her.* And so, I waited. Far from boring, though. The legs, the body, the face, all so perfect. *If she'd only close her mouth when she chews.*

My trance was broken by a movement in the shrub behind her, and unless Adam was creeping up, having realised she was the only woman on Earth, I took a punt that it was young Lucy ready to play a cunning trick with a piece of fruit. I dared not move and tried to be part of the bush as his black beady eyes broke through the healthy green flora like the muzzle of a hunter's shotgun. His expression oozed hatred for his surroundings as he slithered into view, and he was clearly in pain from what I imagined was simply being alive. This told me he wanted this over more than I did. Advantage Jimmy.

'Hello,' Eve said to him.

Well, would you Adam and Eve it? She only speaks English.

'Hello, my pretty one,' replied Lucy with a forced smile. 'Thuch a lovely day.'

Ha! The cunt has a lisp. He sounded like an even camper version of his older self.

'Yes, isn't it,' she said with a beaming smile.

'You are alone?'

'Yes.'

'But where ith the man?' he said, looking left to right for dramatic effect.

'He does not tell, for I need not know,' she said, spitting out a pip.

'You are obedient to him?'

'But, of course.'

I wondered where Adam was myself. If I were him I'd have been banging that chick 24/7, especially if she had to be up the spout before she cursed man to eternal sin. But even though I should've been more assertive with the world so close to doom, my instinct held me back. I didn't know if he'd see me as just another snake or know who I was. I had to play it cool.

I slid out like I had other business, but before my whole body was in the open Lucy spun round and glared at me, and I had to use every ounce of composure to not freeze. And even then I didn't know if playing it cool was the best thing to do. For all I knew, freezing could be the normal reaction to another snake staring at you. Still, I'd made my decision and had to stick by it. I didn't think Eve noticed me as she stuffed more berries in her mouth, but Lucy held his stare for a few seconds before turning back to his task, which allowed my heart rate to drop to a level that let me breathe. I gave them a wide birth and thought about my next move. Not that you could call that a move, all I did was pass by, but Eve speaking English changed things. I now knew I could get her alone and tell her to ignore Lucy and get it on with Adam. I might not have to deal with Lucy directly.

Their voices faded to vibrations as I entered the bracken with a plan to backtrack and curl up nearby. I needed to stake this one out properly. Lucy didn't seem that interested in me, but he still had a good look. I did, however, take comfort from him not having known I was there until he saw me, as it meant I could hide from him.

I slunk in behind the tree, super fucking quiet; if he saw me again so soon he'd know I was up to no good. Their voices were muffled, so I crept up to a branch and, poking one eye over the edge, finally got a proper look at her cleavage. Superb. I didn't want to catch his eye, so if I had to look somewhere it might as well be at her.

'For you know what to eat?' Lucy asked her.

'Am I not free to choose?' she replied.

'You are free to chooth ath you dethire.'

'But I must not desire from every tree.'

'Did Lord thay you mutht not dethire from every tree?'

'He said we may eat from the tres in the garden, but not from the one that stands alone or we will die.'

'You will not die,' he said, looking like *he* was about to. 'Lord knowth that when you eat of it, your eyeth will be opened and you will be like him. Knowing good and evil.'

'But what is evil?'

I rolled my eyes.

'Eat from the tree and you will feel all the wonderth of the world and be free.'

'But why do you insist?'

'I do not inthitht. I only invite.'

'But will there not be time to taste all?' she asked. 'Will the fruit not grow if I desire not from every tree?'

For God's sake. Why does everyone talk in riddles around here? I should've been grateful I could understand them at all, but I was dying to give someone a slap.

Lucy poked his tongue out and had a good sniff, then without another word he disappeared back into the scrub. Eve stood up, puzzled, unaware of the approaching Adam, who too was naked as he ambled through the woods. He stopped out of sight from Eve and casually reached for a piece of fruit before sitting against the tree to munch it.

This was my chance. But as I slid down, I still didn't know what I was going to say to her, if anything. I reached the ground at the back of the tree and glided around, and so wished I was still a man. Sensational.

'You are quite right, my pretty,' I said. 'You shall not eat from the tree that stands alone. You must obey the Lord.'

Her face lit up as she smiled at me, and I was heartbroken I had to tell her to go and bang someone else.

'I shall,' she said.

KEPT IN THE DARK

'Adam must sow his seed in you before you taste the forbidden fruit.'

'Who?'

'Adam. The bloke that's here. *Jesus, sweetheart. How narrowed down do you want it?*

'Is there not time to desire other fruits before we mate?' she said.

'No. You must do it today. Before you are tempted.'

'But—'

'No buts. Just do it.'

My raised voice must've startled Adam because his footsteps came thudding through the woods. I was back in the bush before he appeared. If he saw me, he might think I was the snake Nobby had warned him about and kill me. Eve stood and they embraced, then Adam let go.

Is this guy mad? If he nails her the world will be free of sin, and he goes in for a hug? I looked up to see the sun going down. *She eats the fruit today. Not tonight. Not tomorrow. Today.* I wanted to go over and tell them to get it on before Lucy got back, but couldn't risk scaring Adam and splitting them up. While they were together, Lucy would keep his distance.

Adam wandered into the woods. It looked like he was trying to build a shelter for the night, while Eve continued stuffing her face with berries. She sure liked her fruit. I poked my tongue out and sniffed for Lucy, but got nothing except Adam and Eve. Either he was too far away or I couldn't smell other snakes. But could he? I'd been within smelling distance a few moments before and he hadn't reacted.

Adam continued to move further away as he ripped down branches and threw them in a pile. And as he began to fade into the trees, I half expected Lucy to reappear in front of Eve with more tales of fruit – nothing. Adam was one tree from disappearing and stood on tiptoe to grab what I hoped was his last branch before heading back, but the branch had other ideas. It made Adam punch himself in the face before wrapping itself around him in a helix down his body; then, looking like a coiled spring, Adam and Lucy toppled over into the bracken. I was on my way over, top speed.

By the time I arrived, Lucy had sprung and was nowhere to be seen, and Adam was unconscious in the scrub, but still breathing. I couldn't understand why Lucy hadn't made sure he was dead. It would've given him certain victory. But I wasn't worried about him dying. He didn't the first time, because he still created sinful offspring after the dirty deed had been done, so I left him to wake naturally and went to check on Eve.

I heard no chewing as I approached the berry tree, because she wasn't there. My tongue smelt that she'd set off in the direction of the dreaded tree, so I homed in on her scent and set after her. No problem there, happy to sniff her all day long. I powered through the scrub, slaloming between trees and dodging bushes until I saw her. She was following Lucy. Off to the tree for a little tempter, no doubt.

I kept tail to the clearing, wondering what I was going to do now. This was surely it. Adam was out cold, Lucy was in the chair, and Eve was about to ruin it for everyone. I had to step up, but there was a niggle in the back of my mind stopping me, and I kept my distance until they stopped underneath the tree. Lucy's upper half rose so his head was almost eyelevel with Eve's, and he swayed from side to side like he was trying to hypnotise her. I couldn't make out what was said, but had no doubt Lucy was turning it on, hoping for Eve to snap off a piece of fruit and damn mankind for eternity.

To be fair, Eve resisted Lucy's powers of persuasion and kept shaking her head. But how long could she hold out? If I didn't intervene she was going to crack before the sun went down. And as it had reached the tops of the trees, that wouldn't be long. But what was I supposed to do? Go over and give him a piece of my mind? Naughty Snake. Leave the virgin alone. He could've put me out of action as soon as I intervened.

I decided to go and find Adam and tell him what his dumb wife was about to do. *Poor fella. Where is your Lord now?*

Eight

Adam had gone, but finding him was a piece of piss, the smelly prick. He was on the nose from half a mile away. I knew he'd been grafting, but he was right next to a running stream. *Take a dip!*

Nobby's first human creation was now studying every branch to make sure it wasn't likely to attack him before he ripped it down. He had his back to me, so I slid over and pretended to be a lump of broken tree.

The light was fading fast and I wondered how Lucy was getting on with Eve. He obviously hadn't worn her down yet, or a young Nobby would've turned up to give her and old Ray Mears the good news, or so the story went. I was thinking more along the lines of Nobby staying put, and waiting for his first two humans to croak before he dealt with them. Maybe they would be the first ones to enter the gates of Heaven, or maybe Nobby would feed them to Lucy as kindling for his fire.

Adam returned with another collection of sticks for his house and placed them alongside me and the others, but before he had the chance to straighten his back, I popped my head up.

'Ere, mate, where's your missus?' I said.

He didn't hang around to savour the spoils of his day's work – he was off. I set after him, thinking I maybe should've started with something a little more gentle, but what were you going to do? He checked behind a few trees as though Eve was playing hide-and-seek, then bounded like Tarzan through the woods. I followed, hoping he wasn't about to see his woman ruin his life, but I was breathing out of my arse before we'd got halfway. The skin on my belly was sore and I had to stop before it split open.

Once on my way again, albeit at a steadier pace than the mad rush Adam had me going at, I pictured a few possible scenarios at the tree, and had a pathetic image of Adam crying in Eve's arms with a story about how the nasty snake startled him, with Lucy hiding in the wings tearing his fucking hair out. But I wasn't sure if Adam had even gone there; he could've been taking a dump in the river for all I knew.

Entering the circle of doom, I smelt humans as the grass darkened and the shadow of the tree crept over. Then movement. No talking, just movement. The grass thinned out to reveal Adam and Eve rocking backwards and forwards in each other's arms, with Lucy nowhere to be seen, no doubt hiding in the wings tearing his fucking hair out. I guessed he was wary of Adam because he knew Nobby had warned him about a nasty snake that would try and tempt them. I had no idea what Lucy's plan was, now the love birds were together and threatening to do Nobby a favour, but I had no intention of spending any more time as a snake than I had to. The courting couple were still struggling with first base, and it could've been a while before they sealed my ticket to Heaven. There was a little tender caressing and some sweet-nothings being whispered, but he hadn't even stuck his tongue in her mouth yet. I had to get the ball rolling. If Lucy turned up anytime soon, my money was on Adam abandoning first base and running into the woods, either with or without Eve.

Not giving a toss if Mork and Mindy saw me or not, I headed into the undergrowth sniffing like a bastard with my head up proud. If Lucy did fancy a bit of a chinwag, I didn't want him to find me hidden behind a tree like a scared rat. It would've forced me on the back foot and that was not the Linton way. He needed to know he had an obstacle to overcome before he could have another crack at Eve.

Lucy was going to be smarter than me, I was under no illusions, but I had no choice other than to seek him out. Whether he knew there was another, shall we say, external entity operating in the area was beyond my knowledge. But I assumed he didn't or he would surely have confronted me by now. I'd passed right by the bastard earlier and he didn't seem too fussed. But that didn't matter. If he didn't know who I was already, he soon would.

I climbed up and down trees, rustled through bushes, left my scent on the grass and flaunted myself wherever it took my fancy, but I'd never have noticed him with his perfect camouflage had he not been shivering. And his shivering told me he was struggling. It certainly wasn't cold. He was heading back towards the tree, but in no rush when he should've been. He should've been moving as fast as he could, knowing it might only take Adam a few seconds to find the hole and sow his seed. Then his strained face told me he *was* moving as fast as he could, and as he hauled his sorry arse through the grass, I knew he only had one more shot at Eve before he collapsed. I had to intercept him.

Nine

By the time I encountered him he was in a state of severe desperation. The sun had fallen behind the trees, ready to give light to the part of the world that Nobby didn't care about, and I didn't fancy Adam's chances with his nighttime seduction moves any more than with his daytime ones. If he thought he could produce and spare billions of offspring from damnation by impregnating his woman with a cuddle, then maybe I should've put him out of his misery and killed the sad sonofabitch. That would've at least forced Nobby to start again, but it wouldn't have done much for me.

At first, I thought Lucy was just stupid. Then I realised he was weak... and stupid. He wasn't supposed to live, given his reason for existing was to destroy life, not to become part of it, and his ambush was pathetic for someone of his supposed powers. His fangs barely grazed my tail as I jumped back and landed facing him, ready to flee, not fight. I needed to buy Adam and Eve time. Maybe he was nailing her by now, maybe he wasn't, but I was happy for Lucy to chase me. Not only would I take him further away from Barbie and Ken, but I was confident he wouldn't catch me. As far as I was concerned, my job was done. All I had to do was keep him talking until I heard Adam's climactic groan.

He couldn't have known who I was, of course, but as soon as I spoke he must've known I was as good as money in his pocket, and known that it wouldn't be in his favour to destroy me as he had on his home turf. He needed Eve to eat the fruit so he wouldn't be left on the shelf to gather dust in a cold and peaceful Hell, so he wasn't going to waste energy he didn't have fighting me.

The one thing I had on Lucy was that he didn't know I'd already spoken with him. Thousands of years in the future.

We locked eyes and checked each other out. His eyes were impossible to read: two jet-black ball bearings embedded in his face. I assumed mine were the same. His bark-like skin, as he lay on his belly, gave off a light quiver that I felt he was trying to hide.

He said nothing, but he sure knew I was no ordinary snake.

'So, err, how you getting on with little Miss Perfect?' I said.

'What do you care?' he replied.

I had this guy stumped. Until then, he must've thought he was the only talking snake in the world.

'Well, I know she'd have eaten that fruit by now if I'd been given the job of temptation.'

He wasn't impressed with that comeback, which told him I knew things I shouldn't have.

'How did you come to be here?' he said.

'I'm from the future, and have come back in a time machine built by my Uncle Nobby to save the world. And looking at the state of you, I don't think I'm too late.'

He gave up trying to hide his quivering, and was now trembling all over from living pain. I would've bet Eve's virginity he'd never make it back to the tree to die, never mind get her to eat the fruit the Good Lord told her not to. The cheeky bastard smiled at me, and I smiled back, but my smile was a little more forced. He wasn't finished yet.

He took a slow panoramic scan of the woods, then kept his eyes on mine as he curled up and rested his head on his coils. I didn't know whether he was trying to look cool and composed, or whether he was trying to conserve energy. I didn't think he was going to pounce again, not the way he looked. I glanced upwards. Subconscious.

'Lord cannot thee,' he said.

I didn't answer, but somehow I believed him. Even if Nobby had seen history occur the first time around, which he hadn't, what happened in Eden when I was there would surely have happened instantaneously for him, given that I had *gone back in time*. And the fact that I had to let him know when I was ready to leave the planet of fire told me he had no idea what went on outside his bubble of self-importance.

Lucy gave a condescending smirk, like he knew something I didn't. Truth was, he knew a lot I didn't.

'You appear ath a therpent,' he said. 'You are here to therve me.'

KEPT IN THE DARK

'Fuck off, I'm here to serve me. The reason I'm a snake is because you destroyed my human body. The Lord gave me this limbless one instead. Perhaps he knew how pathetic you were going to be.'

'Why doeth Lord not faith me himthelf?' he said.

'He's been asking the same question of you, but that's not why I'm here.'

'If you were thent to me, then you belong to me.'

'Yeah, well, Mr Lord has other ideas. If I was here to serve you, she would've eaten that fruit two minutes after I arrived.'

He kept his smile. 'Yet I dethtroyed your body. Oneth with me, alwayth with me.'

'Well, apparently not,' I said with my own smile. 'The Lord rescued me from your stinking universe of fire. Twice.' It was surreal telling the Devil about his future house. For all I knew he hadn't even set the place on fire yet; there was no one dead to burn. 'I don't know why,' I continued, 'but he's given me a chance to redeem myself of my gravest sin.'

He stared into my eyes, but he was never going to read them. Not if they were anything like his.

'Lord doeth not care about thin. He only careth whether you believe.'

'Well, he seemed to care about my sin.'

'Which woth?'

'I killed my father.'

For some reason that perked him up and his smile got wider. I started to wish I'd kept my mouth shut.

'I don't know why that makes you smile,' I said. 'The fat bastard died believing in Nobby.'

'Nobby?'

'The Lord.'

'I know,' he said.

'You know what?'

'That your father died a believer.'

He had to be lying, I thought. How could he have known that?

'And your dark soul died not believing,' he continued, 'or you would not have been thent to me.'

'Be that as it may,' I said, 'the humans are mating as we speak, so you may as well fuck off back home. It's over.'

'How can Lord reward you?'

'I'm going to Heaven, my friend.'

'Lord shall only create Heaven for thothe who believe,' he said. 'Thothe who do not believe shall belong to me.'

My heart stopped while his words echoed around my brain, and were soon joined by Nobby's words. *He who does not believe, his deeds are evil and he can do no good. He shall not be worthy.*

Non-believers go to Hell. That's why I went there in the first place; me murdering Fatty had nothing to do with it. It was because I didn't believe, and neither did Mum, which meant she was in Hell too. It also meant that Fatty was in Heaven, which made me feel sick, especially as it seemed I was going to Hell even if I succeeded. Nobby had lied. And even if I had have gone to Heaven, Heaven without Mum would not be Heaven. So I needed to find a way to save her. I had to bank on this happening instantaneously from Nobby's point of view, which meant if I failed and died, I'd be right back where I left him. And as he'd revealed his hidden strength, that being the ability to send me back in time, I now had to get Eve to eat the fruit before she opened her legs, but I didn't want Lucy to know why.

'He sent me to stop you,' I said. 'But he's not all he's cracked up to be, so I think we should talk.'

He kept his head on his coils and his eyes flittered as he tried to keep them open.

'You really don't look too good, mate,' I said, 'so feel free to tell me to fuck off if you want. But before I do, I'm going to watch you fail again at talking that fair maiden into taking a bite to prove your point. I know you're only here out of necessity, and if you fail there'll be no second chance, so unless you want to embarrass yourself in front of me, the Lord and Frank and Betty over there by trying to seduce her with a speech impediment and a headache, I suggest you keep out of sight and let me do the business.'

'You claim to have been thent by Lord,' he said. 'How can I know you will not betray me?'

'You can't. But you don't have a choice and neither do I, so you can either go over there and humiliate yourself or let me have a crack at her, but whether I have a crack on your behalf or the Lord's depends on you. You see, I'm in a bit of a pickle and you're the only one that can help me.'

He screwed his face up, and I had a moment of empathy for his humiliation at becoming the very thing his existence was to destroy.

'Thththththth...' he went with his tongue wiggling away.

He didn't have much going for him at this stage. I could've gone over and tied him in a knot, then used him as a club to batter Nobby with when I got back. But as I needed his assistance to save my world, under the guise of helping him destroy Nobby's, I thought I'd keep him onside.

'I don't know how much gas you have left, but if you want my help you'd better spit something out. You go back over there looking like you do and he sees you, he's going to be away into the woods and she is sure to follow, and we both know you ain't gonna be chasing them. So here's the deal.

'We shall be meeting again. Long after you've shed your skin and slithered off to stoke the fires of Hell, ready to rid the Lord of his rejects. You see, I'm what one might call a chosen one. I know that means nothing to you at this stage, but it will, my friend, it will, and I have as much interest in getting the Lord rattled at the first sin being committed as you. But only if you promise me one thing.'

'Which ith?'

'Sometime in the far distant future, a woman will be sent to you. Susan Linton. You will not destroy her body or even show her the flames. You will send her to Heaven and never bother her again.

'Then when me and you meet again, in the even more distant future, you leave me alone too. I know that's going to piss you off, but it's only two people out of I don't know how many billions. It's either that, or the Lord wins and you shrivel away to nothing.'

'Your wish shall be granted,' he said.

I should've been thankful he was struggling to stay alive, making it easy for me, but I was looking forward to more of a battle, to be honest. I was never going to trust him, but I had to get Eve to eat the fruit anyway, so thought I might as well try a bit of insurance.

KEPT IN THE DARK

I moved away, slowly. Very slowly. Partly because I kept one eye on Lucy, and partly because I only had half my muscles to work with; my lower half was dead. Dead. I couldn't feel it and it had already turned deathly black, but it retained its weight and I had to drag it behind me, wishing it would fall off. Lucy's attack hadn't been as lame as I'd thought.

I heard him set off behind me, even more slowly. Fair enough that he should want to see me do his dirty work for him. *I bet he regrets killing half of me, now.*

Ten

When I arrived back at the tree, Adam had worked out the joys of being with a naked woman and was investigating what felt natural. Eve was silent and not really into it, which was no surprise considering his technique. I could've rattled her bones better even as a snake.

But as it was his first time I guessed he'd fire quickly, so I nipped up to a branch above their heads and knocked down a piece of fruit. It bounced off Adam's head and rolled next to Eve, but Adam didn't break his stride or even open his eyes. I could only assume he knew what was at stake. But then again, why had he waited so long to put the moves on her?

I slid down as Eve expressed a bit of enthusiasm in losing her virginity and out came a few squeals of bodily pleasure. *You go, girl.* I had to act, and as she flailed her orgasmic arms across the grass and brushed the fallen fruit with her fingers, I moved over and nudged it into her hand. Then whispered in her ear, 'You are mating. You can now eat the fruit.'

'But he hasn't sowed–'

'Just eat the damn fruit and keep your mouth shut while you're doing it.'

She took a bite and arched her back in double ecstasy as Adam pulled out and jumped away from his lover. The look on his face was a picture. Eve seemed oblivious to everything but the fruit and lay on her front stuffing as much into her face as she could. Adam's horrified gaze alternated between her and me, and I wasn't sure if he was more aghast at her eating the forbidden fruit, or annoyed that he didn't get to blow his load. I waited for Nobby to zoom down with his little rule book – nothing. The thing was, he wouldn't have known who I was even if he had turned up. He'd have been the Nobby before I was born and think I was Lucy.

Then the real Lucy poked his head through the grass, with droopy eyes like he'd just woken from a drunken slumber, and it was all he could do to drag the rest of his body clear of the thin floppy stalks. Adam's look of horror towards Eve turned to one of fury towards me and he lost it. He grabbed my tail and I was launched through the air to land out of sight in the grass. My bottom half never felt the bump, and the adrenaline that surged through me drowned out the pain in my top half.

I made my way back, and as the visibility through the grass grew, I saw that Adam had given in to temptation and climbed the tree to shake down more sin. Lucy was closer to the tree than me, and I didn't know what he was planning now his wish had been granted, but he didn't look happy. Was he going to kill them this time around? It would've stopped mankind in its tracks, now he knew

Nobby had a card or two up his sleeve. Whatever, he wasn't finished yet.

I upped my pace but my bottom half was a hindrance. I had no control over it and it flopped and caught on every root and bramble as I struggled through the undergrowth like some long-extinct creature that was half-lizard, half-dead. Lucy was also half-dead, but all over, which meant his mind was half-dead. The black-eyed legless weasel flopped forward like a rubber log being kicked along the ground, and although his back end was more use than mine, it was not in sync with the top half and he kept veering off as he tried to keep in line with the tree.

This caught Adam's eye, and he jumped down munching a mouthful of fruit. Eve also caught wind of what was going on and collected an armful from the ground before they both moved away from the tree. But Lucy didn't change direction. Then I realised he needed the tree to get back to Hell.

I launched myself forward with everything I had. If I could stop him getting to the tree I would win on both accounts. I'd destroy the Devil – saving me and Mum from Hell – and still get to give Nobby a piece of my mind.

I made it into the clearing with half the forest tangled around my tail, while Adam and Eve sat down to watch the show with the new tasty treat they had succumbed to. Lucy reached the tree with me bumbling along trying to wriggle free, and he groaned as he lifted his weary tail and flopped it against the trunk.

KEPT IN THE DARK

'I shall enjoy making your mother suffer,' he gurgled, before his face disappeared into itself and his body sprung up to become a fruitless branch.

I wasn't surprised. Why would the Devil keep a promise he didn't have to? His work was done. My work, on the other hand, was not. I had to get out of there.

My upper half was a sausage of pain, with the dead tissue creeping towards my head, but I wanted to die on my own terms, not from the spit of the branch monster. I slid up to Adam and lay next to a head-sized rock near his feet.

'Well, that was a bit silly, wasn't it?' I said.

He stared at me, and I stared back, with the biggest, smarmiest, most sarcastic smile I could muster. He looked at the rock, and then as I had wished, he stood and raised it above his head like he'd just won a trophy. I kept my smile as he shouted what sounded like a beg for mercy from Nobby, and then he started crying.

What's he waiting for? I thought. *The national anthem? Just do it.* But he lowered the rock and held it to his chest like he was ready to play piggy-in-the-middle. Eve jumped to her feet; she'd run out of fruit and didn't look like she was about to scrump for more, and I was happy for her to take the lead as she rushed over and grabbed my dead tail. I felt nothing as I sailed through the air and into the river.

All snakes can swim, but I pretended I couldn't and sank to the bottom. I'd heard somewhere that drowning was a pleasant way to go, all things considered. My head became light and fluffy, but my thoughts were dark and heavy with trepidation about whether Nobby would send me to Hell before I'd given him a piece of my mind and, hopefully, talked him into loaning me his time machine again.

Eleven

I wasn't sure where I was at first. They both favoured the larger office, filled with fuck all except the place where they hid, but my initial prediction proved right and I bounced straight back into Nobby's gaff. He wasn't there and I had no idea where he'd gone, but assumed he'd nipped out for a piss while I was waiting on that wretched planet. He showed up before I got too impatient, and again, neither of us were happy.
'You have failed,' he said.

Wow. This guy's quick.

'Well, not really,' I said. 'You said they had to mate before they could eat the fruit. They were mating. It's not my fault Adam couldn't fire.'

I had to think on my feet and technicalities were my best shot.

'The Dark will soon come for you again,' he said.

'I would've gone there anyway. You promised me Heaven. The snake told me all non-believers go to Hell.'

'I did not promise you Heaven. I said you would be redeemed.'

'So where would I have gone?'

'Nowhere. You would have changed history, and so would have ceased to have ever existed.'

I felt stupid. Of course I would cease to exist if I changed history, and so would Mum; the idea had been niggling at me in Eden. But it still didn't seem like much of a redemption.

'That's your idea of redemption?' I said. 'Blaming me for your mistake, then sending me all round the houses without arms and legs to try and fix it? And my reward would've been to cease to exist? And because I couldn't fix your stupid error you're going to torture me for eternity.' I paused as a thought came to me. 'No, hold on, you're going to let that freak do it for you, the one you are trying to stop. Let me give you a tip, stop sending people to him and he won't be much of a problem, will he?'

'Have you learned nothing?' he said. 'Man has failed me. I gave life, I gave love, I gave freewill—'

'Oh, don't start all that freewill bollocks again. You created the Universe, you created Hell, and you created the criteria by which people are judged, which is believe in me or else. But love is not something I'll let you take credit for either. Love is what people feel between each other, not what they think of you.

'You claim to have the power to prevent people from suffering, but instead of being just and caring and actually doing that, you're offering some kind of bribe, but only telling a few people that can't be trusted themselves. That, my friend, is not love. Maybe if you went down there, you might find out what love really is.'

I was quite pleased with that little rant and waited for his reply, but he stayed silent. He had to know I had him.

'There's one thing bothering me, though,' I said. 'If you knew the Dark was making people sin, then why did you wait until I had lived and died before choosing someone to sort out your mess?'

'You are not alone in sharing the burden of defeating the Dark,' he said. 'But you turned against me by not knowing me.'

There was another? I suddenly didn't feel quite so special. But that they had evidently failed too gave me room to move.

'I'm glad you didn't insult my intelligence by claiming they'd succeeded, or you wouldn't have had to drag me aside.'

'The Dark is cunning and subtle. The fallibility of man means it must be defeated slowly.'

'Well, excuse me,' I said. 'But if you knew man was fallible, why would you put your trust in him to defeat the Dark? Surely an omni-cunt like yourself would be in a better position?'

He said nothing, so I took an educated guess at the other chosen one. 'I bet Jesus got straight into Heaven.'

Again, he took his time. I noticed he was quicker with his questions than his answers.

'He was a believer and he spread my word.'

'Of course, he was a believer. You gave him magic powers. And as for spreading your word — thirty-three fucking years he spent down there, and only managed to convince twelve people he was sent by you before he got himself crucified. Why didn't he live to a thousand and make sure everyone got the message?'

He paused as he got out his little book of excuses.

'He died to show man that his love was my love,' he said, avoiding the question altogether.

'Well, it didn't fucking work, did it. Man carried on sinning long after his farcical appearance on Earth. Or was that all part of your divine plan to strangle the Dark slowly? How's that working out for you, by the way? What are we on now, six thousand years? That may not be long for you, but for the people you're claiming to be doing this for it's many a lifetime.

'Look, we both know what's going on here and if you don't want to come clean that's your prerogative. But at least give me another chance to put things right. You can hardly blame me for what happened in Eden, but if I can't talk Jesus into carrying on past thirty-three I deserve to go to Hell. I'll convince him to stay alive and go around the world spreading your word until everyone believes in you. Then Lucy can go fuck himself. Oh, and by the way, what was with the reptile prank? Can't you give me a human body?'

'You can only possess a body that is not worthy of a soul,' he said. 'You shall redeem yourself as a creature.'

I would be landing on the night of the Last Supper. Then I'd have a few hours to either find Judas and ruin his evening, or find Jesus and talk him into fleeing before he got his collar felt.

Twelve

This one had to be easier, I thought. How many Last Suppers could there be in this town on the one night? And I'd get to meet Jesus. I didn't look at my body for I knew what I was. I could feel my short legs and long tail, and my nose was in a constant twitch. I didn't care what I was at this stage. I was just happy to have left another one of Nobby's planets, where I'd nearly died again from boredom, waiting for the thing to spin away from its white sun. The landscape was completely flat all around with barely a rock in sight.

Landing outside of town was a tactical move, as I feared the locals there might be a bit more challenging than the pair of muppets in Eden. But my vantage point was no better; perched on my hind legs I was no more than ten inches tall.

I could hear and smell the river, which was comforting as I knew it twisted through the town, so I left my scent against a rock and gave my legs a stretch. Carefully, mind; just because there were no people nearby, it didn't mean that nothing else lurked behind the tufts of grass that grew by the side of the dusty track.

From the top of a rock, I looked across what proved to be fuck all except the shimmering heat distorting the horizon, and without much choice but to sit and wait, my thoughts inevitably drifted off to Nobby. The God who gave his son to save mankind. Although Nobby's concept of a son differed from the creatures he created to actually have sons. His idea of a son was to drag some poor bastard away from the joys of Heaven, then send him to some hellhole on Earth to convince every man and his wife he's been sent by God to tell them to believe or else.

Lucy would never create such a world, even if he could, but he was left with no choice but to pick up the pieces of life Nobby didn't want and destroy them, which he'd been doing since Nobby went with the first life that had the potential to know he existed. Lucy had obviously snuffed out the others – if there had been any others. Nobby gave no indication as to whether he'd been down this road before, nor did Lucy boast about previous victories in pissing on Nobby's acceptance of below-perfect life. But there was no need to worry. Jimmy the rat was there to save the day and set everything straight.

I understood why Jesus wanted to clock out when he did. I was sure it was fun roaming around impressing everyone with his tricks for a while, but given that he thought he was going to Heaven if he convinced Nobby of his tale of sacrifice – well, who wouldn't want to trade his miserable existence for the joys of Paradise?

What Jesus didn't know was that what awaited him was a trip to see Lucy. That would later be retold as the

KEPT IN THE DARK

Harrowing of Hell. Where Jesus saved the souls of the damned, then returned to Earth to say goodbye to his chums before floating up to Heaven. But Lucy was still there, and the fire was still raging, so maybe the truth got lost in translation and Jesus didn't really return to Earth. Maybe he'd been a naughty boy and remained in Hell, because if he ended up in Heaven, why didn't Nobby drag him out and send him back to Earth to save himself?

Perhaps Nobby didn't trust him enough to send him back down. It would've made sense, given that Jesus had clocked out early without permission. *He's clearly not up to the job. Let's hand the baton to Jimmy.*

But I was going with the story that he was in Hell. And indeed, about to go to Hell. He may not have cared about a talking rat's future, even less its mum's, but if he thought he was heading for the Dark he would surely change his plans. So I decided to keep my own plight quiet, and focus on informing Jesus about his if he didn't sort his life out.

The sun was setting, but I welcomed this as the town would surely emit light of some kind. I didn't expect a Manhattan skyline, but I guessed they'd at least have mastered fire, so my eyes swept the area until a flicker in the distance caught my attention. I stared until the one flicker turned into two, then three, and within ten minutes I was gazing at what was clearly a human settlement. I scanned three-sixty to make sure it was the only town on the horizon and made my way to the river. The track might have been quicker, but I felt safer by the water.

I scuttled along with my little legs going nineteen to the dozen and found my acceleration and agility were phenomenal. Not that I was impressed, but I was over worrying about my looks and physical limitations, or whether I even had a body. I was in Nobby's pocket and had to make do with what I'd been given.

Although hidden by the long grass at the water's edge, I felt vulnerable, and wondered what predators were out there. Cats? Owls? Snakes? Don't talk to me about fucking snakes, I thought, but had to treat such issues as obstacles, not dangers. Getting eaten was not an option.

The town lights were out of sight in the long grass, so I soldiered on and thought about my plan. What plan? Did I focus on finding Jesus first, or Judas? I guessed Jesus would be the easiest to recognise, if he looked the same as he did on TV. But he was in hiding, getting ready for his grand finale, and according to the Bible, Judas didn't get the order from Jesus to betray him until the Last Supper. So unless either of them were in the phone book, I was going to have to rely on a bit of luck.

After a longer-than-anticipated journey that resulted in a pair of burning lungs and four weary legs, I came upon a town that superseded Adam's architectural shortcomings but was not exactly prime real estate. I couldn't make out whether the buildings were constructed shoddy from scratch, or had once been relatively smart and were just badly maintained. They were stone structures for the most part, but there was far too much wood involved, especially in the roofs, and in the heat, along with the naked flames people used for light, I guessed they must have had a fair few house fires. Maybe Jesus turned the wine back into water at such an event.

The houses didn't have what you would call windows – there was no glass, just a hole with a thin rag for a curtain.

KEPT IN THE DARK

And this was the town where the only man in world history who could've magicked up a few panes of glass lived. So much for loving thy neighbour. A plus for me though – I'd be able to earwig and smell food easier, which would make finding a bunch of lads having a farewell bash easier.

A shadow crossed the road twenty feet ahead and I froze. The grass distorted my vision but I knew what it was, so I held my breath and inched backwards towards the river. Why in God's name was I a rat? Talk about making things difficult. I was doing this to save Nobby's reputation, after all. You'd think he'd have made me something more noble than a rodent. But I had to put such concerns to the back of my mind. There was a cat on the prowl, and I guessed that tins of Whiskers were in short supply in this town. A juicy rat would be most welcome to a hungry stray.

Once my tail touched the water I relaxed, but then there was a squelch as my nose was pushed into the mud and I struggled to breathe, waiting for teeth to sink in. Whatever held me down was too big to be a cat's paw and I feared its owner could swallow me whole. Mission failed. Thanks for coming. See you in Hell. But nothing. The creature's foot moved an inch, allowing me to twist my head and take a breath, then it snorted and shifted enough for me to slip free and dart into the scrub.

I rubbed my face back to normality and crept back to see what had crushed it. I didn't want trouble, I didn't want revenge, it was an accident, it was my fault for walking backward in the first place. The truth was, I knew what the snort was. It was a woman coughing. But my hope of checking out the local talent was dashed when I saw an old lady who looked a hundred bent over the river, filling up a tatty wooden bucket.

'Not like that, dear. Keep your back straight and your legs bent,' I whispered.

Next to her on the ground was a basket of food that didn't look half-bad. The bread looked fresh, the fruit ripe, and whatever else smelt rather tasty. I went in for a nibble. My tiny body was going to need all the energy it could handle.

With her bucket full, the woman coughed and groaned as she straightened up, and I had a good look from behind the loaf I was feasting on. Her face was worn and tired and she was probably younger than she looked. She was missing her front teeth and I suspected the food wasn't necessarily for her. A woman's lot in these times, I supposed. I also realised she was unlikely to give a rat directions to the local Passover so I decided to be on my way.

But not before asking her anyway.

She screamed and dropped her bucket. The water slopped out and knocked the basket over, forcing me to jump down, and she gasped as the food spilled onto the dusty ground and the basket rolled into the river with a light splash. She turned to watch it sink as I ran back into the scrub, then she ran for her life, minus her water and groceries. I couldn't help but feel guilty.

*

The sky was now filled with a million stars and a quarter moon, and I wondered what would qualify as a party around there. The music would be a bit lame, I imagined,

KEPT IN THE DARK

and it was a fair bet the wine tasted dodgy. I crept back to the track and sniffed under every door, listened through every window, and thought again about Lucy and Nobby. In a way, I was flattered the two superpowers of the Universe were fighting for my attention, but I also felt humiliated that they were using me to try and outwit each other.

The Romans were famous for their innovative approach to sanitation, but sadly that didn't stretch beyond themselves. There was horseshit everywhere. Which proved useful, as not only could I hide behind it, but if I were seen, people would be less likely to approach if I was next to a pile of manure.

Up ahead, two men exited a house and walked up the street, and I guessed I might as well follow them. As I made ground, from the safety of the shadows I noticed they weren't talking, just walking with their heads down. Hardly in the mood for a party, I thought. Didn't even have a bottle between them. But they were all I had to go on, and it wasn't as if I expected to find a bunch of pissed-up blokes wearing *I'm with Jesus* T-shirts.

The two men trundled along the road with me staying as close as I dared until they stopped outside a house. I didn't wonder if it was Jesus' gaff. The place wasn't pretty and a wanted man wouldn't hide so close to the main hub. The door opened and a third man emerged, the light from inside giving me a good look at their faces. They all sported beards and wore medallion-like necklaces over their ankle-length dresses, and after a brief and muffled exchange in a strange language, they carried on their way.

It then dawned on me that I had assumed Jesus spoke English. Surely Nobby didn't expect me to use improvised sign language to give the news to his precious son.

The road veered uphill more than I was comfortable with and I began to feel the pace. My legs were collapsing underneath me, my throat was dry, and I knew I could be going in the wrong direction and the Bee Gees were off to milk a cow. But with no other activity in sight, I kept going and hoped they were soon joined by nine or ten others.

I hadn't forgotten about the cat, but soon learned that staying in the shadows wasn't the best strategy to avoid it, for it, too, was hiding in the shadows. All I felt was a paw clasp my back and teeth sink into my neck. Pinned down and helpless, I waited for the bite to tighten, but much to my surprise the animal released its grip and allowed me to crawl away. Crawl being the operative word as my back legs were useless. I dragged my ripped body as fast as my front legs would carry me, searching for a hole to disappear into, but blood was in my eyes and I couldn't keep them open. Then the paw slammed down again.

Fuck! This prick wants to play with me before eating me.

The cat slapped and clawed me a few more times and I knew I had to act. I could hear the river and knew if I could make it there intact I was sure to be safe, so I relaxed my body and played dead. The cat nudged me with its paw. Then again. On the third nudge, I snapped my head around and nipped its nose with my little bucked teeth. The cat screeched and jumped back.

I was off. My injuries were excruciating, but I hoped my unexpected aggression had done the trick and made the cat fuck off. I reached the water's edge and went for the final push, but I was going nowhere. My back leg was caught up. I struggled, but the cat had hold of it good and I prepared to be the first blood sacrifice of the evening as another paw scratched at the wounds on my back. Then I somehow slipped free and wasted no time diving in.

I couldn't see a thing underwater and coughed and spluttered as I tried to keep my head above the surface. The water helped wash the blood from my eyes, but my legs were floppy sticks of pain. Except one of my back legs which I couldn't feel at all. The current was taking me back the way I'd come and I didn't want to have to restart my journey. Too tired and in too much pain, I looked for a safe place on the bank to hide and rest. The other side was too far, and besides, I'd only have to swim back again, so I doggy-paddled towards the edge and looked for the longest grass I could find. At least I tried to, but I kept veering into the middle. I rolled onto my back to see I only had three legs. Old Tinkerbell must have ripped one off in the last attack. No wonder I was nearly swimming in circles. I floated to the bank and hauled my sorry arse out of the water, only to see Tinkerbell six feet away with my leg in her mouth.

What had become of Jimmy Linton? Born into a childhood blighted by a cruel and violent father, that ended when I watched my beloved mother die on the kitchen floor. Then the long wait to avenge her death, in a battle which ended with my own death, only to find out there was more to life than death, and now reduced to a half-drowned, three-legged rat, with a shredded body and a hungry cat on my case.

Tinkerbell's scraggy, moonlit silhouette made her look even more sinister and I knew she was waiting for me to make the first move. But what was that going to be? I couldn't go back into the water as I would surely drown, and I'd never outrun my assailant with only three legs. Part of me wanted to snatch my leg back and give the cat another nip on the nose, but I had to put personal anger to one side. *Maybe later.*

I braved a glance through the long grass and saw a dark lump. I had no idea what it was, but hoped it could offer protection and made a dash. The object took shape as the grass thinned out and I realised it was the bucket the old hag had dropped when I scared the shit out of her. The cat's shadow began to overtake me, but I felt no more than a scratch on my tail as I made it in. Then, squeezing the last energy from my remaining legs, I took off like a crazed hamster until the bucket spun over the bank and hit the water. A wave rushed in and slammed me against the bottom and splinters tore into my wounds, but the force helped the bucket to right itself and head off downstream. I poked my head over the edge to see Tinkerbell staring out at her lost meal.

'Fuck you, cat cunt. Nobody eats Jimmy Linton,' I yelled, before slumping to the bottom of the bucket, exhausted and way behind schedule.

Not that I had a schedule, but I had to take five and check the damage to my body, or what was left of it, but I couldn't make use of the shaft of moonlight flickering around as I rocked from side to side.

The water inside wasn't a problem. There wasn't enough to sink the bucket and I was glad of a drink. The problem was how to talk Jesus out of being crucified. Sounded ridiculous when you thought about it. That was if I even found him. I was sure Jesus was loyal to his flock, and only his flock apparently. He probably wouldn't flee on the advice of a beaten-up, three-legged, talking rat, even if it was to save his life.

The safety of the bucket was welcome, but I couldn't stay there unless Jesus fancied a bit of skinny-dipping before supper. Plus, the river was twisting away from the town, which meant I had to lose the bucket. I hooked my front legs over the edge, whispered something under my breath about Nobby being a cunt, then splosh! I was back in. I adapted my leg strokes to accommodate my missing appendage and paddled slowly to the edge.

It was unlikely Tinkerbell had followed me downriver, but that didn't mean there weren't other creatures on the hunt, and I froze at the slightest sound until my paranoia settled as I headed towards the nearest building with light. I had to make sure I wasn't bleeding to death. It sure felt like it.

The house was the last in a row at the bottom of a daunting hill that rose and faded into the dark sky. Faint light crept through the edges of a curtain dangling over a hole in the wall. I clambered onto the ledge, not knowing what I might expect to find in a two-thousand-year-old living room. *They might have a cat.* Taking no chances, I listened and sniffed before taking a peek. It was pretty basic. The room was about twelve feet by twelve, dimly lit by a couple of flames housed in fittings on the adjoining wall to next door. It had a high ceiling and a tall window in the other three walls, each draped with a grubby curtain, and shoddy wooden furniture was scattered about the floor. In the corner was a bed with a woman lying on it. It was the woman I'd encountered by the river. The woman whose bucket had saved my life. Her eyes were closed, but I got the impression she wasn't asleep. It also looked like she'd been crying.

Once I was confident she was alone, I crept passed the curtain and dropped to the floor. My stump took more weight than I'd intended and I let out an involuntary squeak. The woman stirred, and I waited for her to settle again before dragging myself behind a box to examine my injuries. There were deep lacerations on my back, and although they were nothing compared to the lashing Jesus was going to get if he didn't play ball, they needed attention.

With one eye on the woman, I searched for a makeshift bandage. It was easy to stay hidden, but I left a trail of blood, so it wouldn't be hard for anyone or anything to find me. It also meant I was losing blood, and I was sure that rats don't have the eight pints humans do.

With no bandage-like material lying around, and certainly nothing rat-sized, I crept back up to the window ledge and nibbled at the curtain in silence. The last thing I needed was for the woman to see me again and scream the place down. As I gnawed away, I looked down at the box I'd hidden behind. It held four bottles that looked like wine of some description, but I had no desire to taste it as I wasn't confident about the grape quality there. Then I nearly bit through my tongue as the door flew open and a man burst in. He looked agitated, but not as much as the old lady who rose from her bed, gabbling away in her foreign tongue, and I wondered if she was reliving her adventure by the river. She made a talking gesture with her hand and threw her arms in the air. *I guess so.*

I couldn't help a chuckle, but stopped when the man struck her face with the back of his hand. She dropped like a stone and blood splattered over the wall as he followed up with a loud and aggressive rant, which I assumed to be peppered with Arabic swear words, then he wrenched her from the floor, yelled some more, and pointed for her to pick up the box of wine. Once she'd done so he pushed her out the door and followed after her, slamming the door behind them. A surge of anger washed over me as memories of Fatty hitting Mum filled my head. Only this time it was *my* fault.

Now alone and in peace, I nibbled, gnawed, ripped and tore at the curtain until I'd severed a sizable strip, then winced as I wrapped it tight around my body and tied the frayed ends together as best as I could with my little paws – not easy without opposable thumbs – and leapt out the window.

Thirteen

The feuding couple had disappeared, which didn't matter as I couldn't see the point in following them, not with one of them a woman. Unless she was there to clean up the supper after they retired to the garden. Plus, I felt I'd already done enough damage to their evening, so I took a breath and started up the hill, and as I limped along I wondered what I was going to do now. Being a snake was a walk in the park compared to this.

By the time I reached the brow of the hill, I was ruined. My legs were being eroded away by the ground, my stump throbbed like crazy and my pea-sized lungs were burning holes in my chest. But then as the road levelled out more buildings came into sight, giving me a little boost. Several clumps of people were milling around, but not enough to make a dozen. Not to mention some of them were women. The biggest group of men together was four; they stood at the side of the road as though waiting for a bus. I noticed that three of them were Barry, Maurice and Robin. Eight missing.

KEPT IN THE DARK

A rising hum over the hill made me scuttle back towards the brow. People were coming, a few of them by the sound of it. I waited in the grass. *This could be interesting.* A halo of fire emerged on the horizon and the hum turned into footsteps as a dozen men appeared with fiery torches. Twelve men, tall and strong. Just what I was looking for. I watched them approach, thinking I surely couldn't be that lucky.

I wasn't that lucky. They were soldiers of some kind, with somewhere to be as they marched past – fire in one hand, sword in the other, wearing red blouses and metal-clad skirts. Were they looking for Jesus too?

The bus queue men glanced at each other and took it as their cue to disappear between two buildings. I was safe behind them within a few seconds, and when they each picked up a box filled with food and drink from behind a wall and headed into the darkness, I knew they were up to something clandestine. If it wasn't a jolly-up with Jesus, it was either to do a job or go dogging. I put my faith in Jesus and wished I could get close enough to hop in one of the boxes and save my legs. I felt vulnerable and feared that things with better night vision than me were out there.

We came into a dry field with the odd tuft of grass which I used to keep myself hidden. *They ain't milking no cow at this time of night in a field with no cows*, I thought. *There must be a hideout near here.* A group of men carrying food and booze, walking into nowhere on the very night of the Last Supper. That was good enough for me.

The four men stopped when they were a long throw from the town, and from the shadow of a lone tree a further seven men appeared, each with their own box. Again, no verbal greeting took place, and in silence they waited. Eleven. *They must surely be waiting for the twelfth.*

And so they waited. And waited. After half an hour the men looked as frustrated as I felt, and I wondered if the missing one, if there was only one, was Judas, and his absence was due to his desire to earn a few quid by letting slip the whereabouts of the said Messiah.

I heard the approaching footsteps before the others, and as the twelfth man came into sight, with a little old lady struggling behind, I saw it was the couple from the house. She was still carrying the box of wine with a loaf of bread now balanced on top, and I guessed if it was Judas he hadn't been paid yet, or he would've surely replaced the dropped hamper with something a little more generous than a loaf of bread.

Once within whispering earshot, the final edition to the equation broke the vow of silence his associates had been observing and uttered a few disgruntled words. His tone was subdued, and given the reaction from the other eleven, who finally decided to use their gift of speech to communicate, I got the impression all was not well between them. Were they complaining about him being late? Or quizzing him about *why* he was late? Either way, I was convinced they were the twelve in question and knew I had to stick to them like glue. The brief conversation petered out and the woman-beating latecomer grabbed the box from the old lady, who gladly flopped her arms down and trundled back the way she came.

The rest of us continued away from the town. Soon the odd tree began to pop up and block the moonlight, making me forever nervous about what was out there. There was also a breeze, strong enough to carry the scent of smoke, which I took to indicate human presence. Or hopefully the half-human, half-chosen one. I overtook the box-laden party-goers with a shortcut through taller grass and hoped Jesus was already there. *Surely he wouldn't turn up late for the Last Supper.*

By the time the divine hideout, a small house, came into view, I was exhausted. My back was only held together by my refusal to fail, and I was reduced to dragging myself along with my front paws. A regular rat would've resigned itself to being carrion long ago. But I was no regular rat, and as I scraped down the home straight, I focused on what I was going to say to Jesus if he was there.

The house was silent, with a glow through a side window and a thin line of light under the front door. The gap didn't look big enough for me to squeeze through, but I wasn't going to climb any more walls; maybe my reduced body mass could make it. I stifled my cries as I stretched out and stuck my nose under the door. The welcome smell of sweet fruit and freshly baked bread tickled my nose, but I couldn't detect the sweat of a man who was soon to be crucified. The blood on my back acted like a lubricant, and with a grimace and a groan, I slid through the gap and darted to the nearest corner of what proved to be a large dining room.

Fire fixtures on the walls gave a low glow to the room, which featured a long table, beautifully handcrafted from wood, standing proudly in the middle. It was strangely low, with plates, bowls and goblets all laid out ready for a feast. Down one side was a line of lumpy cushions. *Why no chairs?* I thought.

I tiptoed through the room, though not sure why, as I didn't expect Jesus to be particularly aggressive, even towards vermin. At the far end was a door ajar and I sensed a presence on the other side, so I crept up and poked my head through. It led onto a veranda, and there, in classical moonlight, stood Jesus. He wore a sack-cloth dress no better than that of his disciples, and stared into the night desert. I didn't know how I knew it was Jesus, I just knew. Or maybe I just hoped.

I stared at the back of the Messiah's head and shivered. Something about Jesus was disturbing, yet compelling. I held my stare until he broke the ice.

'Why is a creature with clothes and speech?' he said in crisp, clean English, still with his back to me.

I couldn't believe my ears. 'Are you talking to me?' I said.

'Indeed, I am.'

'But I never said anything.'

'But you have come to talk, yes?'

'I've been sent by the Lord.'

Jesus spun around and glared at me. Not the reaction I expected, but it told me he wasn't impressed. He was tall and slim, with a bushy beard that covered his cheeks and hung down his neck like a wizard's. I wondered if it was his regular look or a disguise.

'The Lord?' he said. 'But why does he send a creature?'

I shivered again. 'Yeah, that's what I'd like to know. Anyway, he said you need to have a word with yourself.'

'I pray daily. The Lord knows that.'

'No, I mean about the miracles and stuff. Apparently, you were only supposed to use them in emergencies, and instead travel the world preaching the word, and let's be honest, you have been taking the piss a bit. In thirty-three years you've barely left town. How the fuck is anyone else supposed to get the message?'

'But I cannot abandon my flock,' he said.

'Your flock is supposed to be all of mankind, not just the sorry bunch of losers that follow you around. It wouldn't be so bad if you used your powers in the spirit of love and compassion for all, instead of a sideshow for those who happened to live nearby.

'I mean, let's take the walking-on-water stunt. What did that achieve for mankind? Don't get me wrong, it was a neat trick and I hope it got you laid, but it did fuck all for anyone else. And the water into wine episode? How many lives did that save? Oh, and let's have a look at the feeding of the five thousand. Why only five thousand? It didn't save the world, it only fed your flock for a day.

'Anyway, the bottom line is you either fuck off and preach to the rest of the world, or he stops granting the miracles and you get crucified before going back for a bollocking.'

I wasn't sure if Jesus understood every word I'd said, but I hoped he got the drift.

He hadn't. He stared down at me, as though trying to decide whether to squash me with his sandal or give me a piece of cheese.

'Let me put it another way,' I said. 'Have you been to see the Dark yet?'

'I am a believer. I shall go to Heaven.'

That's one advantage Jesus had over me. He had direct knowledge of Nobby's existence, through his miracles if nothing else, so he had every reason to believe he would end up in Heaven. Whereas I had nothing to go on except a loud mouth. If in my lifetime Nobby had let me know he existed, I would've sure used it to spread the word. Probably.

But the last place I wanted Jesus to think he was going was Heaven.

'No, you're not,' I said. 'Your mission won't be over if you die. You're going to Hell to try and save the wretched non-believers, but you will fail and remain at the mercy of the Dark.'

'The Lord would not let such an act be taken against me,' he said. 'I shall not be forsaken.'

'Do you really want to take the risk? Nobby won't save you.'

'Nobby?'

'The Lord. Look, I'm not just passing on the message. If you don't do as he says I'll be in as much trouble as you. I mean, look what he's done to me already. I'm a fucking rat.'

'You have not always been a rat?'

'As it happens, no,' I said. 'How many talking rats have you seen? I used to be a man… look, it's a long story but we have to work fast here or we'll both end up in Hell.'

'But I am awaiting guests.'

'Yeah, I know, they'll be here any minute. It's that Judas prick that's gonna stitch you up.'

'Judas Iscariot?'

'If that's his name.'

'What do you know of him?'

Nothing, really. But I wasn't going to let him know that.

'I'm from the future. I know everything that you don't,' I said.

'Should my brethren turn against me, the Lord shall grant me the strength to forgive.'

'You won't have time to forgive. You'll be taken away and killed, then the Lord will send you to the Dark. Trust me, we both have a lot to gain if you leave now and a lot to lose if you don't.'

He looked up at the stars, as though waiting for Nobby to confirm or deny my story. On hearing nothing, he shifted his attention back to me.

'If you are from the future, you will cease to exist if the future is altered,' he said.

'I know, that's why I'm here. It's better than going to Hell.'

I didn't expect Jesus to care much if a rat ended up in Hell, even if it could talk, and I didn't blame him for being suspicious about taking advice from one. Not to mention he had good reasons for calling it a day on Earth, at least until now, but this was about more than saving me. I needed my mum to cease to exist as well.

'Why will the Lord send you to Hell?' he said.

'Because he's a fucking nutcase. His excuse is that I died a non-believer, but he's given me a chance to save myself by talking some sense into you.'

'The Lord will not forsake me.'

'Yes, he will,' I said.

'No, he won't.'

'Are we really going to do this?'

It was turning out harder than I'd anticipated. He had every right to think the rat was full of shit and that he was going to Heaven. He was Nobby's chosen one. Why would Nobby send him to Hell just for dying too early? This made me think he was going to Heaven after all, and Nobby had passed the buck onto me for some reason. A non-believing murderer who should've been rotting in Hell from the moment he died. At least according to Nobby's logic.

'I am sorry, but you must leave,' he said. 'My guests will not take kindly to a creature so strange.'

It was clear Jesus wasn't about to change his mind anytime soon, and as the guys would arrive any second I had to change tact, and hope to identify Judas and stop him blabbing. How I would do that, I had no idea. I didn't expect Jesus to give any introductions, and even if he did, I couldn't see Judas taking any more notice of a talking rat than Jesus had. Besides, I assumed Jesus only spoke English because he was Jesus. Everyone else spoke bollocks, and I didn't see why Judas would be any different.

A knock echoed through the house and stopped me from replying. Jesus smiled, then walked over, knelt down and touched my back with his palm. A warm sensation went through my body as the pain subsided; my wounds healed, and my leg grew back. I looked up, and for a moment felt guilty about giving him a hard time for his other miracles.

Nonetheless, I knew I'd outstayed my welcome, although I had no intention of leaving yet. I nodded in

KEPT IN THE DARK

sincere appreciation, then walked away in fake obedience as Jesus made his way to welcome his guests. Then I doubled back and hid among the cushions by the table. Jesus placed his hands on the shoulders of each man as they entered, and I guessed a full hug would've been on offer if the men weren't hampered with a box. Except the one who turned up late, when Jesus made the effort to lean over and whisper in his ear. Was he telling him to betray him, or to not betray him? Or maybe it wasn't Judas, and Jesus was having a quiet word about him only bringing a loaf of bread when everyone else had made the effort.

The twelve guests unpacked their boxes and spread the food over the table as they made small talk with Jesus, but I didn't think it wise to join in; for all I knew, Jesus might flip and give me my injuries back. He would've known I was still nearby, but what else could I do? Go and play in the sand and wait for the inevitable?

Jesus circled the room to light more wall fires and I wondered why he wouldn't put on a show on his last night. Light the room with a snap of a finger at least.

When they had all finished their chores, the disciples chose a cushion one by one, with Jesus in the middle and six of them either side. I had to continually alter my hiding position as they shuffled their backsides around. *Strange way to eat dinner*, I thought, but they seemed to have made themselves comfortable.

They filled their goblets with wine and their plates with food, and I couldn't help but notice Jesus' lack of table manners. The others weren't exactly eating as though they were dining with the Queen, but Jesus was shovelling his food and chewing with his mouth open like a bear. Bits caught in his beard without so much as a polite wipe of his sleeve, and he sure could put his wine away. I shivered as it reminded me of my father, who would eat and drink in very much the same way. Although if Jesus knew he was going to be crucified it was understandable he'd want a skinful beforehand. Another similarity was the grunts and hocks he and his followers made when they spoke. It sounded like my father when he sleep-talked after he'd drunk himself unconscious. Their language replaced vowels with coughs.

But that was where the similarities ended. Everything else was very much the opposite. Instead of healing my wounds, my father would inflict them. Instead of inviting friends around for dinner, he would go down the pub and fight them. Instead of walking on water, he was terrified of it, refusing to even step under the shower. And he was positively petrified of rats.

The atmosphere loosened after everyone had settled and had a drink and I could have done with one myself, but the rancid, vinegary stuff they were throwing back didn't smell like any wine I'd ever tasted. How hard would it have been for Jesus to knock up a few bottles of decent claret for this special occasion?

I lost sight of him when one of the guests repositioned himself, so I slunk around the back of the cushions and up to a beam in the roof, and looked down and wondered if he'd given any consideration to what he'd been told. I didn't think so, and with my now redundant bandage wrapped around my neck like a cloak, I floated down onto the table. Everyone stopped eating and stared.

KEPT IN THE DARK

Right. Which one of you fuckers is Judas?' I yelled.

'They will not understand your tongue,' said Jesus, his own tongue beginning to slur as the disciples diverted their gaze to their leader and his apparent ability to speak rat.

'Then you tell me which one he is,' I said.

'You shall stay silent and hidden or you shall leave. Such a creature is not welcome at the food table.'

I found that ironic, given Jesus' display of pigotry.

'I'll leave when you leave,' I said. 'Which had better be soon, or by the time you've pissed out that disgusting wine you'll be strung up on a cross.'

'Your tone is one of a desperate soul, but my duty is to the Lord and my devotion is to my brethren. None of whom shall I forsake, just as they shall not forsake me.'

'You just don't get it, do you? Never mind forsake, how about for fuck's sake?'

Suddenly, Jesus disappeared into thin air and simultaneously I felt something grab my tail. Before I knew anything else I was flying through the window to land a good thirty feet away. Although I was relatively unharmed and had to give Jesus credit for the trick, I was not a happy rat.

So what now? The only two people that could save my skin were in that hideaway. One couldn't speak English, and the other was a pissed-up, stubborn animal abuser with magic powers. If I could've spoken their lingo, I would've told the Romans where Jesus was myself. Wankers.

The town lights were out of sight through the trees. I could hear the faint chatter of humans when the wind blew the right way, but there wasn't much point in heading back there as I couldn't understand what anyone said. Not to mention I didn't fancy another few rounds with Tinkerbell. I could've crept back to the party, but wasn't sure how far Jesus' rat radar reached, and felt if I got caught again I could end up in the next town. My only option was to stay put and wait for everyone to leave, especially Judas. I still wasn't sure which one he was, but I took a punt it was the one who turned up late with only a loaf of bread and some wine. Only a lying, disloyal pig would hit a woman. And Jesus did have a word in his ear.

My suspicions grew twenty minutes later when that very man left the party and headed towards town. Which told me Jesus hadn't listened to a word I'd said.

'I know where you're going, you sneaky little shit,' I said under my breath as I waited for him to pass.

He headed back towards cat territory, so I stayed close, as I would've sooner had him see me than Tinkerbell. But although I'd identified Judas, I still had to stop him from squealing to the Romans.

Fourteen

The town was awash with legs scissoring in all directions and I did well to avoid being trampled as we reached the main street. The chatter of local gossip created a growling hum under the flaming torches that were crammed into the crevices along the stone walls, giving a spooky flicker to market stalls that stretched down one side. Off-beat drum music pounded nearby with people happily wailing away like they were being tortured. Early busking, I guessed. I darted under the stalls and struggled to pick out Judas' feet among the blur of sandals as he hurried along.

The line of stalls ended with the last building and I welcomed the thinning crowd as the hum faded with the lights. But the terrain changed to grassland full of dips and mounds with rocks hidden in the dark ground, and I had to tread carefully. I was forever grateful to Jesus for my new leg, unless Judas had already stitched him up and was off to hang himself in the woods, in which case I may as well have been running on a hamster wheel for all the good it would've done me.

After a few minutes, we came to an expanse of sandy ground with a building two hundred feet or so ahead. It was surrounded in darkness but looked way more up-market than the knocked-up huts in town, which meant it housed important people. Something was about to go down inside and I had to stop it.

Judas reduced his speed to a hasty walk now his destination was in sight, and I was happy to follow suit as I was about to have a heart attack. I had a sniff for water. My top lip was stuck dry to my gum, and as I prized it free with my tongue, the moon went out as if by a light switch and I was airborne before I registered the talons in my back. I twisted my body as far as my ligaments would allow, then there was a jolt and a screech and from ten feet up I dropped. The air rushing against my lacerated back felt like stabbing needles and I hoped the few scraps left hanging from my assailant's claws were enough to keep it satisfied.

My legs were running before I landed and only stopped when I ran head-first into a rock. I dug my petrified paws in the dust, hoping it would swallow me up. The sky appeared empty, but I was too paranoid to move and had to assume Judas was now inside, ready to break Nobby's heart for a few silver beans. But whether I was going to see it, never mind stop it, was anyone's guess. Judas might soon be on his way out with a smile, thinking about the guilty pleasures he could now afford. Or they could still be in there, negotiating the deal over a cup of tea and a biscuit. All I could do was get there safely. Whatever it was that had attacked me was probably not too far away, and I could've been the only rodent running around like an idiot, asking to be eaten.

After my heartbeat settled and my crushed nose stopped throbbing, I crept through the long grass to within twenty feet of the building. There was no light from inside and nothing but silence in the air. Outside the entrance was a large trough with sand scattered on the ground around it and, across the top, a wooden frame with a dozen golf-ball-sized holes in it – I wondered if it was some kind of torture implement. It made good cover as I closed in and scanned the building, which was about sixty feet wide and hard to tell how far back it stretched. Slits for windows, too narrow for someone to enter, sat high above either side of a wooden door embedded in the stone-block wall. The roof blended with the dark sky, but looked made from tiles of some sort. Outside the front door was a stone porch, and crouched in the corner was Judas with his head in his hands.

What did this mean? Was he deliberating over what he was about to do or feeling sick about what he'd just done? Maybe he'd missed the guards and was kicking himself because he'd already spent some of the money on tick. Maybe he'd gone in there and killed them all and was just plain shitting himself. I had to assume he was still waiting for them, but I couldn't tell him not to do what Jesus had asked him to, and even if I could've he was never going to betray his Messiah. If you know what I mean.

I had no idea how much time I had and thought of ways to stop him, like loosening a roof tile and letting it slide onto his head. But even if I managed it without him hearing, there was no guarantee it would've put him out of action. He could've just ended up with a bump. And I couldn't scare him off. A rat had jumped in front of him while he was eating and he'd almost seemed pleased, so seeing a rat as he was coming to terms with having to seal the fate of his magic friend would hardly send him running for his mum. I stayed hidden and wondered what I'd missed.

Nothing, as it turned out. I heard the soldiers before Judas and stayed in the shadows as their torches illuminated the corner. It was the same dozen I'd seen earlier, plus another man who led the way. He didn't look like a soldier, but it was clear he was in charge and his clothes looked more like a collection of expensive house rugs than the ragged garments everyone else in town wore. The night air was cooler, but it was still warm. He must have been sweating his bollocks off under that lot. The Chief handed his torch to the man behind who went in line with the others, and one by one they doused the flames in the sand trough and placed the handles in the holes in the rack above. *Fair enough.*

One soldier kept his torch alight and led the way to the door, but they still hadn't seen Judas, who I thought was brave if not stupid to be standing in the shadows ready to surprise a bunch of men with swords. He finally stepped into the torchlight, and the soldiers stood poised as he addressed the Chief. *What if they slice him up?* I thought. My work would be done. Then the Chief put a soft hand on Judas' shoulder and said a few smiling words, and everyone relaxed as he unlocked the door and pushed it open.

KEPT IN THE DARK

The last man in swung the door behind him and I threw myself in the corner of the threshold and tensed my body. My scream as the heavy wooden block crushed me was drowned out by the chattering of the soldiers, and I felt blood squirt out of my wounds and spray the doorframe, but I did my job and the latch never caught, and I stayed as still as a hooker's body as the fireman went ahead to light the fancy fixtures that decorated a long hallway.

Once the way was sufficiently lit, they set off single file with their boots crunching along the stone floor, so I left the door ajar and caught up. There were casual mutterings, but also an atmosphere of business. Or maybe that was biased, based on previous knowledge.

They might be off to play poker. Maybe Judas decided to try and win the cash instead.

The parade halted at an archway, and the fireman raced around with his torch to reveal a large windowless hall with a high ceiling, decorated with faded green paint that was a downgrade from Dulux. The stone floor was bare of any furniture, and each wall housed its own dark archway. Two soldiers peeled away to stand either side of the one opposite as the fireman led the rest through. I detoured around the shadowy walls to avoid the eyes of the bored-looking guards, and was soon back in pursuit down a dark tunnel with a rough wooden floor. Passages sprouted off on both sides and the men disappeared into one.

I followed the scent of smoke and the echo of their boots as I zigzagged through the maze, gaining with every second. Abruptly the clatter of their boots stopped and I upped my pace to see them piling through a door at a dead end. I had to dig my arse into the rough floorboards to stop crashing into it as it slammed in my face.

I pulled out the splinters lodged in my backside and sniffed under the door. I didn't know how sniffing would help, but it was my best sense and it just seemed the natural thing to do. I didn't know if silver had an odour and wouldn't have recognized it if it did, so all I got from what wafted under the door was confirmation that it was too early in human history for showers and deodorant.

The dim light emanating from around the edges of the badly fitted door never made it to the first corner and I followed my own scent back in the dark. Maybe there was an outside window into the room. I bit the ankle of one of the archway guards then sped across the hall and along the hallway. The door was still open and I slipped through the gap without a thought for anything else. I then saw that I had plenty else to think about when I near-on crashed into an owl with an injured wing, flapping around on the porch. Guessing it hadn't mistimed a telegraph pole or been hit by a car, I sensed a predator nearby. And a big one if it had brought down an owl. Shreds of skin hung from the owl's talons and I realised it was what had given me a ride in the air earlier.

The bird kicked off with a noise that didn't sound like a mating call, and I got the strange impression it was asking for help. *On your bike*, I thought, *especially if there's a bigger monster out there*. I gave it a wide berth, and nearly jumped out of my shredded skin when it began squawking like a distressed parrot. *This could alert whatever attacked it, and if it's big enough it might fancy me as a starter*. I had to shut the damn thing up.

KEPT IN THE DARK

But retrieving my strips of skin from the razor-like claws that lunged at me was no easy task, and I picked up a few more nicks and cuts to go with the lacerations on my back. Changing tack, I jumped in the trough and tunnelled under the sand, wincing as it ground into my cuts, then resurfaced and returned to the owl. I picked my moment, then climbed on its head and shook myself, spraying the sand into its big round eyes. It flopped on its side, blinking like a bastard as I wrapped a stretch of my skin around its beak as best as I could. Without warning, the owl slid backwards and I jumped down to see Tinkerbell plucking the thing alive, right there on the doorstep. The owl tried to cry out, but I'd done a good job considering. Although it had now been a waste of time.

The cat continued to rid the owl of its feathers with one eye on me. I hoped she liked owl more than rat as I bounded back inside. Tinkerbell, perhaps confident her larger prize wouldn't go anywhere, bounded in after me. But I didn't have time to play Tom and Jerry all night and had to lose her. We raced across the big hall and passed the guards, who hollered and cheered as the cat and mouse zoomed into the dark.

Going back to the occupied room was suicide. I needed confinement and prayed for a rat-sized, cat-proof, box to crawl into, but all I found was another door. There was a gap at the bottom, but as I squeezed under, the door came with me, creating an opening at the side. I tried to push it closed, but it was too heavy, so I looked for a hiding place.

Moonlight crept through two small high windows to reveal the silhouettes of strange ornaments on a shelf that went around the walls of a small storeroom. Not my cup of tea, but they looked valuable as bits of gold and silver shone from them like fairy lights. At this stage I couldn't be sure Tinkerbell was still chasing me; she might have gone back to the owl and to hell with the measly rat. But I'd made a similar mistake earlier and wasn't about to repeat it.

I climbed some scattered boxes on the floor to the shelf and tried to scale the slime-covered wall to a window, but I slid back down with lumps of goo on my paws and struggled to wipe it off, keeping an eye on the door. I didn't know if the gap was big enough for the cat, but it wasn't going to take much to make it big enough. A paw appeared and tapped the floor, as though I would be stupid enough to hide just inside. Then a pair of flared nostrils followed and the door edged open a millimetre at a time. I had to do something and snaked between the valuables on the shelf to the corner behind the door. It was no use hiding in one of the pots – not only would I risk being stuck and missing all the fun with Judas and Jesus, but Tinkerbell had already proven to be a tenacious hunter and would no doubt happily go through every pot, vase, box, nook and cranny in the room until she found me.

The uneven floorboards catching the underside of the door and slowing Tinkerbell's progress bought me a few seconds to panic and climb inside the nearest vase. It was about two feet tall with thick sides and lumps of shiny metal embedded in it told me it was heavy, so I poked my head over the top and grasped the rim with my tiny paw fingers.

KEPT IN THE DARK

'Come on, Tinkers,' I said as I rocked back and forth like a madman.

I dismounted when Tinkerbell was a cigarette paper away from squeezing in, and as the vase toppled, I listened for the crash to leave her trapped and in pain. But all I got was a dull thud followed by a yelp as the door caught the cat's tail as it closed.

Now I was in big trouble. The vase was blocking the gap under the door. Tinkerbell had nothing to do except turn the place upside down and find the little shit who had her locked in there with a sore tail. I shat myself, literally; a few pea-sized pellets rolled onto the shelf. I flicked one at Tinkerbell with my tail and thought about my old leg digesting in her stomach as it sailed through the air. The cat wasn't to know the leg had once belonged to the rat that just flicked a lump of poo at her head, but as soon as she retrieved the object that caught her ear, she seemed to recognize it as coming from food. I flicked another, in the hope it would cause a distraction long enough for Jesus to fly through the window and save me.

Perhaps unsurprisingly, the cat was enjoying the game of poo-ball, swiping her paw at the shiny droppings that flew through the air. I teed the last one, then strained for more, as Tinkerbell, assuming the game was over, began her route to the source of the amusement. The only way down for me was the way I'd come up, but that would mean a direct collision. I could've jumped, but if Tinkerbell was able to see the poo glisten, my blood-soaked body would stick out like a hotdog covered in ketchup. I thought about hiding in another vase, but Tinkerbell was now on the shelf, systematically pushing everything in her path to see what she'd flushed out. I would have to stand my ground and fight to the death. It would've been my death, no doubt, as a rat anyway, but I reckoned I could put a fair dent in Tinkerbell's pride in the process.

The family silver continued to crash and smash onto the floor as the distance between us narrowed, and only stopped when we locked eyes. The room fell silent bar the fading echo of the last thing to hit the floor and it became another stand-off, during which I again got the impression Tinkerbell was waiting for me to make the first move. But I was happy to stand and stare for as long as it took for someone to open the door.

Tinkerbell lifted a paw and stretched out her claws. I wondered if the situation in the other room was just as tense, or had they gone out the back to follow Judas to the garden. I stretched my own paws and readied myself, then the silence was broken by footsteps down the hall. Tinkerbell leapt from the shelf meowing like a scared kitten and scratched at the door. I didn't know if the men would hear it over themselves, but if they didn't, she would soon be back on the shelf. More pissed off than before.

The cracking of boots outside rose, as did Tinkerbell's desperation pleas, and sure enough the footsteps stopped outside. *Tinkerbell! You beauty!* She stepped back and licked her paws with a soft purr as the door opened and the man with the torch entered. She was through his legs before he had a chance to look down. I couldn't believe my luck. Not only had I escaped a sure-fire death, but my target was right outside.

KEPT IN THE DARK

The Chief entered next and barked a few words when he saw the mess. Two soldiers dragged Judas in, swords at his throat. It wasn't clear if a deal had been struck, but Judas looked as bewildered as the rest of them and put his hands up as if to say, 'Fucked if I know.' The Chief rummaged through the boxes for what I guessed he thought Judas might have nabbed earlier, hence the mess, which was when I began my stealthy descent. Whatever it was, the Chief found it and put it in his robes which allowed the soldiers to lower their swords; then it was my turn to escape through their legs without being seen. I hoped that Tinkerbell had returned to her meal on the doorstep, but stayed close to the soldiers just in case.

Once back in the big hall, the other guards rejoined them and they all headed down the hallway to the front door. I wasn't sure what the score was between them, but thought that where they went next might give me a clue. I didn't see what the Chief had hidden about his person, but if it was the silver in question, it meant that Judas was still on track to betray his Messiah.

*

The owl had gone; a trail of feathers and blood led into the dark. The soldiers relit their torches as the Chief said a few stern words to Judas, which gave him the all-clear to leave. But he followed the trail around the corner, and I had no intention of being drawn into another confrontation with Tinkerbell, so I left the Chief and his men to enjoy the rest of their evening and set off around the opposite corner, hoping to meet Judas somewhere around the back.

Fifteen

The building was bigger than it looked from the front (I'd realised that from inside), and when I'd almost done a full circle of it, instead of finding Judas, I stumbled upon Tinkerbell tucking into her evening meal by a tree. She was chewing with a screwed-up face, as though owl wasn't the sweetest meat she'd ever tasted, and one look at me was all she needed to go straight to the second course.

'Oh, for Christ's sake,' I screamed. 'Would you just leave me alone.'

Then, for the umpteenth time that evening, I was forced to run into the unknown to flee from that bastard cat.

The long grass was my best ally in the open, but the rustle and footfalls of Tinkerbell were never far behind and I needed a secure hiding place before a paw landed on my back, which would've hurt, given that the cuts I already had were still kicking up.

I shot sideways through a hedge and up the nearest tree. How I found the energy I didn't know, but I now had to rest. *Surely Tinkerbell isn't still onto me.* I dragged myself to the end of the lowest branch and hid among the dark of the leaves, then sensed I had other company. Below me was a group of men in silent prayer. It was Jesus and his cronies. Spread out a few feet apart, almost in formation. I didn't have the heart to tell Jesus that Nobby couldn't hear prayers, his or anyone else's, much less answer them, so if he wanted to talk to Nobby he'd have to wait until he died like everyone else. Which hopefully wouldn't be until I'd changed time enough for me and Mum to never have existed.

I couldn't see Judas, yet he had set off before me. Did he detour for a quick pint the first time and was simply following history, and would he be here soon? Or had he encountered the owl and the pussycat en route and changed direction, and, possibly, his mind? Maybe he saw the blood sacrifice the owl had made and couldn't bear to see his Messiah go through the same thing. The latter scenario was the more appealing, but I knew I was clutching at straws.

I could hear what I thought the river tinkling nearby, like a little waterfall, and then Tinkerbell's head appeared under the hedge and took a moment to suss out the weirdos staring at the ground while praying to Nobby above. Or maybe they were praying to Lucy below. Who the fuck knew? Then, apparently seeing them as no threat, she looked up at me, and I wondered whether, if she knew what was going down with the humans, she would think twice or go in for the kill anyway? No doubt in time I'd find out.

She scrambled up onto my branch and waved her nose in the air as a light breeze swept across the garden. I gripped a leaf to maintain my cover, but the scent of the blood seeping out of me must've carried and Tinkerbell edged her way over. With my cover blown, I let go of the leaf and steadied myself on the thin end of the branch. It wasn't going to take Tinkerbell's weight and it was a fair drop to the ground, even for a cat. But that didn't seem to deter her. She gave me a look that said, 'You're fucked now, rat.'

Everyone's attention, including Tinkerbell's, was directed to the rising sound of marching boots. I peered over the hedge. The usual suspects were there, all swords and fire, heading towards the garden. They stormed in and everyone from Jesus to Tinkerbell froze as the Chief scanned the prayer bods under the tree. I assumed he expected Judas to be there, like he was the first time. Had I done enough? The spilling of Judas' food for the supper. Interacting with Jesus. The storeroom calamity. All my doing. And none of the other disciples looked like they were going to tell tales to the Chief any time soon.

The waterfall sounding splashing stopped and was replaced by the swishing of sandals through the grass as a figure appeared from the shadows. Judas. He was rearranging his dress and I assumed he'd taken timeout from his prayers to take a piss against the tree. Everything was still in place for history to repeat itself. The Chief caught his eye and raised his eyebrows, waiting for the kiss that would seal Jesus' sacrifice. Not really a sacrifice, though, was it? At least not from Jesus' point of view. Not if he ended up in Heaven.

Judas stood without a twitch, right underneath me. I figured he hadn't yet been paid and would need some front to ask for it now. I also imagined that he'd be reluctant to wait till afterwards for payment, as they didn't look like the most trustworthy of fellows.

I turned back to Tinkerbell, who seemed as interested as everyone else in the proceedings below. Maybe she did know what was going down. I stood on my hind legs, clenched my paws into fists and grinned. 'What are you waiting for, cat?'

She kept a sure foot as she upped her pace along the branch and I held my nerve until the branch began to spilt. Then I jumped on Judas' head and dug my claws into his eyes. Boy, did he scream. I let go as he raised his hands to protect himself; then there was a snap and a screech and the branch caught Judas' shoulder on its way down. I hopped in one of his sleeves and felt the jolt of Tinkerbell landing on him as I made my way around his elbow and down his torso. I stopped between his legs. Then I bit down. Judas hit the deck before my teeth had penetrated his foreskin. There was no scream, just a sharp intake of breath.

I guess Tinkerbell saw the wriggling. She wrestled her way inside Judas' collar to follow me down, but her claws got tangled in the fabric of his dress and I heard empathetic mutterings and felt hands feeling around outside as a couple of the disciples tried to save Judas from the unprovoked attack by the creatures that shared the garden. It must've looked like Judas was being tickled by his mates as they tried to grab hold of the struggling mass.

As soon as I smelt Tinkerbell's breath, I released my grip and slipped away into the grass. Judas howled as

Tinkerbell's teeth replaced mine, and his hands left his eyes to deal with the continued attack on his genitals. His instinct was to wriggle around, but he seemed to know that any sudden movement on his part might make the cat hurry along with her meal. His screams dimmed to a whimper as he waved away his mates and, lifting his dress, gripped Tinkerbell's head and held it in place to try and stop her chewing. His eyes were closed, his face scrunched-up. As he squirmed, Jesus and the rest of his clan scuttled over to see what all the fuss was about, followed by the Chief and two soldiers. Their torches lit up the scene and poor old Judas was compromised. I pissed myself, literally; a little puddle formed in a depression in the mud at my feet. *If Judas was in two minds about hanging himself the first time, it's going to be easier now.* The two soldiers also folded up on the spot and beckoned their comrades over. Even the Chief gave a smirk – until he saw Judas' puffed-up eyes. I could read his thoughts: *how's this guy supposed to give Jesus the fatal smacker if he can't see?*

Tinkerbell must've smelt my puddle because she let go of Judas' tackle, but I was halfway up Jesus' leg while she was still sniffing the ground. Jesus stepped back from the others, who were still staring at Judas, no doubt thinking he was surely going to Hell. I popped my head out of Jesus' collar.

'It's me,' I said.

'I know,' he said. 'Why do you invite the creature?'

'The fucking thing keeps chasing me. Can't you do something?'

He didn't reply, and all I heard was snickering as the soldiers watched Judas squirming on the ground. The

KEPT IN THE DARK

Chief was doing no such thing, waiting for Judas to get up and give the fatal kiss, but Judas wasn't going to be in the mood for kissing anytime soon. Tinkerbell sniffed the air near where I'd left my scent, then followed her nose and looked up at me. But this time I wasn't worried. I was cuddling up to Jesus. He had magic powers. The cat didn't care and launched herself up at me. She hooked her front paws into Jesus' dress and snapped her teeth an inch from my head, while Bee Gee Barry ran over and grabbed her tail. Hard as he pulled, there was no give in the claws embedded in the scraggy but tough hessian cloth the chosen one had picked out of his wardrobe to impress on his big night.

'I cannot alter time for you,' said Jesus. 'You must remove the creature.'

'Yeah, I'll jump out and lie on the grass, so it can rip the rest of my skin away and send me to Hell. You're the one with the magic. You do something.'

Jesus did fuck all except wriggle, so I bit his earlobe to see if my chosen counterpart could feel pain – nothing. Interesting.

Tinkerbell did a double take at Jesus' face, then jumped down and disappeared into the night as Jesus and eleven of his disciples turned to face the Chief. Judas was still on the grass, wincing and whining as he held his wounds, and although they probably weren't as life-threatening as the ones Tinkerbell had given me, they were hopefully enough to keep him down until the Chief and his men had fucked off to re-strategise.

I kissed Jesus' neck myself in relief. Mission accomplished. All I had to do now was wait for the Chief to lose patience and lead his men away, then clock out as a rat. Jesus would still be alive, and it would be all over for me and Mum.

As Jesus looked down at Judas' discomfort, I couldn't help wondering why he didn't go over and heal his wounds? Then Judas could've given Jesus a big smacker to say thank you. I hoped it was because he'd seen sense.

'You made the right choice, JC,' I said.

'I did not make any choice. Another shall betray me tomorrow.'

'Do what you fucking like, mate. I'll have ceased to exist by then, and so will my mum.'

'Why is it important for your mother to cease to exist?'

'She died a non-believer and went to Hell.'

'If she went to Hell, then she will remain in Hell, for she is outside time. There is only one way–' He was interrupted when Judas' cries turned to words. I needed him to continue with good news to prevent his other words sinking in, but the only voice I heard was Lucy's in Eden. *Oneth with me, alwayth with me.* My mum would remain in Hell no matter what I did. All my work as a snake and rat had been for nothing.

Unless – '*There is only one way...*' – but before I could push Jesus for more, Judas raised his voice and began a repetitive babble.

'What's he saying?' I said.

'My Lord, my Lord. He's calling for me.'

'You wanker. You told him you were the Lord?'

'No. He thinks I'm the Son of God. They all do. They've seen my miracles. I told them I'm the King of the Jews.'

KEPT IN THE DARK

I didn't know if Judas was calling to give Jesus the kiss of death, or for Jesus to give him the kiss of life. But I didn't care. I could save myself but not Mum; that wasn't part of the deal. But I sure as hell couldn't save her if I ceased to exist.

'If you're so hell-bent on dying in some kind of bogus sacrifice,' I said, 'why don't you just give yourself up?'

'Because they think I've been claiming to be the Son of God, and no man claiming to be the Son of God would give himself up to be killed. They would think I was covering for the real Jesus. Besides, the Lord told me to stay here until all men believe. Only then can I offer myself as a sacrifice to show my work is done.'

'But the Lord will know anyway.'

'Not if my disciples spread the word that I died for their sins.'

I had to give the guy a bit of credit for being more honest about his scam, but he was adamant he was going to Heaven, and I hoped he was right, because I now had to get Judas back on his feet.

'They will,' I said. 'Now, why don't you heal Judas? Then he can rise and kiss you.'

'I can't do it from here. I have to touch him. Then they will believe I really am the Son of God and will not kill me.'

'What if I distract the Chief while you heal him? They'll think his wounds weren't as bad as he's making out.'

This was going to be hard to believe. Judas had covered himself up, but his dress was soaked in blood and it seemed his eyes were in less pain if he kept them closed.

He was curled up in a ball, but at least he'd stopped jabbering.

'Wait here,' I said. 'When you see the Chief and his men distracted, go and sort Judas out.'

Jesus planted a kiss on my back as I hopped out; again, I felt the warm sensation sweep through my body as the skin on my back closed up. Another gift from the magic box that Nobby gave Jesus. Maybe that was why the talents of the chosen one were downgraded by the time Nobby sent me down to sort out his mess, if all Jesus did was get the masses hammered on water and cure pests.

I didn't want to be seen, so I skirted around and cut in for a sideways approach. The Chief was too busy being impatient to notice me creep up, and the soldiers looked more worried about not getting to perform the crucifixion they'd been promised.

Not wanting to venture into another sweat-soaked adventure inside a dress, I gave the Chief's little toe a nip. The one that hurts the most. There was a yelp. He sure felt pain. His foot instinctively lifted away from the danger and lined up a shot at squashing me, which was when I raised the sharp splinter of wood I'd dragged over. I held it vertically, then hopped to one side as his clumsy foot came down. He lifted it again with an almighty roar, then dropped on his backside and glared at his soldiers to make sure they weren't laughing again. I wanted to nip his other little toe just for a laugh myself, but I didn't want him to be in too much pain and miss the kiss of death.

He panted and winced as he eased out the slither of wood that was pinning his sandal to his foot, then used the hem of his skirt to dab the wound. It didn't look too bad.

KEPT IN THE DARK

The wood had been sharp enough to penetrate his sandal, but had barely managed to pierce the thick skin on his sole. What little blood there was soon transferred to his clothes, and he was back on his feet as Judas was being helped to his by another disciple. Both me and the Chief looked over, he no doubt to see if Judas kissed anyone, while I wanted to see if he could even walk. Which he could, straight over to Jesus, to embrace him with a peck on the cheek.

The Chief gave the biggest smile of the evening and nodded, as if to say 'I thought as much.' But his smile changed to a frown when Judas turned to the disciple who had helped him up and gave him a peck too. The Chief's eyes flittered between the two recipients of a kiss while Judas just stood there, staring like an idiot, oblivious to his mistake. Jesus gave a subtle cough, but it took Judas a few seconds to cotton on and give a slight but deliberate nod in Jesus' direction.

I was back on Jesus' shoulder with seconds to spare.

'You have done well, my son,' he said.

I'd done it for me, not him. But I needed to keep him onside, so I had to take the praise. 'Thanks. Now, what were you saying earlier? My mum will remain in Hell, and there is only one way...?'

'There is only one way to save your mother. But I cannot help you change time.'

Before I could respond, the disciples surrounded us in a protective circle as the soldiers charged, and I had no choice but to jump down and dart into the long grass before a sword was placed against Jesus' throat. Judas, who I guessed had to keep up the charade in front of his fellow disciples, grabbed the soldier's arm and yanked him away. The sword fell on the ground and Judas picked it up.

He glared at the smug Chief, whose smirk disappeared when Judas sliced the blade through the soldier's ear. The Chief uttered a few reluctant words as the soldier fainted, then tossed a small cloth bag at Judas' feet. It rattled as he picked it up, and after checking that his friends had seen nothing, he was gone. Jesus soon had another sword at his throat and was led through the gate, and I now had to get him alone again before they strung him up. I hadn't finished with him yet.

Cries filled the air that I took to be jubilation at the capture of the said Messiah, and I stayed put as the shadows released floods of people keen to join the hysteria. A thousand waving arms accompanied delirious chants, while a few desperate fans wept at the impending slaughter of an innocent man. Whether any of them believed he was the Son of Nobby was another matter, but protests against the sword-wielding soldiers and their supporters fell on deaf ears, and the only thing they got for their efforts was a kick in the shins or the threat of a sword. I let the crowd go ahead. Either of the soldiers' strategies would've been fatal to me.

Sixteen

I never understood how Jesus suffered for our sins, even if he had felt pain. Did he really think no one would ever sin again after he died? Even though he left without convincing everyone of his divinity. Did he really expect Nobby to buy his tale of sacrifice? Which turned out to be a non-sacrifice passed off as a token of forgiveness, so the people who died believing would be forgiven because of the so-called sacrifice Jesus had made, regardless of the sins they had committed while alive.

Once the mass of feet thinned out, I followed the roar and torchlight to a large courtyard outside a palatial building, but Jesus was invisible through the legs of a thousand nutters river-dancing to the beat of 'KILL HIM! KILL HIM!' or whatever it was they were shouting. I needed to be on the roof.

There were no drainpipes, as the Romans, although ahead of their time in regard to drainage, didn't feel the need to install them, given the rain Jesus failed to conjure up day after day, so I went inside to negotiate my way up. Frantic roars echoed along the corridors as I leapt up stairs and across window sills until I reached the top. There was a hill in the distance, and the silhouettes of two crosses stood out in the moonlight. And if I wasn't mistaken, people were milling around underneath, some of which were trying to hoist a couple of poor fellows onto them. I had no interest in the prelims and hoped they'd stick Jesus in a cell while they deliberated over his appropriate punishment.

I peered over the front edge of the building, impressed by what an organized affair it had become, given that it had been knocked up spontaneously in the middle of the night. The courtyard was lit up like a concert arena, with the thousands hungry for an impromptu crucifixion jumping around like pill-heads at a rave on one side, and the fifty weeping idiots on their knees pleading for the life of an innocent man on the other. To whom I had to give credit for taking such a moral stance, but they weren't going to cry away the desires of the majority, who were there to demand entertainment, not justice. Directly below was a balcony with wide steps leading down to the noisy spectators, and I noticed there wasn't a handrail in sight. It must've been thirty feet up, and I wondered if they'd run out of materials, or if it saved the efforts of the soldiers when they tossed people over the edge.

The crowd hushed to a whisper as a man walked out. He wore a bright red dress that stood out among the grey and beige of his minions, who bowed and fell silent as he sat in a chiselled stone chair. *Ah, Pontius. Ready to bang the gavel.* Talking of which, I still couldn't see Jesus.

Then the roaring resumed as a man was dragged out by two guards. A shackled and frightened man covered head to foot in grime, who didn't appear to know what was going on. And neither did I, because it wasn't Jesus. Had he transported himself to safer ground and stitched up some poor bastard who'd been asleep? They shoved him in the middle, and the crowd roared again as the old Chief from the garden appeared with a smile.

Then the proverbial roof collapsed as Jesus was brought out. Wearing what his guards must've hoped were anti-magic shackles. The Chief gestured for him to be manhandled alongside the other prisoner before waving his arms to calm the raging crowd.

I wished I could've understood what was being said, but it seemed like an early version of the X-Factor. Down to the last two. Cast your votes now. The Messiah or Mr Smelly. The disciples waved to attract Jesus' attention like a bunch of school kids wanting to be picked first, shouting what were surely pleas for him to save himself, and justifiably too, as it was fair to assume they'd seen a magic trick or two in the time they'd spent with him. And even if the only trick they'd seen was Jesus transporting himself across the room to stop me ruining his little dinner party, it would've been enough to make them wonder why he didn't transport himself to a more enlightened part of town. There weren't many other hands in the air for Jesus unfortunately, and the ones that were got spat on by the opposition. I went through the losing crowd looking for Mother Mary, although none of the women looked like virgins.

Mr Smelly got the nod and was released from his shackles, then he was down those steps to embrace his family like he'd just won Wimbledon. The crowd upped their chant and I felt it was a call for immediate sentencing, followed by immediate punishment. Pontius stood and raised his arms to silence them before going into a rant. Far too long for me. The bloke just wouldn't shut up. *What's wrong with you?* I thought. *It's like four in the morning. Let everyone go home to finish their night's sleep, get some yourself and proceed with a fresh head tomorrow. Jesus obviously isn't the Son of God, otherwise he would have fucked the lot of you by now, which means locking him up for a few hours won't be a problem.*

But that wasn't the way they did things there – night, day, before breakfast, if there was a good old-fashioned crucifixion to be had, any time was a good time.

The crowd retreated to create a circle as Jesus was released from his shackles, shoved down the steps and thrown to the ground. One soldier produced a whip and snapped the dust to gee things up, while two others laid the boot in and goaded the crowd as Jesus rolled into a ball and pretended to be helpless. Then the whip guy let Jesus have it and blood splattered over the faces of the nearest spectators who revelled in it like it was much-needed rain. *These guys need to find themselves a football*, I thought; being entertained by this sort of thing at any hour is not conducive to a healthy society. But there was Jesus, being dragged, thrown, kicked, punched and whipped, and all the while putting on an admiral performance at feigning pain. At least I assumed he was feigning it. What lunatic would have gone through this when he could've had the bastards struck by lightning at will?

The beating continued, as did the roaring crowd, and I got bored. It was the same thing over and over. Whip, slash, ouch, blood everywhere, big cheer. Whip, slash, ouch, blood everywhere, big cheer. So my mind drifted back to Nobby and what Jesus might say to him about what had happened. I was going to have enough trouble lying about how I'd failed, without his cowardly chosen one ruining it with the truth.

Jesus had become deathly pale and I wondered how much blood he had left before he reached the point where not even a miracle could save him. He was still bound by the laws of biology so would bleed out sooner or later, and probably sooner going by the flappy gashes over his almost-naked body. His dress was long gone, and all he had left on were a few strands of his iron-age boxers. I saw a bit of a dangle and wondered if he'd ever used it other than to take a piss. Should've had the pick of the crop with his powers.

The soldiers continued to pass the whip around until the sun broke the horizon and the Chief addressed the crowd again, his words received with the cheer he'd hoped for. First light also revealed that Jesus' blood disappeared when it left his body. Not even a stain in the sand. I looked at those who had welcomed the magic blood – there wasn't a drop on their faces or clothes.

The whip was finally retired and Jesus lay flat on his back. The gaze of the crowd then shifted as two burly men dragged out a trunk of wood each from a barn-like building in the corner. Another followed with a hammer and a bag of nails. *Here we go. This is what they came to see.* The roar resumed tenfold, and I could've sworn I saw a Mexican wave go through the crowd as the wood crashed next to Jesus. The gorillas got to work nailing it together, and as each slam of the hammer lifted Jesus into the air, I wondered if he was about to fly away, or was just eager to get on the damn thing.

When the last nail had been driven home, the men heaved the cross upright and gave it a shake to make sure it wouldn't collapse under the weight of a man. A man who had been considerably heavier before they'd emptied half his blood into the sand. Two soldiers ushered them away and yanked Jesus to his feet by his scrawny arms, at which point I knew I'd have to wait until he was on the cross before I had one last go. They spat in his face and laughed along with the crowd, and I was dying for Jesus to spit back, but as he'd spent his life telling everyone else to turn the other cheek, he had no choice but to stay calm. *Nobby would be proud of you, son.* Another soldier appeared with a cutting from a bush and I chuckled as he tried to fashion it into a crown. *Aren't them thorns a bitch when they catch you?* It was too far away for me to judge the end product, but the soldier proudly jammed it on Jesus' head and said a few words to the delirious crowd.

Jesus didn't complain when they ordered him to pick up the cross, but the lack of reaction from everyone else when he did made me question my own sanity. *For fuck's sake. How stupid are these people? It took two gorillas to drag that thing out here, it must weigh a ton, and Jesus walks off with it like it's made of cardboard. If that doesn't tell you he's got superpowers, what will?* But everyone from the Chief, to the soldiers, to the baiters, to the handful of worshipers, never batted an eyelid, and instead spread out to line the streets like it was a Royal Coronation.

KEPT IN THE DARK

I raced down behind the building with an ear on the crowd. The morning was at half-light and the torches had become obsolete, and I was worried they might have a few crucifying hills dotted around. Jesus might not have been feeling the pace, but I certainly was; I didn't have the energy to run up and down the wrong hill if the murderous scum took a detour with their prize.

I breathed easy when they picked the hill that already had the two crosses on it. Screams rang out, and I saw the same guys still struggling to hold the convicts in place while a couple of others drove nails in the poor bastards' hands. *Got room for a third?* I thought as I nestled in the long grass to watch the support act. I wondered what they'd done, and although no crime could warrant retribution of this kind, I hoped it was something worse than claiming to be the Son of God.

The main crowd arrived at the foot of the hill and Jesus remembered he was supposed to struggle and dropped to one knee, only for a soldier to encourage him up with a brace of whip-slaps across his back. I made my way up for a closer look at the two sideshows that were about to share their last moments in the limelight with Jesus, and thought about running up to tell them not to bother the Messiah for any favours as he was in enough trouble as it was. But they didn't look in a talkative mood anyway.

Jesus was huffing and puffing like a racehorse by the time he made it to the top, but I concluded it was because he was running on a near-empty tank of blood, rather than the inconvenience of lugging the best part of two trees up with him. He dropped the cross in between the dying criminals and flopped to the ground, probably wishing they'd get on with it so he could get back to Heaven. One of the gorillas he put to shame with his display of strength that went unnoticed, grabbed the bag of nails and the hammer, while the other two stretched Jesus' arms out and bound his legs together before laying him on the cross. Extra cheers went up as the nails crunched through his hands and feet, and the soldiers from the earlier crucifixions slapped their heads at the realisation that it was easier to nail the convicts down before raising the cross.

Once they were confident Jesus wouldn't flop to the ground as soon as he was upright, half a dozen civilians were summoned to help winch the cross into place, and as he rose between his new friends, a woman squeezed past the guards and threw herself at Jesus' bloody feet. *Ah, here she is. Better late than never.* It was hard to tell how old she was, like every other woman there, but she was in her fifties, at least. Plenty old enough to be his mother.

Mary waved her arms up and down as she wailed away on her knees, perhaps wondering what her precious son had done wrong, which made me wonder if she knew who he was. If she'd been a virgin when she conceived, you'd think she'd have known something wasn't right when she missed a period or two. Unless Nobby had found some way to brief her, which was possible, but after the fiasco with Eve, he had tended to favour the male side of his creation to carry the burden of knowledge.

So although it was possible she was pleading for Jesus to use his powers to escape, it seemed more likely she was trying to work out how it had all gone wrong, and had little idea what her boy had been up to around town.

KEPT IN THE DARK

Feeding the masses on conjured-up fish, bread and wine, while she toiled at home. If I ever found out that Mary had to earn her keep in a way that jeopardized her health – which looked to be the case based on her withered complexion and lack of teeth – I would've had even less respect for Jesus. For if I'd been given such powers, my mother would've led a far more privileged life, and wouldn't have spent her days ploughing fields and milking goats or whatever it was Mary did. Not to mention that I wouldn't have clocked out voluntarily at thirty-three in such a humiliating manner to leave her to wonder what she'd done wrong.

Although, to be fair, Mary's joints moved quite freely for a woman of her age, so maybe Jesus had at least blessed her with a holy ointment so she could flail around in relative comfort.

It also didn't escape me that, had Mary been aware of her flesh and blood's true origin, she would and should've been the proudest mother in the world. The Good Lord had planted in her his very own seed. Okay, Nobby still wasn't ready to trust a woman to do his dirty work for him, but that she had been used as a vessel for the chosen one was surely progress.

But if Mary did know, why would she weep? They weren't tears of joy, that's for sure, and Jesus didn't look like he was about to set her straight any time soon. He was looking down at her, but I got the impression he was preoccupied with the paradise he thought awaited him when his last drop of blood disappeared. After all, Mary was a believer, so would get there eventually anyway. She was allowed a few minutes to say goodbye before being thrown back into the crowd, where her sobs were drowned out by the boos and chants of the locals.

This was my cue. I shot out of the grass and up the cross to Jesus' shoulder, which was pure gold for the crowd, who laughed and cheered as I stood on my hind legs and milked it by giving them a wave.

Jesus didn't look too well, regardless of his lack of pain receptors. His face was a sickening white against his blood-drenched body. I hoped he was alert enough to have a conversation. I needn't have worried.

'Leave me to die with dignity,' he said.

I was having none of that. Dignity, my arse. Nailed to a cross while being heckled by a bunch of peasants, when he could laser them dead with his eyes probably, and right in front of his mother. That was not a dignified way to go.

'You need to tell me how to save my mum,' I said.

'I cannot help you. The time has come for me to return to the Lord. I am sacrificing myself for the sake of mankind.'

'You lying weasel. I saw you out there pretending to be hurt. You knew the only way you could die was if they literally drained the blood out of you. You may talk Nobby around to the idea it was to show your love for man, but I know better. And I might just have to tell him what his little boy has been up to.'

Jesus forced his head around and looked at me in a condescending way I didn't expect. 'All believers go to Heaven,' he said.

'Yeah, well, I wasn't a believer, which means I'm going to the Dark. Besides, you aren't going straight to Heaven. Oh no, my fallen friend, your mission is not quite over, because after a three-day holiday in Hell you're coming back here.'

'But why?'

'Jesus, mate, because you've fucked it. All the people down here that have been lucky enough to see your sideshow of magic are wondering why you don't save yourself to show your true divinity. And so am I. And so will Nobby when he finds out. So tell me how to save my mum and I'll pretend I worked it out for myself.'

'You need to return to her life and make sure she dies believing,' he said.

'Nobby won't send me back to save a non-believer, even if it is my mum. He couldn't care less.'

'Then I cannot help you. You must leave me to die.'

It was no use badgering him. He wasn't going to gain anything by not helping me. But there was something else I needed him to do, that required badgering him.

'Right, here's what's going to happen,' I said. 'When you get back, you will not mention anything about me to Nobby. Because if you do, me and Lucy will come and get you. I'll tell Lucy you weren't really a believer, and as you have magic powers, he'll be rather keen to get his hands on them.'

Jesus' face went whiter. Which told me he was falling for it.

'Lucy?' he said.

'Oh, get with the programme. The Dark wants you. And to be quite honest, I'm not even sure it's Nobby who's gonna send you back. It could well be Lucy, in which case I'll be more than happy for you to tell him what I've been up to. I'm on first-name terms with him, so maybe I'll have a word if you keep your mouth shut to Nobby.'

I was now right in Jesus' ear to be heard over the crowd, who had every reason to think I was literally chewing his ear off.

'But I cannot lie to the Lord,' he said.

'Really? So you're going to tell him the sacrifice you make tonight is to get yourself killed so you can get out of this god-awful place and into Heaven, because you couldn't be bothered to carry on spreading his word? Come on, you won't have to lie anyway. He's not going to ask if there was a rat in the picture, so you won't have to tell him there wasn't.'

Jesus half closed his eyes and I hoped he wasn't about to clock out. Then he managed another dab of magic to reverse-drain enough blood to his head and carry on.

'Why are you not with the Dark if you did not believe?' he said.

That was the question that had me stumped.

'I did go to the Dark,' I said. 'Twice.'

'Yet you say it was the Lord who sent you back.'

'Yes, but not for another couple of thousand years. You might think that's a long way off, but death goes on forever and ever and one day me and Lucy are gonna come looking for you.'

By this stage I wished he did feel pain, so I could give him a nip on the nose to make him wise up. How hard is it to keep your mouth shut? And for a fellow chosen one too. Where was the brotherhood?

KEPT IN THE DARK

Jesus opened his mouth and I waited for a confident 'Okay'. But instead, he blasted some local talk that gave the crowd another reason to cheer.

'What did you say?' I asked, thinking he must have told the nasty men to go fuck themselves.

'I told them I forgive them, for they know not what they do.'

'Are you kidding me? They just tortured you, then nailed you to this here cross, and you're telling me they didn't know what they were doing? Do you really want everyone to walk away and spread the word that the Son of God ran out of miracles, so was unable to save himself, and they now have to live the rest of their sorry lives riddled with guilt that it's their fault because they were born in sin to begin with?

'Now you know as well as I do that Nobby will have no choice but to run with it, but I'm not impressed one bit. And now you've passed the point of no return, which means so have I. So, do you forgive me?'

'What for?'

'For this,' I said, before I jumped on his head and relieved myself down his face.

The crowd couldn't believe their luck. *I wonder if this will make it into the Bible,* I thought as I gave my little fella a shake and hopped back to Jesus' shoulder.

'Now, what are you not going to tell Nobby?' I said.

'That I have seen you.'

'Good boy. And I shall say nothing of you to Lucy.'

But Jesus had one last trick up his sleeve yet, and he used it to gather a sky-load of black clouds that plunged the town into darkness. Lightning crackled as driving rain washed the blood from his body into thin air, and I shivered as I looked at his eyes one last time. One twinkled with the promise of Heaven; the other was glazed over with the dread of Hell. While I wondered what possessed Jesus to use his encore miracle to make sure his mum had to walk home in the pissing rain.

*

I sat at the foot of the cross and wondered who would take Jesus down and put him in his tomb. The dead criminals hung either side, with blood still dripping from their bodies into the rain-soaked mud, while Jesus' blood continued to vanish as soon as it hit the ground. Not even a ripple in the puddles. I watched the crowd disperse, then glanced back up and saw there was no need to take him down. He was gone. The nails were still in the wood, but they had no one to hold, and the local undertaker now had an easier morning. I guessed he spun the Chief some yarn about putting Jesus in the tomb to grab the extra cash.

I didn't need to hang around for three days to see if he reappeared. There was no resurrection. No tomb to be empty. I shrugged and made my way back down the hill.

*

It didn't take long for Tinkerbell to find me by the river. I'd gone there via Jesus' hideout. I had a chicken leg strapped to my back and a length of thick string from a frayed cushion tied to my tail.

On the highest part of the bank, I made a noose in the loose end of the string and rested the drumstick inside it, then hid behind a rock and squeaked into the morning air. Less than a minute later, Tinkerbell's curious head poked through the grass, like it had to be a wind-up that a lump of dead meat had called out. *Come on.* I thought. *Just do it.* She crept over and sank her jaws in as I clung to the rock and rolled over the edge. My own tail jolted as I hit the water and dropped the rock. A bigger splash followed, pushing me further under, and muffled screeches and gurgles disorientated me as Tinkerbell tried to scramble up the wet muddy bank. I slammed into the bank and wrapped my tail around a root, ignoring the pain as I had no need to conserve energy. There was another splash as Tinkerbell fell back in, and my lack of oxygen began to replace my adrenaline.

My head became fluffy as my grip on the root loosened, and I wished I could've stayed in that state forever. But I knew a fate worse than death awaited as me and Tinkerbell sank lifelessly to the riverbed, unless I could talk Nobby into letting me use his time machine again. I didn't know what for, but I had to bank on him still being reluctant to let Lucy have me.

Seventeen

Nobby had left his office again. At least Lucy showed himself straight away, and he had a lot more to be getting on with in his little life-cleansing room. What did Nobby have going on that couldn't wait?

I'd got to know him better than he'd got to know me, and he had nothing to lose except face. I, on the other hand, was not only fighting for my existence, but also for common sense. The kind which Nobby wasn't familiar with. He had no idea what he'd created; at least he didn't until I had a word in his ear, and even then he still shirked responsibility. And it wasn't like he was going to come around anytime soon. Lucy had him by the bollocks and he wouldn't let go.

He thought if everyone believed it would defeat the Dark, but he didn't care about the people being sent there, or about the sins believers committed. I was only in Heaven for a short while, but I never felt Nobby was there before I got dragged out, and I never felt that I or anyone else needed him when we were already in Heaven. So although believers were correct in their belief and were reaping the rewards, they were never going to meet him, and had no need or care to, because Mr Nobby had his hands tied, and could only dictate to a few random humans what they had to do to stop Lucy ruining his Universe. And that he had an office out the back that only chosen ones were allowed into by force was none of their business. And why should it have been? He gave them what he promised.

Nobby turned up without a hint of an apology for his slapdash attitude towards punctuality, ready to exchange excuses about the failed mission and what we were going to do about it. He said nothing. Was he waiting for me to speak first? I doubted it.

'You have failed again,' he said, when he remembered who I was.

I could've said the same thing, but he was willing to talk, which meant he hadn't finished with me yet. Which was good, because I hadn't finished with him either.

'Yeah, well, at least you're not complaining I never tried,' I said. 'At least you don't want to. I gave it my best shot, but even if I'd been a man I couldn't have changed his mind. You chose the wrong person to give those powers to. And before you start prattling on about how he sacrificed himself for the sake of mankind, you knew he'd spun you a yarn or you wouldn't have sent me back to sort it out.'

It was quite comical that he had no idea what had happened. I felt like pushing him on it, but was happy for him to think I believed he saw everything. I didn't need him asking awkward questions about Eden and Jesus, and if I wanted to continue the chase I had to tread carefully.

'Jesus was sent to give knowledge of me to man,' he said. 'But the Dark was not defeated, and another was sent to complete my message.'

Another? How was he going to explain this one?

'And who might that be?' I said.

I had an inkling, but any religious education other than Christianity I picked up at school was forever slapped out of me at home, and I didn't want to embarrass myself by guessing. It could've been Hitler for all I knew. I also didn't want to antagonize him with further blasphemy, as he seemed a bit touchy about that sort of thing, but there had been another poor sod between me and Jesus who had failed to play his part in Nobby's grand plan.

'With every failure of man, the Dark has become stronger,' he said. 'Which has tainted the soul, and can only be cleansed by undoing the web of time. And only that which has perished in its path shall be worthy in its defeat.'

I didn't understand one word of that. Not one. If only he'd put his hands up and said 'Jimmy, I fucked it. Please help me sort this out and I'll give you a wild card into Heaven.' Respect given immediately. But it appeared that he who could create shall not be told what to do by that which he had created, at least not directly. But everybody's vulnerable to a little manipulation, and this stubborn and arrogant creator of failure was not going to be any different at the hands of Jimmy Linton. The chosen one Nobby wished he never chose.

'So there's yet another who's failed you,' I said softly. 'Is he in Heaven too?'

'The angel did not fail. He was given the perfect word, but again man fell to the Dark.'

What? He's been handing out angels? And all he gives me is snakes and rats?

'So Jesus did do the right thing, and it's the angel that needs correcting?' I said, wishing I had eyelids to flutter.

'The angel completed his mission, but the message was corrupted by the Dark.'

By the Dark. Everything ends with the Dark. This bloke couldn't take the blame for a fart when alone in a lift.

'You say the message was corrupted, and not the angel?'

A believing soul cannot sin, and so cannot be corrupted,' he said. 'The angel was to show man that my love was greater than the Dark.'

I waited for the follow-up explanation as to why this angel hadn't managed to do this, but, as I said, I had got to know him better than he had got to know me and knew it was just as well he didn't try.

'So, you want me to go and find the angel? What did it get wrong in translation to make the Dark appear?'

'The angel gave the final revelation to man,' he said, 'but the Dark had become stronger with every sin and infected the message.'

I could take no more. Something wasn't right about this whole thing. It was just one excuse after another. But although this was complete nonsense, it was quite refreshing from Nobby. He still couldn't admit any of it was his fault, having now passed the buck onto some angel, but he was more open about what he knew, or at least about what he'd been told, and that only made manipulating him easier.

'Okay, then, let's get this over with. What's the angel's name? And you'll have to give me a bigger body this time.'

'I have no need to care for the creatures as they cannot harbour a soul. You will find your strength.'

In other words, he didn't give a shit about things that couldn't worship him. And as for finding my strength, my instincts as a snake and rat were only of any use at getting me into trouble, so anything smaller than a bear this time wasn't going to cut it, especially as he'd made it clear that this was my last chance at redemption.

The angel's name was Gabriel, and I had to make sure he gave the correct revelation so some other poor chosen one could go on his way filled with the joys of the Lord, instead of the joys of the sword. But I had no intention of changing history this time. I just had to find the angel. *Angels are kind and pure, helpful and wise. If anyone knows how to save my mum, it will be an angel.*

Eighteen

I kept my eyes open this time. Not that I saw much until I reached Earth, but the Good Lord had granted my wish and made me something substantially bigger than in my previous outings. Not only that, I'd also scored a pair of wings, which made my descent more comfortable than the head-rush I was used to.

The Earth's curvature gradually flattened out as I glided through the atmosphere, and I noticed another feature of my new body. Forget the fucking wings, I could feel what was between my legs and hoped I fancied horses as well as women.

Mountains cast shadows upon the ground as I followed a river across a desert like a border on a map until it ran by a town. A far cry from the planet I'd just left, where I'd spent my time dodging ice bullets being shot from turquoise coloured glaciers that crashed into each other like dodgem cars.

A flash of silver caught my eye. A lake, a little away from the main hub, and, unless I was mistaken, a few other horses were there. *This should be a laugh*, I thought. All the flying had made me thirsty. And horny.

The horses didn't flinch as I swooped from the sky like a dragon. Not every day you see a flying horse, mind; they could've at least acknowledged it. I landed, trying to look like I'd done this before, tucked my wings in and strolled over, doing my best to look humble. Not because I was worried about hostility, I had wings; it was out of respect for my fellow beasts. It was the first time I'd encountered a creature of my own kind since being downgraded by Nobby. Except for young Lucy in Eden, of course, but I had to show him a different kind of respect. I'd also never given any thought to banging another of my own kind, but seeing as I was hung like a horse, I thought I might as well test the water while I was there.

But as cocksure as I had been with human females, I wasn't sure how to approach a horse. *What's the deal? Do I have to do a dance or something, or do they just take it?* I took my fill from the lake and winked at the nearest mare. She held my stare, then stuck her arse in my direction and swished her tail. *Was that a green light?*

I strode over and mounted her. *How are you supposed to do this without any fingers?* I thought as I tried to shoehorn my dick into her with my hoof. The mare reared up and butted me on the nose. I didn't see it coming and went down. *I guess it wasn't a green light.*

Feeling I'd outstayed my welcome, I scrambled to my feet and set off towards the town. About fifteen minutes, I reckoned. I thought about flying, but wanted to keep any interactions with the locals to a minimum, and landing and taking off all over the place might have encouraged people to change their plans for the day. So I set a steady pace on foot. This time, I needed history to repeat itself from the word go, at least until the angel Gabriel had given the message. Only then would I seek his advice.

I figured it would be easier to find the chosen one first, then stalk him until Gabriel turned up. I didn't think I'd find Gabriel hanging around in bars. He'd arrive, locate the chosen one with magic powers, deliver the revelation and then scoot. Even an angel wouldn't hang around there for too long. Not when there was a Heaven waiting.

Boy, was I wrong.

I reached the outer buildings of town, catching the stares of a few locals. I assumed that a horse sporting wings was not a common sight there. But no seventh-century sand farmer was going to interrupt me and I headed downtown.

The sun had dipped behind the mountains by the time I reached the main street, and warped silhouettes danced in the curtain-covered windows of the houses as I plodded along. That I couldn't see any faces was neither here nor there. I had no idea what the chosen one looked like anyway, and knocking on doors and asking might attract unwanted attention from residents who wanted to adopt a talking, flying horse.

Nobby's verbal map of the area wasn't exactly tattooed on my brain, but I tried to piece together the fragments I'd caught. I remembered that he'd said something about a cave. A cave on a hill. The chosen one went there to meditate or something. Or so Nobby had said. *Meditate? He'll get the trance of his life if a flying horse turns up and starts yacking on about God. Maybe I could wait until dark and hide behind a rock. I could pretend to be an angel. I had the wings for it. Just give them a flap now and then. Piece of piss.*

Looking up at the mountains, all I saw was mountains, nothing but fucking mountains, any one of which could've been hiding the blessed cave. I ambled along like a lost tourist. Left or right? *Why didn't I listen?* I tossed a coin in my head and turned left, to see a mob heading towards me waving what looked like gardening tools – odd, since they didn't look like they were off to tidy up the shrubs. I didn't need this for a variety of reasons, but couldn't help a smile. *Unless their spades and pitchforks can make them fly, this should be fun.*

They slowed up as I nonchalantly unfolded my wings, then speeded up as I jumped and flapped like a dancing humming bird, unable to keep all four legs off the ground at the same time. I had to make a break on foot; at least I could outrun them. I galloped towards the nearest mountain and didn't stop until I was halfway up it. I wasn't out of breath – I could've run forever – but I was embarrassed by my pathetic attempt to fly in front of a bunch of strangers. *Why didn't I take off?*

So what now? I was stuck on a mountainside in the middle of the desert, with a bruised ego and dust up my nostrils. I couldn't go back into town with Farmer Giles and his merry men on the hunt, and my wings didn't work. *Why didn't I listen?* I couldn't even remember the name of the mountain – Mount Hurrah, or something. Not that remembering it would've been much use; the peasants still loitered on the edge of town with their makeshift weapons, probably aghast at losing what would've surely made them rich, so going back to ask directions wouldn't have been wise.

The sun was as good as gone, and I scanned the hills in the hope of seeing a neon sign saying 'The Chosen One's Cave'. Stars spread from horizon to horizon, except in the east, where black clouds were on their way to stop the moon splaying the shadows of the mountains across the valley. I'd often stared up at the stars as a child and wondered what it was all about, and had wondered about prayer. I never said any, because what did I expect to happen? *Is there really a God who can get me out of this? All I have to do is pray. Then does this God not know? Will I embarrass God by telling him? And if God does know, why would he have to hear a prayer before helping?* So I had no God to pray to. Only a Devil to hide from.

Now with the knowledge that there was a God, as well as a Devil to hide from, I still knew there was no use in praying. Even if Nobby could hear prayers, he couldn't answer them; he'd already rolled the dice. Besides, what sort of God would want one of his subjects to point out an error in his creation, which he needed to break his own rules to rectify. Who are we to question what happens in his world? Our job is to worship God or be torn apart. Whatever else happens is just bad luck.

I dragged myself away from my ever-growing anger at Nobby and focused on the town, which had turned an eerie black after a hasty cloud invasion and was only recognisable by its few flickering lights. I had to go back down. These simple folk might have an early night if there was a storm brewing. But any ground vision was eaten up by the darkness of the valley and my hooves slid in the sand and stumbled over rocks. Coordinating four legs came naturally as a horse, as it had as a rat, but that didn't mean I was a natural at walking down a steep, pitch-black mountainside strewn with loose rubble. I didn't even have any horseshoes on.

'Where are you, oh chosen one? I know you live here. God told me,' I bellowed, then listened to the echo as the ground under my front legs gave way, forcing me to my knees. I scrambled up in time for my back legs to slip and cause a mini-avalanche, which I soon found myself a part of. I covered my face with a wing, unable to do anything except try and enjoy the ride as my legs flailed for anything to slow me down. If I lost a leg as a horse, it really would be all over.

After far too long and a thousand cuts and bruises, the hill went into decline and I rose to finish the race on my own terms. My heartbeat slowed as the gradient levelled out, then it stopped altogether when the ground beneath me disappeared. I closed my eyes and shook my head at my luck as I plunged into a dark abyss like the coyote from the Road Runner. Embarrassingly, it took me a few seconds to remember I had wings.

'I have to run before I jump,' I said to myself as I soared through the air once again, swooping as close as I dared to a rock face searching for caves. A rumble of thunder gave my senses a nudge. If I didn't find it tonight, I at least needed to find shelter. Fuck sleeping in the rain, and I guessed there'd be no room at the inn. I headed towards the town and picked out the torch lights of people who might've been looking for me, so I changed course

KEPT IN THE DARK

for the outskirts and searched for an empty outhouse to lay my weary head.

A few spots splattered on my back. Then a few more. Then the heavens opened in a torrential downpour. Rain pounded my body from every angle and my wings became heavy as I powered through the cold, grey, swirling mass. I closed my eyes and would have to guess when it was safe to open them.

The hit was most unexpected, although I should've been more aware, but in any case, what were the odds? Dazed and in pain, I tumbled through the clouds with the wind knocked out of me and opened my eyes to see what looked like a man with wings spinning towards the ground. *Fuck, it's Gabriel!* Conceding that the collision was unintentional, I swooped down to see if he was okay, but, upon seeing me, the streamlined angel shook his head, repositioned his wings and took off like a bullet.

The rain wasn't going to let up anytime soon, so I caught my breath and landed ungracefully in a dark corner of town. I gave my wings a shake and tucked them in tight. Now I was under pressure. The angel was in town and he didn't seem as fussed about the rain as me. *He must be on the hunt for the chosen one too.*

Thunder and lightning banged and flashed like a rock concert from Hell as I dripped through the sodden streets, worried about what sort of reaction I'd get from Gabriel, if and when we met. He was a messenger from God, so you wouldn't think he'd be hostile; but I was also a messenger from God, and right then I felt like giving someone a bloody good hiding. I wasn't physically scared of Gabriel – I saw how big he was, the size of a man, while I was a horse. No contest. I was more worried he wouldn't speak English and, God forbid, wouldn't know how to save my mum.

My caution in finding a roof over my head took a hit when a boom of thunder shook the building next to me, sending a pocket of water from a badly designed roof cascading over me like a schoolboy prank. I barely flinched, being already wet through, but my patience snapped and I kicked open the nearest door, not giving a toss who was in there. It was pitch-dark with no commotion. *This will do*, I thought as I nudged the door closed with my backside and flopped to the ground. I closed my eyes, but my intense desire to sleep was overwhelmed by the thousand thoughts and problems spinning around in my head. My death was becoming harder work than my life ever was.

I didn't get any sleep that night. I assumed the dead don't sleep. Why would they?

After an eternity of darkness, listening to the storm pass and thinking about the vicious circle of life my death had become, first light gained the strength to reveal a wall no more than six inches from my nose. I could also see the window behind me, and the outline of a man lying below it. I hoped to Christ he wasn't one of the crazy gang from the night before. I needed to make a quick and quiet exit. But manoeuvring my legs in the semi-light wasn't easy, not to mention then having to open a door that was sure to creak and squeeze my fat arse through it.

I folded my front legs in one by one and prayed I wouldn't clip the man, and was ready to jump and bolt if need be. The growing light was welcome as it made my movements safer, but it could've been the fella's alarm clock. He might've had a busy day planned repairing the storm damage.

I rolled onto my front knees in silence and with some tenacity, but when I tried to rise one leg at a time I found that's not how horses stand, especially new ones. They need room for a roll and a stagger to stabilise themselves, and it's not safe to be lying next to one. I changed tactics and tried to open the door with my hoof. Maybe I could gradually slide along the floor. Having no toes didn't help, but I persisted long enough for the sunlight to make the man's wings visible.

Was this good or bad? It had to be good, surely. It was him I was looking for. But it was a bit too sudden, not to mention unexpected, and I was reluctant to say anything at first. Gabriel wouldn't have known who I was, assuming I was a regular horse that had taken shelter from the rain just as he had. If I kept my wings tucked away, that was. *Maybe I should just keep my mouth shut and follow the bastard wherever he goes.* But I could never keep my mouth shut.

'Gabriel?' I whispered.

Gabriel sat bolt upright and stared at every spot in the room except my face. He was unhealthily thin, with a pasty face, a red nose and a hairdo like he'd had a night on the tiles and got lost on the way home. He rubbed his eyes and shook his head. He was, without a doubt, hungover. It was hard to tell how old he was – maybe fifty, maybe eighty. A pair of tan-coloured trousers a few inches too short was accompanied by a filthy string vest that had seen better days. His grubby white wings were at the ready and he looked worried. I shivered, and thought he looked familiar, then remembered this was over a thousand years ago and I'd never seen an angel before.

'Gabe?' I said, trying not to laugh at Nobby's attempt at creating an angel.

'Would ya be a talkin' fookin horse dere?' he said in a strange Irish accent.

'You have come to seek the chosen one?'

'If ya mean d'prophet, Oi've already spoken wid him.'

'What do you mean you've already spoken with him?' I said. 'You only got here last night.'

'Oi've been here f'two weeks already.'

'Two weeks? Then why are you still here?'

'Oi can't remember d'message.'

My desire to face the day head-on took a dip. 'Where did he get you from?' I said.

'Oi was in Heaven and got dragged off ta see d'Lord. He said he was goin' ta send me back ta deliver a message, but Oi can't remember what it was.' He unfolded his wing to reveal a bottle conveniently lodged in its feathers, then took a generous swig and let out a long breath that hit me like a punch in the face. 'D'you know what it is?'

I looked him up and down. This had to be a wind-up, surely. *This is what Nobby sent to give mankind the recipe for eternal life? A drunken Irishman?*

'So what have you told the prophet?' I said.

Gabe looked at the floor, then took another swig. I waited for an answer, but didn't expect a coherent one.

'Oi gets confused when people talk ta me f'too long,' he said. 'Dere was so much ta remember.'

'I'm not surprised if you keep knocking back that stuff. When did you last see him?'

'Tree days ago. Oi'm supposed ta meet him t'day fa d'tird and final revelation, but Oi've no idea what Oi'm talkin' about.'

I'd noticed that, with each successive mission, the living standards of Nobby's so-called 'chosen ones' declined. Adam and Eve lived in Paradise, albeit with a catch, Jesus had to make his own furniture, the prophet had to work from a cave, Gabe had the memory span of a fish and I was beaten whether I believed or not. So much for progress. We really didn't get any favours from the Good Lord.

But Gabe had already given the first two revelations, which was welcome news. I just had to make sure he gave the same third revelation. But as I'd already changed today's timeline by inadvertently becoming Gabe's roommate the previous night, I didn't know what damage I'd already done. Gabe also couldn't remember what he was supposed to tell the prophet, and had seemingly been making it up as he went along, so I didn't know if he even knew what he was going to say to the prophet at this stage, or what he would've done had I not turned up. I didn't think he would've spent the morning with a pen and paper, trying to recall what Nobby had told him. My bet was he'd have sat around drinking, so at the very least I had to let him carry on doing that, but I was still going to stick to my guns and wait until he'd given the final message before I picked his brains about how to save my mum. If I asked him about the message beforehand it might change. But picking his brains was going to be a problem. I'm surprised he managed to pick his own brains to save himself. I also needed him to think I wanted him to give the correct message, as I assumed Nobby would want to know how Gabe got on, and needed him to give a good account of my efforts.

Nineteen

It took a good five minutes to fly over the mountains to the cave of worship, and I had to give the prophet credit for hiking up there in the hope the piss-head angel would return with more tales of questionable morality. At the cave entrance Gabe looked worried and I wondered what damage he'd already done.

'When are you to return to the Lord?' I said.

'When d'message has been given' – he paused for another swig – 'and yee have arrooied. Den Oi need–'

'Me? How the fuck do you know about me?'

'Have ya not come ta take d'prophet back?'

This was priceless. 'As it happens, no,' I said. 'I'm just here to make sure you don't screw up the revelation, but it looks like I might be too late. Why didn't you write it all down?'

'Oi lived a tousand years ago or more. No one could read or wroite.'

'You still haven't said how you know about me.'

'D'Lord told me ta tell d'prophet, dat he would be goin' ta Heaven on a flyin' horse when d'message had been delivered.'

'So you remembered that bit?'

'Well, it did sound a bit strange.'

Things weren't going well. My hopes of an all-knowing, all-caring angel were disappearing with every word he spoke.

'How long will we have to wait for him?' I said.

'He'll be here at nightfall.'

'Nightfall! But it's like eight in the morning. Am I going to have to sit up here all day with you?'

'Nope, Oi need anoder drenk. Wait here,' he said before he emptied the bottle down his throat and flew off, leaving me to shake my head.

So what was I supposed to do now? Okay, I'd found the cave, but I didn't fancy an all-day session with the flying booze-hound before the prophet turned up.

Gabe returned after twenty minutes with several bottles tucked in his feathers and offered me one. I was surely tempted, but I knew if I started at that hour I might as well concede defeat. I did, however, need water, and the view was ample to pick out yesterday's lake.

'I'm going to get some water,' I said. 'If anyone turns up, don't say a word about me. Got it?'

Without waiting for his reply, I started my run-up and soared into the air, and as I glided on the thermals, I kept a sharp eye out for a man on his way towards the cave. Hopefully a man more sober than Gabe.

The same mare I'd put the moves on was by the lake again, but my equine sex drive had wavered since I was last there so I left her well alone. I took my fill of water and splashed around, wincing as the water washed my cuts from my tumble the night before, then gave my wet wings a couple of minutes in the sun and headed back.

*

Flying low behind the cave, out of sight, I thought about what to do with Gabe. I had to keep him there until the prophet showed up, then hope to God that he gave him the same third and final revelation.

I landed with soft hooves and crept around the side, not expecting to hear anything as I knew he was alone. I just wanted to feel in control, if only for a few seconds.

'Oi can see ya, y'know,' said Gabe.

I dropped my haunches and stepped around to the front. 'You could see me? How?'

'Oi dunno. Oi can just see tings.'

'Don't tell me he gave you special powers.'

'Oi guess he did.'

'So what else can you do?'

'Well apart from bein' able ta floy, Oi'm invisible ta everyone here except d'prophet. Which is handy when ya need a drenk.' He chuckled as he opened a fresh bottle of Arab grog. 'So, d'ya have a name dere?'

'I'm Jimmy.'

In a strange way I was warming to this guy. It was still scary that he was responsible for the future of mankind, but I liked his style and thought again about having a drink. Then I remembered what he'd said about me taking the prophet back. Did that mean I'd have to carry the bastard? Nobby had sure kept that one quiet.

'Take me back to when the Lord gave you the message,' I said. 'Surely you weren't drunk then?'

'Oi'm always fookin dronk,' he said, tipping his head back with a guffaw. 'It's Heaven, f'fooksake.'

I fell to the ground in fits. I tried to stand but my legs collapsed and I lay giggling like an imbecile. It was the first time I'd laughed properly since I was in Heaven myself, and figured that although the mission may be near-on impossible, I could at least go out having a blast.

We polished off the rest of the booze and I sent Gabe to steal some more, given that he was invisible. This gave me a few minutes to sober up and check my surroundings. The cave entrance was no more than four foot high and not much wider, which was a problem with my long legs, and I didn't want Gabe to find me stuck and have to listen to his smart-arse remarks for the rest of the day. I dropped to my knees and stuck my head in. Before sunlight gave way to shadow, I saw clear marks where the prophet had knelt to lap up the wise words of the archangel Gabriel, and I wondered what drunken bollocks he'd taken as gospel, ready to spread to the world.

The air was cooler inside the cave, and I let it lower my brain temperature until I heard Gabe flapping behind me. I edged back into full sunlight, which was now uncomfortably hot. I didn't relish the thought of drinking all day in this heat, but couldn't risk missing the prophet. I was also jealous of Gabe being able to sit inside the cave while I had to sit outside sweating my bollocks off. I tried to take my mind off the heat by asking Gabe what he knew about Nobby.

'Can you tell me anything at all about what the Lord said?' I asked as I rearranged my bottle in the tips of my feathers.

'Oi wouldn't know much about dat,' he replied. 'He's not an easy man ta follow.'

I had to respect that, although Nobby could've at least made sure Gabe knew what was riding on this. As it was, Gabe didn't seem to care who lived or died as long as he had his bottle.

'If you can't remember anything,' I said, 'then what have you been telling the prophet? And more to the point, why has he been listening to you?'

'Oi'm a man wi'fookin wings, so Oi am. If he can believe dat, he can believe anytin. Besoides, he's no broighter dan Oi am, so Oi'm sure he won't remember it eider.'

I could only wonder about the conversations Gabe and the prophet had been having. An alcoholic and a desert peasant discussing religion and philosophy before the centuries were in double figures.

'Did you see anyone other than the Lord before he sent you back?' I asked, wondering if Lucy had whispered a few words in Gabe's ear. It would've explained a lot.

'Not dat Oi recall,' he said.

I took that as a no. Even an eternally drunk person would remember the briefest of encounters with Lucy.

'So what did you do when you were alive?'

'Oi got dronk?' he said with his now trademark laugh. 'Now Oi'm not sayin' dat bein' dronk is an easy way ta live ya loife, but it's a dam soight easier dan bein' sober, dat's f'sure.'

Gabe's laugh was infectious, and I bellowed along, encouraged by the potent liquor. It tasted vile, but I was past the point of no return and it gave me the confidence that only alcohol can.

'What time do you reckon it is now?' I said.

'Fook knows. But he said he moight be a bit oily t'day.'

'You said at nightfall.'

'Yeah, dat was before Oi saw him in town dis marnin.'

'What? You've seen him today? Since we've met?'

'Aye. He kept y'man busy whoile Oi lifted deese here bottles.'

Maybe I wasn't warming to him after all. I just stared, not knowing whether to laugh, cry or kick him.

'Did you tell him I was here?'

'Well, Oi moight've done.'

My heart sank. I didn't know anything about this prophet, but I didn't think he'd necessarily like the idea of being taken away by the flying horse that Gabe prophesied, even if it was to Heaven. Maybe if he lived to a ripe old age first. But now? With the rest of his life ahead of him? If he changed his plans due to worry about being taken, the final revelation might not be given at all. I had to get him back in the picture.

'Right, I want you to go back down there now,' I said. 'Not when you've finished your drink, now. And tell him that I've gone back to Heaven and he's still to meet you here, and that he's to come alone.'

It was also possible the prophet was one of the spade-wielding maniacs from the night before, in which case, news that the horse with wings was still around might alter his objectives. For all I knew, the only reason the prophet hadn't tried to kidnap Gabe was because no one else could see him, so they wouldn't believe him. But now many had seen a horse with similar appendages to Gabe, and if the prophet had half a brain, he would dismiss Gabe's teachings as the crap that they were, and instead use him to capture the wonder horse and earn himself a few quid. He could be rounding up an army right now. Or maybe the prophet was indifferent to the presence of such a creature, and was busy at home trying to piece together the rambled mess the thirsty angel had charmed him with. But I was taking no chances.

I hurried Gabe into the air and looked for a hiding place. The problem was that Gabe had a radar for me like Jesus. I had him onside now, but after what he was yet to drink and maybe a bit of persuasion from the prophet, who knew what he might let slip.

The sundried bushes scattered around the cave were too small and bare for a horse to hide either in or behind. Other than the cave, which I couldn't fit into, there was nowhere I could conceal myself. Of course, if the prophet was on his way to capture me, all bets were off, because there wouldn't be a final revelation. Mine or Gabe's.

Gabe returned and assured me that the prophet was still pucker. It was in Gabe's interest for the prophet to come alone as he still had to give the third instalment, and if he didn't he'd be in trouble with Nobby. But I doubted whether Gabe was aware of any consequences through his drink-glazed perception of reality, and wouldn't have been surprised if he happily welcomed a gang of baying men to listen to his tales of worship.

We carried on drinking, with me standing in the baking sun scanning the hills, while Gabe sat in the cave and waffled on about everything from the Lord and trying to remember what he'd said, to trying to remember what he'd told the prophet, to how wonderful Heaven was. Like I didn't know. Every now and then he went on about his dear old mother. She had lived a hard life but, never mind, she had made it in. Nearly everyone did back then. I thought about this and realised that, as time unfolded through the ages, more people had started to doubt Nobby's existence, which was why, I guessed, he began sending down chosen ones to try and steady the ship. But with all his supposed wisdom he thought it was about worshipping him, and that if you believed you could not sin.

I felt sorry for Nobby in a way. He thought he'd done the right thing, but had no idea what he'd created. And that included Lucy. Nobby couldn't have created Lucy intentionally, but that didn't mean he wasn't responsible for whatever grievance he had against him.

I didn't pay much attention to Gabe's ramblings. Occasionally I picked up something about Nobby, but most of that was irritation at Gabe referring to him as the 'Good Lord'. And I didn't need to know what he'd already told the prophet – it had been said. Nobby had said I would land the day before the final revelation was given. But it seemed he didn't know Gabe was already here, and two-thirds in with his bastardization of it.

Gabe necked the bottles as fast as he flew back to replace them and I couldn't keep up. I'd always liked a drink, and was embarrassed I was five times the size of my drinking partner. But I had to hand it to Gabe, he sure could put it away, although his speech had turned to mulch and he'd become a bit touchy.

Eventually, and after we'd pissed a small river down the side of the mountain, the sun started its descent and I struggled with double vision as I locked my eyes on the track, and my ears on any noise outside of Gabe yacking on about having been the best man in town back in the day. Someone had to appear soon, surely. Other than Gabe, who dragged his drunken arse out of the cave with something on his mind.

He put his bottle down and began a mock boxing match with a narration of some fight he'd had many moons ago. I wanted to bite his wings off and kick him down the mountain, and hoped the prophet turned up before he walked back. Maybe I could revert to my old plan and pretend to be an angel. I'd always been good with accents. An Irish one was my bread and butter.

These stupid thoughts soon left my mind, but I had to do something about Gabe's erratic behaviour; he was scrambling back up off the ground after being floored by the momentum of his own left hook that had missed my nose by a whisker. I wasn't sure if it was wise for him to go for more booze in that state, as he might get lost, and I still couldn't be sure the prophet wasn't on his way up with a lynch mob. At the very least I had to keep Gabe there, because so far the prophet had lapped up every word he'd said, and he'd be the only one able to save my skin should it all go tits-up.

'Okay, Gabe, it's getting dark,' I said. 'I need you to stop drinking and pull yourself together.'

Not a wise thing to say to a drunk Irishman whose fists were already clenched. I should've known better.

'Would ya be tellin' me what ta do dere?' he slurred as he picked up his bottle and stuck his neck out.

I wasn't worried about him using the bottle to hit me; it was still half full, and his punches would've been laughable to a horse. I didn't speak or move and hoped my silence would calm him down. But Gabe wanted an answer.

'D'ya not have a tongue dat works, or are ya just plain fookin stoopid?' he said, before he glugged the bottle dry and threw it to one side. He took a step forward with both fists raised.

'For God's sake, Gabe, I'm not here to fight you,' I said. 'We both need to straighten up and get ready.'

'Is dat roight?' He took another step forward. 'And how do Oi know ya haven't been sent boy d'Devil himself ta take me away ta Hell?'

'If that was the case, I would've taken you already.'

'Oi'd like ta see dat.' Another step. 'Cos if it's a foight ya be wantin', it's a foight yel be gettin', but yel not be standin' after.'

'Let's not do this now,' I said. 'I like you and you've nearly finished your mission. You could be back in Heaven before morning and fight whoever you like, but right now you have–'

My plea was cut short by a lunge at my head and I took a step back with my long legs. Gabe landed flat on his face as blood splattered from his already bright red nose and vanished as soon as it hit the sand. I couldn't help but laugh at the sorry sight of the man Nobby had picked out of Heaven to spread a new message to save himself from further humiliation. He sure did pick'em.

Gabe sat up holding his nose. He didn't look in pain, but I didn't know if it was from the drink or because he was an angel. I'd sure felt pain on all my missions, but the spread of special powers to the chosen ones had not been consistent. But at least it stopped Gabe from being a dick.

'You okay, Gabe?' I said, ready to kick him if he tried it again.

He flicked the blood from his hand and lay on his back laughing. 'Would ya look at d'state o'me?' he said. 'Bless d'Good Lord.'

I looked at the mess in front of me and wondered what the prophet would think when he saw God's messenger paralytic with a busted hooter. The prophet knew I was there, or at least had been, and could be excused for thinking it was me who'd thumped Gabe.

Gabe scrambled up and wiped more blood off his nose, then picked up a bottle. It was empty. He peered into it with one eye, then launched it into the fading sky, where it seemed to hover momentarily before plunging and smashing out of sight. Half in despair, half amused, I watched him drop to his hands and knees and go through the empties one by one.

'We're all out, mate,' I said.

'Fook dis, Oi'll get some more,' he said as he staggered to his feet.

'No, Gabe. He could be here anytime now. You need to sort out what you're going to say to him.'

'Me? Oi tought yee wanted ta take over from here.'

'Yeah, that was before I found out you told him I was here. He's gonna think I've come to take him.'

'Now woy would he tink dat?'

'Because you told him a flying horse was going to take him to Heaven, remember?'

'No, Oi didn't. Oi was supposed ta, but Oi'd forgotten all about it til yee turned up.'

I took a moment to process this information. It was good news, but until I'd met the prophet and sussed him out for himself I was still going to have to play it carefully. Gabe brushed himself down and rubbed his fingers through his hair, then flapped his wings, ready for flight. But I had no intention of letting him go anywhere.

'Actually, Gabe, there's another couple of bottles in the cave,' I said. 'I put them in there earlier to keep them out of the sun. They're right at the back.'

Gabe had his wings tucked in and was wobbling towards the cave before I'd finished the sentence. And as he rummaged in the dark, finding nothing except more empties, I sat and blocked the entrance with my backend.

'Would ya fook off,' he said. 'Oi can't see a ting as it is.'

'Sorry, Gabe, but we need to stay here.'

I didn't know if he had a special power for getting out of caves, but it was all I could do.

'Oi won't tell ya again. Fook off.'

A bottle bounced off my arse, followed by a thud and a yelp as Gabe hit the wall.

'Oi can't even see where ya are. Would ya just fook off.'

'You need to calm down,' I said. 'You can have another drink later. Right now, we have to get ready for the prophet. What do you think Nobby's gonna say if you go back having failed after he's sent someone down to help you?'

Gabe fell silent and I wondered if I'd touched a nerve. Because the setup, as I understood it, was that if you believed you went to Heaven. No questions asked. And that was where Gabe had been prior to this little outing. But Gabe's hesitation made me wonder if he had in fact met Lucy.

'Who d'fook's Nobby?' he said.

'The Lord.'

Gabe chuckled. 'Dat fits. And what d'ya call his girlfriend?'

Girlfriend? Does he mean Lucy? There really could be more to this sacred angel than meets the eye. I realised I knew nothing about Gabe except that he'd lived over a thousand years ago and got dragged out of Heaven to try and save Nobby's arse.

'Tell me about when you first got to Heaven,' I said.

'Well, it was great at foist, but' – he began to shiver and his eyes filled with tears – 'Oi'd rarder not talk about d'fire.'

My stomach churned. This sounded all too familiar. 'Why didn't he destroy your body?' I said.

D'Lord saved me before he had d'chance. Oi'd been sent dere f'failin' d'Lord d'foist toime. But den he sent me back here ta troy again wid a new message f'man. Well, f'one man. D'foist person Oi talked ta was d'only one dat would see me.'

'And that was the prophet?'

'Aye.'

'So this is your second outing under Nobby's orders?'

'Aye.'

I stared at the sky. A few stars were out and I wished I could fly around the Universe for eternity and never have to see, think or worry about Gabe, Nobby, Lucy or my life ever again. The meaning of life had become more complicated by its foolish simplicity and I wished I could give it all up. But I knew that was the booze talking. There was no Universe to fly around in, only one to struggle in, and struggle I must.

'So how did you fail the first time?' I said.

There was a clink of bottles and Gabe's laugh echoed around the cave.

'Would y'moind if Oi asked ya a question dere, Jimmy?'

'Sure.'

'Would ya moind movin' y'fat ass so Oi can get out?'

The air had cooled now the sun had gone and we sat and stared at the moonlit track, neither of us sober enough to make a flight reconnaissance. Gabe couldn't see his hand in front of his face, and I couldn't be arsed. I realised that kidnap wasn't on the cards now I knew how to fly, and if that was the prophet's new agenda, all I could do was wait and go out having fun.

'I would've thought that, after you failed the first time, he would've chosen someone else,' I said, secretly wishing I'd let him go for more booze.

'Me too,' he said. 'But here we are. Moind yee, he brought y'man Jasus back f'ra second go after he failed as Moses, so Oi guess he tought Oi deserved anoder shot.'

I was over being shocked by new information, especially when it came to what Nobby had been up to, but it seemed he'd been repeating his own mistakes with the same two unfortunate chosen ones. Insanity is doing the same thing over and over and expecting different results. Einstein said that. Apparently. How could Nobby create someone who was so much smarter than himself? Maybe he thought that everyone who believed in him was the same, and would behave the same. And as a result, there I was, on top of a mountain, dressed up as a horse, as pissed as a parrot, waiting for Nobby to yank me back into reality and threaten me yet again with Hell.

'So what was your first mission?' I said, not sure I wanted to know.

'Well Oi kinda knew, but it didn't quoite make sense,' he said with a furrowed brow. 'Oi was supposed ta make a boat, and put only animals in it.'

Here we go, I thought. 'Let me guess. Two by two?'

'Fooked if Oi was countin' 'em. Most o'dem looked d'same. Only four-legged ones, he told me. How was Oi supposed ta get all dem bastards in dere? Oi was only one man.'

'Didn't your family help?'

'Dey tought Oi was as mad as d'noight and told me so. And Oi couldn't blame dem. How was Oi supposed ta make a boat big enough ta carry all d'beasts d'Good Lord made? Never mind round'em up from d'lands and get dem on d'fookin ting.'

I was having a ball at this stage. Nobby's comedy show had rolled into another town. 'So what happened?' I said.

'Oi built d'fookin ting. Took me a hundred years or more and was d'finest ting Oi ever accomplished. D'animals weren't best pleased, but Oi was a fair hunter, so Oi was. D'heedens Oi'd been told ta abandon ta d'mercy of d'flood looked on from d'hills as Oi forced moi wife and children on board ta weder d'storm. D'clouds gadered, d'rains fell, den d'fookin ting sank in d'droydock.'

Boisterous laughter filled the air and I thought about sending Gabe to get more booze and to hell with the prophet. The mission was fucked anyway.

'Oi could see d'animals breakin' out o'dere cages and trashin around in d'water,' he continued. 'Most o'dem made it, but some couldn't swim, like d'monkeys.'

'But monkeys only have two legs.'

'Dey have four tings touchin' d'ground when dey walk. What's the difference?'

'Did your family survive?'

'Aye. Except moi firstborn, but he was a wee shite anyway. Oi wasn't on d'ting at d'time, so dey had ta save demselves as Oi can't swim. Oi had built it whoile on d'drenk and it didn't look too stable. But ta be fair, Oi'd never even seen a boat before, never moind built one. Besides, Oi wasn't too keen on spendin' God knows how long sailin' d'seas wid a load o'stinkin' beasts and not a drop ta drenk.'

'So you wouldn't have gone anyway?'

'No, Oi would've gone. Oi had nout ta lose if d'flood was on its way, but Oi at least wanted ta see if it floated first.'

'So what happened then?'

'D'heedens beat me ta det as soon as dey stopped laffin, and d'next ting Oi knew Oi was in Heaven. But Oi got d'feelin sometin wasn't quoite roight and was hauled away ta'da place Oi'd rarder not talk about. Den y'man

KEPT IN THE DARK

Nobby showed up and saved me. Oi was grateful ta say d'least, but he's a hard man ta understand and all Oi could do was agree wid everytin he said in d'hope o'goin' back ta Heaven.

'It seemed ta do d'trick, until he dragged me aside again wid anoder mission. Oi wasn't happy, but it was eider dat or be sent ta d'oder place. Oi tried real hard ta listen ta d'message, but Oi was as dronk as a mule and just agreed so Oi could get on wid it. D'next ting Oi knew Oi was flyin' troo d'clouds towards dis place. But Oi'm scared, Jimmy. Oi've messed dis one up too and Oi'm scared Oi'll end up in d'oder place.'

I empathised with Gabe's concerns, but he knew what his first mission was, which meant he believed. That he screwed it up and was about to do the same here was irrelevant. His hand was already stamped to get back into Heaven. But I couldn't work out why Gabe had been to see Lucy at all. He was a Nobby believer whom Lucy should've had no claim on.

'But why did you go to the Dark if you believed?' I said.

'Cos Oi disobeyed d'Lord. He told me not ta have any children wid a heeden. But Oi had tirteen.'

'Don't worry, Gabe, you'll be fine,' I said. 'And anyway, you haven't lost this one yet.'

I wobbled to my feet and nodded to a moving halo of light down the track.

'He's alone,' said Gabe.

I relaxed. The booze was wearing off and the thought of playing hide-and-seek with a bunch of nutters didn't seem like fun anymore.

'Okay, tell him to go deep inside the cave,' I said. 'Tell him he needs to for the final mesmerising revelation. And clear those bottles out quick. I don't want him to know you've been on the piss all day.'

Gabe crawled back into the cave and threw out the empties while I kicked them in the scrub and flicked dust over them. It was dark, but the visitor had fire that might glisten off the glass. Gabe would have his work cut out explaining how he'd drunk the whole lot by himself in one sitting.

'Your face is a mess,' I said when he reappeared. 'Put your wing in front of it. Tell him you got sunburnt. I'll be around the side, so for Christ's sake don't let him go round there. If he needs a piss, send him the other way.'

A human bark came from the direction of the torchlight. Gabe barked back, without a hint of an Irish accent.

'What, you speak Arabic?' I said.

'Did ya expect him ta be turnin' up speakin' fluent English now? He can barely say his name in his own language.'

'What did you say to him?'

'Oi asked him if he brought d'booze.'

My dismay for Gabe kept growing. Also respect. And if the bar was open again, I thought I might as well carry on too.

I nipped out of sight as a torch came into view, then stole a peek to see the shadow of a man appear. I also saw that Gabe didn't cast a shadow. I'd never noticed it before. *Makes sense*, I figured. *If people can't see him, why would he?*

KEPT IN THE DARK

The prophet and his messenger gabbled away in low voices as I leaned against the cave with my nose and one eye poking out. Gabe's wing covered his face as the prophet rocked backward and forward on his knees with his hands together in prayer. *Jesus*, I thought, *Gabe's sure done a number on this one.* I wished he'd usher him into the cave as arranged so I could ask him what the prophet had been saying. Plus, I needed a drink. The prophet had brought up a box of the local hooch and Gabe had already cracked one open.

The prophet cut a sad and pathetic figure as he worshiped away to Gabe, who looked disinterested as he swigged relentlessly from behind his feathered appendage. I was dying to show myself and tell him to sort himself out. I couldn't focus as it was, and not being able to understand a word the hysterical prophet was saying made my head hurt.

Gabe squeezed out the dregs of his umpteenth drink of the day and bent down for another. I gave a little snort, and he picked out two bottles and slid one towards me. It hit the side of the cave and smashed.

'Oops. Le'me get dat,' Gabe said to the prophet, who didn't bat an eyelid as Gabe staggered over.

'Would you just get him in the cave,' I whispered.

'He won't stop talkin' long enough f'me ta tell him.'

'Then give him a slap.'

'Oi can't do dat. He's over dere singin' moi praises, God help me, so he is. And he keeps apologisin'.'

'What for?'

'Oi dunno. Sometin about not believin' me.'

'Well, get him in the cave and find out. And get me another drink.'

Gabe staggered back over and almost fell into the prophet, who ogled him like a doe-eyed schoolgirl as he grabbed his torch and rose to his feet, giving me a good look at his face. He didn't look too bright, as Gabe had said, but he could be guilty of nothing, at least not yet.

None of this was the prophet's fault. How was he supposed to have made one ounce of sense from what Gabe had told him? Even if he'd been given the right message, it was unfair to expect him to spread it successfully by himself. This didn't say much for Nobby's confidence in his chosen one, if he wanted the masses to hear it from a regular human instead. He was a sturdy young man, but still looked knackered from the hike, and I bet it wasn't the first time he'd been told to bring booze either. All he had in front of him, regardless of what happened that night, was a lifetime spent trying to convince everyone that an angel had given him the Word of God. And if I didn't set him straight, which I wasn't going to do, there would be disastrous consequences.

Gabe, who had either forgotten to cover his face or couldn't be bothered, exchanged a few grumbled words with the prophet, who closed his eyes and bowed his head as Gabe brought a bottle over.

'What's he doing?' I said.

'He's got a bad back, so Oi said Oi would cure him.'

'And can you?'

'No. Can yee?'

'No.'

KEPT IN THE DARK

Our laughter brought the prophet out of his trance. He fell back on his knees with his hands in the air, crying what I assumed were more thanks and apologies to Gabe, who blessed him with a sign of the cross that I was sure was the wrong way. It seemed to work, though, and he dropped to all fours and crawled into the cave with a wince as his back spasmed up.

I moved into view. 'Right, find out why he's sorry,' I said.

Gabe sat crossed-legged at the entrance and muttered a few words. This prompted more machine-gun-like barking from the prophet, which made me wonder why Nobby hadn't equipped me with a tongue for the local language. I'd had the same problem last time and reckoned there'd be some excuse like *He who has sinned shall not be sowed with the speech of something, something.*

Gabe cut him off and got a quick word in, then turned to me.

'He says he's been troyin ta convince everyone he's been chosen by d'Good Lord since Oi turned up, but no one will believe him. Dey make fun o'him ta d'point where he's started ta doubt it himself. Den last noight a horse wid wings was seen dancin' in d'town square. Dey said it couldn't floy, but it ran like d'wind and snorted bolts o'lightnin' from its nose and farted tunder as it galloped up d'mountains ta bring d'rains dat fed d'lands. He tought dey were teasin' him until Oi told him about yee oilier. And now all he wants ta do is say sorry f'doubtin' me and beg forgiveness.'

'So forgive him and let's get on with this.'

Gabe flicked another bottle from the box with his wing and said a few words into the cave. The prophet wailed again, so piteously that I wanted to drag him out and put him out of his misery. One blow from my hoof and he wouldn't be awake to be forgiven by anyone.

'Okay, give him your final speech,' I said.

'What d'ya mean?'

'For fuck's sake, Gabe. You're God's messenger, remember? The idiot upstairs that's gonna send us to Lucy if we don't get this right? The one who gave you power to steal booze without being seen? Ring any bells?'

'So what is d'last message?'

'What are you asking me for?'

'Did d'Good Lord not tell ya what d'message was before ya came?'

'Yes. But I'm fucked if I can remember.'

We folded up and clinked bottles.

'So what were you going to tell him before I showed up?' I said.

'Oi was gonna tell him d'one last toime ta learn ta read, so he could wroite it all down before he forgot it. And dat d'Good Lord loves him wid all his heart.'

I waited for the rest, but it was soon evident no more was coming.

'Please, tell me that's not it,' I said as Gabe stared at the floor. 'You mean to tell me that I've been sitting up here all day in the scorching heat, drinking this disgusting stuff, and listening to you slur your way through everything from how you were the best man in town with your fists, to sinking the Ark before you even got on the fucking thing, and all for two fucking sentences?'

KEPT IN THE DARK

A bark came from inside the cave and Gabe poked his head in. 'Would ya fook off in dere. Oi'm prayin' ta d'Lord ta cure ya back, so Oi am.'

I assumed Gabe was unaware he'd said it in English as there was no follow-up translation, but it shut the prophet up whether he understood it or not.

'Well Oi kinda knew Oi'd messed up after d'fiost meetin',' said Gabe. 'But Oi was annoyed at havin' ta come back, and don't tink Oi was speakin' too kindly of d'Lord at dis stage.'

'So why didn't you start again the next time you saw him? After you'd calmed down.'

'Cos d'foist ting Oi told him was dat every word Oi came ta speak was d'unchanging word o'God. Oi could hardly go back d'very next day and say d'opposite was now true. He may be an idiot, but he's not stupid.'

'So what did you tell him about Nobby?' I said, trying not to laugh. I realised I'd been more interested in Gabe's biblical stories than in what he'd told the prophet.

'It's all a bit hazy as Oi'd been on d'drenk,' he said. 'But Oi sure let him know what happens ta anyone dat doesn't do as d'Good Lord says. D'poor fella sure started ta listen up when Oi told him dat, Oi don't moind tellin' ya.

'Oi told him dat if dey rejected him, dey would be punished wid terrible agony in dis world and in d'hereafter, wi'not a soul ta help'em. And dat anyone who makes mischief in d'land would be crucifoied. Like y'man Jasus. But when it came ta rememberin' d'message, moi moind went blank and Oi had ta tink on moi feet a bit.'

I pictured the scene. The prophet sitting in the cave getting five minutes away from the missus, when out of the blue Gabe crawls in. Bottle in hand, breath like a barrel of scotch, and ready to let off steam about Nobby before making up the greatest tale since Jesus. The saying *Alcohol is the root of all evil* took on a more profound meaning as I thought about what might've been achieved had Gabe turned up sober.

'Oi told him about d'joys o'Heaven and d'fires o'Hell,' he continued. 'And dat only dose who believe wid be saved. Which Oi knew ta be bollocks, seein' as Oi believed and didn't feel saved at all. All Oi want ta do is rest in peace and get dronk. Is dat too much f'ra'man ta ask?'

'Well, that's it then, we're fucked,' I said. Secretly wanting to punch the air. 'Tonight is the night that the final revelation shall be given, and it consists of two sentences. Two sentences with which you have to convince the prophet to do the opposite of what you've already told him without contradicting yourself. And you can't remember what you've already told him. Good luck with that one.'

I was aware my voice had risen and that the prophet would know someone else was there, but that didn't matter, it was all over bar the shouting. As it stood, history was on course to repeat itself, and I now needed to pick Gabe's brains in case he disappeared in a puff of smoke as soon as he'd given the last two mesmerising sentences.

'Listen, Gabe,' I said. 'My mum's in Hell. She died a non-believer. Please tell me there's a way to save her.'

'How did she die?'

'My father killed her. So I killed him. I thought that's why Nobby sent me to Lucy, then I found out it was because I didn't believe. Which means my mum is in Hell too.'

He screwed his face up. 'Ya been ta see Lucy as well as Nobby too?'

'I went to Heaven first, then got thrown back and forth between them. But for some reason Nobby doesn't want Lucy to have me, even though I died a non-believer.'

'How did yee die?' he said.

'Some old man killed me. It's a long story.'

He hesitated, and I wasn't sure if he was waiting for the long story, or thinking about how to save my mum.

'What did Nobby do when ya told him ya killed yer farder?' he said, which told me his wheels were turning in my favour.

'He sent me to Lucy, who then destroyed my body.'

'And what did Lucy do when ya told him ya killed yer farder?'

'He sent me back to Nobby, who then sent me back in time to fix his fuck-ups.'

'Back in toime ta me?' he said.

'Not exactly. It's another long story.'

Again, he hesitated. And again, he fortunately wasn't interested in the long story.

'Ya need ta get Nobby ta send ya back ta save yer ma, and make sure she dies believin',' he said.

'I know, but Nobby won't send me back to save someone who didn't believe. Especially if there's nothing in it for him.'

It wasn't going well. He was telling me nothing I hadn't heard from Jesus.

'Tell Nobby,' he said, 'if ya go back and stop yer farder killin' yer moder, den yel have no reason ta kill yer farder.'

'Why would Nobby care about my father?'

'Oh, he'll care. Oi'm an angel, don't forget. Oi know more dan ya tink.'

I had no choice but to believe him. I had nothing else to go on once I got back to Nobby. That was if I got back to Nobby, as he did say it was three strikes and you're out. Gabe's was the final revelation. There were no more chosen ones for me to chase around.

I also wondered what would happen to Gabe. Yes, he was a believer and would return to Heaven, but he'd still have to go through a debrief. And just like with Jesus, I didn't want him blabbing about what had happened. Especially that I'd been on the sauce all day, and had made no effort to sort out the poison that the prophet was about to infect the world with. And as Gabe was just as likely to forget what I told him as what Nobby told him, I decided to use the threat of Lucy, as I had with Jesus, to make him listen up.

I took a step back in case he attacked me again. 'Listen, Gabe, if Nobby finds out I was here he'll send me to Lucy, unless I tell him you'd already given the wrong message before I got here.'

A wet patch grew around Gabe's groin area, and I knew I should've approached the subject with a bit more subtlety. I had to relax him before he became doubly incontinent.

'It's okay, Gabe. You're going to be fine, as long as you don't say a word about me to Nobby. He won't ask you about me, so you won't have to lie. Just tell him you gave the prophet the message and you'll be back in Heaven before you know it.

Gabe's bottom lip began to wobble. 'Oi trust ya, Jimmy. Please don't le'me go ta d'Dark.'

'Don't worry,' I said. 'I have as much to lose as you. We're in this together.'

Gabe smiled and I knew I had him onside, but I also knew I had to end the night before he forgot everything I'd just said.

'Right, give y'man the rest of the good news so we can get the fuck out of here.'

I didn't wait to make sure Gabe completed the revelation. I wouldn't have understood it and even Gabe was unlikely to forget two sentences, which meant my work was done. I certainly had no intention of carrying the prophet anywhere. By the time Gabe had crawled into the cave I was airborne.

*

Under normal circumstances, flying while drunk wouldn't be advisable for a horse, especially at night. But it does have its advantages, especially when the horse in question wants to die. There were no dark clouds, no pelting rain, no heavy wet wings and no angels to crash into. The town was dark and asleep and the only light came from the stars and a half-moon that glistened off the lake. I didn't want to take any humans with me, and didn't want to be breakfast, lunch or dinner for whatever scavengers found my corpse splattered on the side of a mountain the next morning.

There were no other horses near the lake to get spooked, and no nighttime ramblers to have a story to tell their grandkids. I lined myself up over the water, closed my eyes and plunged yet again to my death.

Twenty

Talking to Nobby had become so painful that I wanted to throw down my cards as soon as he bothered to turn up. But he wanted to drag it out and just stared, and I stared back, and it reminded me of the stare-outs I'd had with Tinkerbell, only Nobby didn't have claws or teeth, just a broom handle stuffed up his arse.

He'd created that which he did not know but thought he did. He'd then recruited two random people from a world that had not only been proven to be imperfect, but which was by his own admission, and doing, full of sin, to persuade everyone to use the freewill they'd been gifted with, by him, to believe in him or be sent to Hell. What a clown. And there he was, no doubt about to pass the blame squarely back onto me. And why? Because he couldn't find Lucy... but I could.

'You have failed again,' I said.

If he'd had a face, it would've been a picture. That I had spoken first was guaranteed to piss him off no end, but to throw his own line back at him with such insolence was a sure-fire way to get sent to Hell. But as I said, he wanted to drag this out, which meant he was still reluctant to let the Dark have me.

'You have returned with further blasphemy,' he said. 'And have again shown yourself unworthy.'

'So what am I doing back here? I thought it was three strikes and you're out.'

'Man sinned through the wishes of the Dark,' he said, again reluctant to give me a straight answer, 'and so I gave him away to repent. But to repent, one must first follow me and deny the Dark.'

'Why?' I said. 'Why do people have to know you exist to survive death? Why did you give them freewill on the condition they use it to believe in you? Life consists of more important things than believing you exist. Life is the experience. If in death people either go to Heaven or Hell based on whether they believe, you are denying that the human experience exists. It makes me wonder why you bothered with the world at all. Would it not have made sense to create Heaven, fill it with souls and be done with it?'

'Life has to exist for it to die,' he said. 'And only in death can man be judged. You were given a life, and now you are being judged.'

His narcissism was ever more nauseating. Lucy's brutal honesty, by contrast, sounded refreshing.

'Oh, that life. I remember. The one where me and my mum were slaves, so I couldn't use the magic you never gave me to show everyone the wisdom of your ways.'

'All men are free.'

'Oh, for fuck's sake, Nobby, that's not how it works down there. Have you even read the books they've put

KEPT IN THE DARK

your name to? Man has been enslaving man since Eve proved you were full of shit, so for a man to enslave his wife and child is not that uncommon.'

The dozy bastard looked puzzled and his game was peeling away in sheets.

'You were enslaved?' he said. It was like talking to a dementia patient.

'Now you're catching on. I was under the control of Fatty. My father, before you ask.'

'Did Fatty not tell you of me?'

I couldn't believe I got him to call my father Fatty.

'He did, as it happens. But my mum didn't, and I'll always believe her over him.'

'Redemption can only come from remorse,' he said. 'Yet you have shown no remorse for your sin.'

'Remorse,' I said. 'What the fuck do you know about remorse? I don't feel remorse because I shouldn't. You should've shown mercy to my mother and justice to my father, but you didn't. I've been trying to make up for my so-called "sin" since I died, while you sit here pretending it's all part of your plan. How about extending your plan to show a bit of compassion? I killed my father because he killed my mother. She died a non-believer and I don't have to guess where she is now.'

Then he dropped the bombshell. Together with an insult that made me turn in my grave.

'Your mother should have listened to your father,' he said. 'Then she would be in Heaven with him.'

It was my turn to fall silent. I didn't know whom I hated most at that moment. Nobby for delivering such an ignorant and hurtful statement, or Lucy for stitching me up. Lucy was always going to renege on our deal, but he must've known Nobby could send me back again when I found out.

I got back to work.

'Seeing as you care more about Fatty than my mother, and I care more about her than him, maybe we can reach a compromise.'

He said nothing, but I got the impression he was willing to listen.

'If you send me back to stop my father from killing my mother, I'll have no reason to kill my father,' I lied.

Strangely enough, Gabe was right: Nobby bought it hook, line and sinker. But although I understood why Nobby was keen to iron out the creases of history from his point of view, I couldn't for the death of me fathom why he'd chosen me, and I certainly didn't know why he didn't want Lucy to have me, to the point where he would send me back to my own life when there was nothing in it for him.

The brief didn't take long, and I didn't bother asking to be an animal of sufficient size to take down the fat one, as it would have fallen on deaf ears anyway.

Twenty-One

Lucy hated life and wanted to destroy it, which sounded like the epitome of evil, and he was, but I think Nobby should've gone with it so he could start afresh, instead of trying to fix a poisoned Earth with the band-aid of a chosen one. He let his guard down and broke his own rules so early in history that it was no wonder man progressed to sin.

First of all, Eden was supposed to be sin-free. Well, it wasn't, was it; there was a bastard tree right in the middle, riddled with sin. Then there was Nobby's alleged author of sin, Lucy, prowling around. I'll let him off that I was also there, also riddled with sin, but he broke one of his own commandments when he lied to Adam about dying if he and Eve ate from the tree.

Lucy knew they wouldn't die. If he'd thought for one moment they would, he would've stuffed a piece of fruit in Eve's hand as soon as look at her. No, he wanted them to eat the fruit of their own accord to show that Nobby had lied about them dying if they did so. He knew Nobby would tell Adam and Eve not to eat from it, and wanted them to question why they were required to use their freewill to worship the Lord or be damned. Especially when Nobby had already lied to them. Lucy thought that if he got them to sin at such an early stage it might encourage Nobby to cancel the poisoned Earth and start again on a new planet, hopefully with a less egotistical attitude. But Nobby was as stubborn as he was stupid and couldn't admit when he was wrong. Especially after being exposed by Lucy.

So when Adam and Eve lived on and realised that Nobby had pulled the wool over their eyes, Nobby had to come up with an excuse. One that he called mercy, which was a suspension of the justice he wasn't aware of. If Nobby could show mercy to people who'd eaten a piece of fruit after he'd told them not to, he should also show mercy to those who had never learned of his existence, or weren't given sufficient evidence to allow them to believe.

But he was powerless to stop non-believers being dragged away to Hell. A Hell that he was unaware of until I brought him up to speed. So I guessed part of his message was for people not to ask questions, and just accept that if they believed they would know not to sin. And I didn't blame Nobby for letting people believe he saw their every move and heard their deepest thoughts. He was insecure enough without worrying about people pretending to love him out loud, but in their minds thinking he was an idiot.

I saw it as nothing short of blackmail. *You shall believe in me or be damned.* Which translates into *Believe in me or I'll blame you for sin and make you suffer for my mistake.* When he didn't even know what sin was, if it ever existed in the first place. If there ever was an original sin, it was when Nobby failed to do the required safety checks on his creation before he pressed start.

But Nobby had a plan. Oh, yes. He had a sneaky feeling that Adam and his good lady wife might be vulnerable to whatever it was that interfered when he created his perfect world, thus making it imperfect, so just in case things didn't go as planned, he gave himself a bit of insurance by putting aside a special soul all ready and packaged. With not so much a message of goodwill to all men, but a message of goodwill to himself, by way of telling everyone to believe or else.

For it was he who gave the wonderful gift of life, and so it was he who should be worshiped. That some would die without receiving the message and not be eligible for Heaven, or that some might endure unspeakable suffering before getting in, or that some might not be convinced by the idiots who had the responsibility of making sure everyone was on the same page, wasn't his concern, as long as there came a time when everyone believed, thus proving him perfect. What happened in between would soon be forgotten.

So after Adam died and told Nobby what had happened – perhaps helped by a quick visit to Lucy – he dusted down the soul and sent it into action in the form of Noah. And to be fair to Nobby, he couldn't have known that Noah was going to hit the bottle as soon as the opportunity arose, for Nobby hadn't known that alcohol existed. It was rotten fruit. The work of the Devil. And Nobby had to pretend, to himself if no one else, that Noah had succeeded, to save himself the humiliation of having to admit that it was a stupid idea to expect a hundred men to build a boat big enough for the task he'd set, never mind one man.

Then Moses was given a go, this time with a strong message for man. Well, a message for the men who weren't chasing him and his followers. But that didn't matter, for Nobby had given this chosen one magic powers so he couldn't be beaten to death as Noah had been. And, I have to say, that parting a whole sea so that he and his followers could escape the bad guys was more impressive than the trivial tricks he subsequently pumped out as Jesus.

Moses of course failed to spread the message effectively, but he was smart enough to go back with a tale of burning bushes and stone tablets bearing the ultimate words of wisdom, the latter surely a result of the fumes he inhaled from the bushes. What actually happened on that mountain not even Nobby knew. He liked to pretend that he not only saw what took place, but had orchestrated it as part of his plan. But I knew different. Nobby couldn't have set a bush on fire from where he was, any more than he could've spoken to Moses through it.

Then there was poor old Jesus. Poor old Jesus, my arse. He lived thirty-plus years as a magic man with an entourage that would follow him around, singing his praises to all and sundry, believing that no matter what happened he'd end up in Heaven because he was a chosen one. Jesus wasn't stupid; he may have been lazy and a coward, but he knew what he was doing – i.e. he knew that he had to put on a show hoping it would convince Nobby he'd given it his best shot. But he was also aware that his message was bollocks and not enough people were buying it, and in the end he couldn't wait to clock out. I didn't blame him.

All this crap about his death saving man from sin was some yarn he spun to make his death seem poignant, so he could collect his eternal season ticket to the royal box. He could've lived forever, or at least until everyone knew of Nobby, but instead he found someone who would happily sell a friend down the river for the right price. Sounds rather extreme, I know, but I was fucked if I could work out what went on in the heads of those lunatics. Any society that believes that all sins, crimes and other misdemeanours should be punishable by a torturous death, as ordered by God, has a lot to learn. But this was what Nobby let happen, despite Lucy's early interruption to show him the folly of his ways.

Then, for some reason, Nobby dragged Noah back into the picture and sent him down to Earth as the Archangel Gabriel. Not exactly a home run, let's be honest. The poor fella was on a hiding to nothing from the moment he had his first drink as Noah. Lucy had that one covered.

I thought about all the people who had ever lived and who were now in either Heaven or Hell, courtesy of Nobby's divine plan, and could only wonder how many of them would've made a better chosen one than the clowns Nobby so irresponsibly picked out with no background checks whatsoever. Neither Nobby nor Lucy were as smart as they made themselves out to be. Sure, they were powerful and determined, and you could argue that you need a level of intelligence to become powerful and determined, in some form at least, but their problem was that they couldn't see a use for their power beyond serving themselves. At least, Nobby couldn't. Lucy was just a cunt who didn't care about his power, as long as Nobby didn't use his to create substandard life, because life as Nobby would have it consisted of nothing more than people kissing his arse. But any God that demands worship cannot be worthy of worship.

The freewill Nobby gifted mankind showed that love cannot be forced, only felt. He was a coward who was unable to feel love, so he lashed out at those who did feel it. And whether he liked it or not, or was willing to admit it, he was ultimately responsible for everything including: my smart-arse remarks, Gabe for being a drunk, Jesus for being a coward, Moses for getting stoned, Noah for being stupid, Eve for eating the fruit and Lucy for being a cunt, as well as for disease, natural disasters, war, suffering, slavery, psychopaths, rats, snakes, spiders and anything else that might want to harm you, bite you, kill you, eat you or otherwise piss you off. Why would God allow a world where he'd have no choice but to stand by and watch the horrors unfold? Does he have the freewill to not watch? To pretend it's not happening? To convince himself it's okay to do nothing about it? Can he simply forget?

Twenty-Two

Normally, every time I left Nobby's office to go on one of his errands, I was aware of Lucy before I re-entered the Cosmos. I could never see him, hear him or feel him, but I always sensed him, like he'd been looking over Nobby's shoulder wearing an invisibility cloak. This time, however, I more than sensed him. This time I *did* see, hear and feel him.

He'd watched me pass through each time, knowing he couldn't stop me from going back to Earth. But he also seemed to be savvy to the 'three strikes and you're out' rule, which was why he assumed I'd be staying with him this time. I didn't know if he knew what I'd been up to, although it did occur to me that he'd now remember me from Eden.

I wasn't looking forward to re-engaging with the stubborn dick, but needs must, and I was interested to see what sort of mood he was in. Not a word was said at first, but I knew what he was thinking. At least I hoped to God I knew. Three strikes and you're out. But there could be no more than one strike on this side of the fence. This was it. The last chance saloon. The one where Jimmy Linton lives in Heaven or dies in Hell by the success or failure of his final mission.

The last words I'd heard him speak as a snake were on repeat in my mind as he loomed into view, reminding me that he hadn't made good on the deal. Mum wasn't in Heaven and I was back in Hell. But not for long.

'You have done well,' he said.

I didn't reply. This cunt had promised me a lot more than a pat on the back.

'Lord shall not come for you again, for you belong to me.'

I still didn't reply. I belonged to no one but me, and certainly not to this wannabe God. But if he had been looking over Nobby's shoulder, he obviously hadn't heard what was said, or he'd have known it wasn't over yet.

The silence continued as he waited for me to confront him about welching on our deal. But I wasn't going to give him the pleasure of gloating. It was me who was about to gloat.

'You've shot yourself in the foot I'm afraid, Darth,' I said when I could hold my tongue no more. 'Nobby's sending me back to my old life.'

'Lord sent you to me, for he knows you are mine.'

'No, he's just pissed off I'm no longer any use to him, now he's run out of chosen ones for me to chase around. He certainly doesn't want *you* to have me. Your race has run its course, my old son.'

'Why would Lord send you back to Earth again?' he said. 'He has been defeated.'

'Yes, and so have you. The only one who still has a horse in this race is me. I talked him into sending me back to save my mother so I don't have to kill my father.'

Then it was his turn to gloat. I don't know why, but he thought he'd somehow got one over on me. And although he couldn't stop me from going back, I suddenly felt vulnerable.

'You have a short memory,' he said. 'Your mother will stay with me.'

'Not if she dies a believer.'

'How will her belief be changed if she died with no care for the truth of Lord.'

That had been on my mind. But first, I had to hope I was an animal big enough to save her from Fatty.

'That's for me to worry about,' I said. 'Although I would turn my father into a non-believer if I could, you'd be welcome to that fat bastard. He's a bitch, much like you are, but he's in Heaven and you're in Hell.'

'You shall not obey Lord's instruction to stop you from killing your father,' he said.

'You do realise he died a believer and is in Heaven? Why would you want him dead?'

I didn't know what it was about Fatty that had the Masters of the Universe so at odds about his existence. Indeed, given that destroying life was Lucy's hobby and profession, you'd think he'd be glad I killed my father. But Fatty went to Heaven, which may have been Lucy's beef. Almost understandable, but Fatty was just one among many to die a believer, and would almost certainly die a believer again if I saved him. Which I had no intention of doing. I knew he'd still end up in Heaven, but there was nothing I could do about that. This was about getting my mum out of Hell.

'My wishes are not your concern,' he said.

'Bullshit. I gave you your wish when I got that dumb broad to eat the fruit. That was the deal, but you didn't meet your end. Now if you don't mind, I have to get going. And by the way, I'm going back as a werewolf this time so I'll do what the fuck I want.'

'Only Lord can send you back, but it is I who chooses your form as it was I who took your body.'

The sneaky shit. He'd been following this all along. No wonder Nobby was so blasé about me being reduced to animal life; he had no control over it anyway. I didn't know if he knew Lucy was pulling the strings or whether he'd convinced himself it was all part of his divine plan. But one thing was for sure: I wasn't going back as a werewolf

PART TWO

Twenty-Three

After several months of planning, Susan had only come up with a bunch of clichés she had learned from the endless books she read. Steal a key to get another cut and return it before anyone notices. Create a diversion to sneak off and return without being seen. Naturally, she must cover her tracks and leave no fingerprints, although her prints weren't on file and hopefully never would be.

Her indulgence in a world of fictional crime fashioned in the safety of someone else's imagination was what kept her going to some extent. It was a place to hide and compare someone else's world to hers. And although she never read a book where she didn't empathise with the victims, she rarely read about someone who had a harder time than she did. One would assume that didn't include murder victims, but that was not necessarily the case.

Like every other keen reader, she always tried to work out who the culprit was before the end, and although she never solved the case before the detective, she liked to think she was only one or two steps behind. Now she would be the culprit in real life and would have to stay one or two steps ahead. She'd often thought about writing a crime story of her own, to create a crook and defeat him (or her) and give inspiration and hope to other real victims. But she wasn't writing a script where she could decide what happened, and she couldn't be a fly on the wall in every room she needed to be in. Not to mention the fact that there were several crimes she had to commit, each one more difficult than the last, ending with one less family member. But this was what she had to do. There were no more alternatives. This time he *had* to go. Everything else had failed. She'd tried poison, but he seemed to have an indestructible constitution.

To think some people did this sort of thing for a living was inconceivable to her. To get a kick out of it even as a one-off, never mind a lifestyle, seemed counterintuitive to living a productive life. But here she was, painstakingly plotting a mini crime wave that would destroy her family in the hope that freedom would rise from the ashes. But it wasn't a real hope, it couldn't be, as any sense of hope had been driven out of her. Not by broken promises, but by promises never made in the first place. He had never given her reason to hope for anything.

All she had to do was steal some keys. No one would get hurt and she'd have a few weeks to prepare for stage two. Or pull out. But that would require either a mental breakdown from her, which wouldn't be unexpected, or a major change from him, which would be very unexpected.

It was to be done on a parents' evening at the school, and she'd convinced her husband their son needed to be there. He didn't, but she wanted to kill two birds with one stone: to get her son out of the house, and to use him in case she needed a diversion. The boy was oblivious to his mother's secret agenda, which was just as well, as part of the plan was to have him arrested for a crime she committed.

Her son was the only pupil there that night. What other fifteen-year-old would gladly go to a parents' evening? They sat opposite the head teacher, Mrs Poleglase, and Susan feigned interest in the rundown of her son's academic achievements, or lack thereof, while her eyes roamed under the desk.

There was an open handbag with a bunch of keys resting between papers and pens. Just begging to be stolen. She'd done her homework and knew which keys she needed to steal, and had two keys of the same make in her pocket. They were never going to open the school and she didn't care if they did. If all went to plan, they would never be used. She hadn't planned how to actually acquire the keys; she wasn't a master criminal and would have to rely on a bit of luck, and now there they were, only three feet away. She sent her son out under the guise of wanting to talk to his teacher in private, in the far-flung hope he would get bored enough to set off the fire alarm.

Mrs Poleglase rambled on about how her son needed to buck his ideas up if he wanted to make something of himself. As she listened to this waffle, Susan felt the urge to stick her foot out and drag the bag over. The teacher couldn't see from the way she was sat forward, and if anyone else looked over they would hopefully think the bag was hers.

But her foot was going nowhere. This was new territory for Susan. Being humiliated at home was part of life, but to get caught stealing so blatantly at her son's school in front of everyone, including her son, would have killed her. She had to find another way.

She excused herself and rushed to the toilet. Staring into the mirror she felt cowardly yet proud that she couldn't commit a crime. Then she remembered what this meant, as if she needed reminding. The trauma of her life, along with the stress of the situation, built up, and a warm blood rush forced her fist into the mirror. Glass shattered around the sink and blood trickled from her hand, and she looked up and thanked God for another bit of luck.

Mrs Poleglase was out of her chair with words of concern before the first drop of blood hit the classroom floor. She handed Susan a tissue from her handbag before searching for a first-aid kit. Susan sat in her chair with a reassuring wave and smile to the onlookers, and had enough time to swap the necessary keys over without leaving her seat, never mind the room. She also slipped a pen in her pocket that would come in handy later. Maybe she *was* a master criminal.

The cut wasn't bad, nothing a wipe of a tissue and a band-aid wouldn't fix. Mrs Poleglase advised her to go to the hospital, but if she could survive the cuts and bruises she picked up at home without hospital treatment, then a nick to her hand wouldn't be worth waiting in A&E for. It did, however, give her a chance to get away early. She was under no official curfew, but if they weren't back by the time his stomach started rumbling, not even a sob story about a cut hand would save her. But there was a second part to this evening's plan she had to complete first. The easy part.

Her son didn't ask why they didn't go straight home. He would've sat in the classroom until morning if it meant being out of the house, so going to Margaret's was a treat, and a rare one. Margaret was Susan's best friend and like a second mum to him. She was also the only person Susan's husband was wary of, which was why they were all but barred from seeing her. But tonight, Susan had a bit of time on her hands. Time her husband thought was being spent at the school. And the look she gave Margaret when she asked her to mind her son for an hour was all Margaret needed to not ask questions. Susan would tell her when she was good and ready.

She had acquired the address during the conversation with Mrs Poleglase that had been cut short. It was easy to pretend you used to live down the same street as someone who'd not been there long. *Oh really? I used to live down Summerlands some years ago. What number are you?... Thirty-two. I was at number six.*

There were two cars parked in the driveway at 32 Summerlands. She had no idea which one was her target. So she let two tyres down on each. They hissed as she poked the stolen pen in the valve and she was scared her son's teacher would appear over her shoulder.

*

The next day, on her lunch break, Susan walked into town and got two keys cut from the cobblers, then caught the bus to the school. She'd initially planned to use the excuse of having left something behind the night before, but now that cliché was not needed. She had the genuine reason of thanking the teacher for her first aid.

KEPT IN THE DARK

Lunch break at the school coincided with her lunch break at work. She entered the staff room to find several people there. Most importantly, Mrs Poleglase, who rose from her chair with an awkward smile. Susan thanked her for her efforts the night before, and then made small talk, waiting for a story about thugs having let her and her husband's tyres down, making them late for work this morning. It never came. This didn't mean she hadn't been late for work and hadn't needed the keys to get in, and as there was no story about stolen keys, Susan assumed she'd been successful. But that was last night's plan. Now she had to put the keys back. And again, the bag was only a few feet away under a chair.

She prolonged the conversation with trivialities about her son, the weather, how her car hadn't started that morning, and Mrs Poleglase stared and nodded, clearly eager to end the chat and get back to her lunch. Susan needed another distraction and recalled a scene in *Fawlty Towers* where Basil pretended to faint to avoid an awkward situation, and although she had no intention of dropping to the floor as Basil had done, she had learned the value of using people's empathy as a means of diversion the previous evening.

She rolled her eyes, faked a dazed look and let her leg buckle.

'Oh, my,' she said. 'Would you mind awfully if I sat down? I feel a bit dizzy.'

She made a beeline for the chair and sat with her head in her hands. Everyone stared, and the keys couldn't be swapped back with so many eyes in her direction. Someone handed her a glass of water and she glanced at her watch as she sipped. There was still ten minutes until lessons started. She should have timed this better.

'Would you like me to call someone?' asked Mrs Poleglase.

'No, it's okay, thank you,' said Susan. 'I just need to sit for a minute. I get a bit flustered when I'm in a room with lots of people I don't know.'

The room was empty except for her and Mrs Poleglase within twenty seconds. Susan didn't know where she'd heard that one and hoped it was her own, but either way, it worked a treat. She gulped the water and held out the empty glass.

'Would you mind if I had another one, please?'

Mrs Poleglase looked at her own watch as she made her way to the sink. Susan put her hand in the bag. She couldn't feel any keys. And thought that if she hadn't driven in today and needed her keys to open the school, she might not have brought them. Maybe her husband had put the two spares on one car and driven her to work. Her keys could be in his car. And once the swap was realised, she would backtrack her movements to the parents' evening. Would the police want to interview everyone who'd been there? Would they ask the cobblers who had had keys cut recently? Susan dealt with a barrage of details not covered before the teacher returned.

'I have to go back to class now,' said Mrs Polglase. 'But you can stay here until you feel better if you like.'

Susan took the water but didn't see the point in sitting there by herself, even if the handbag was left behind. Mrs Poleglase grabbed her coat from the back of the chair and slung it over her arm. It rattled.

KEPT IN THE DARK

'No, thanks, I'll be fine,' said Susan. 'But if you could be so kind as to walk me to the bus stop, I would be grateful.'

'Of course,' said Mrs Poleglase, struggling to hide her growing impatience.

Outside the school gates and a stone's throw from the bus stop, Susan again let her leg buckle and fell into the teacher. She grabbed her coat as she went down.

'Just give me a minute, I'll be okay,' she said. 'Could you see if the bus is coming.'

Mrs Poleglase walked to the kerb and Susan did what she needed to do.

'I'm fine now, thank you,' she said as she rose to her feet and held the coat out. 'I'm so sorry if I've made you late for class.'

'No, that's no problem,' said Mrs Poleglase. 'Are you sure you're going to be alright?'

'Yes, thank you so much.'

Mrs Poleglase walked away and Susan got to work on the keys. She'd practiced this in her build-up and had them back in their original formation before their owner had disappeared through the school gates.

'I say,' she called.

Mrs Poleglase turned to see her waving the keys in the air.

'Oh, thank you,' she said. 'I don't know what I would've done without those.'

Now Susan had the keys with no credible link back to her. But the next crime would require a lot more work and courage.

Twenty-Four

This was the one where I really could save the world. At least my world. Outside of that, there was no world. Maybe it was solipsism, but I never felt an obligation to sacrifice myself for the sake of mankind. It would achieve nothing I would be aware of, and no one would be aware of what I'd achieved.

Maybe that made me a arsehole, along with Nobby and Lucy, but I was and could only be a product of theirs and the acceptable conditions for life they couldn't agree on. If they could've communicated in some way, perhaps more people would've earned a golden ticket into Nobby's fun house. And I make no apology for playing the advantage to ensure I got another chance after the misery I'd endured the first time. But it was simply not good enough for Nobby to create whatever he could, and then run with it because he was unable to admit where the fault was. He'd put no consideration into the possibility that man would use freewill to think for himself, which would result in a unity far stronger than the worship he demanded.

KEPT IN THE DARK

As soon as I opened my eyes I knew what I was. The multiple vision gave the game away. I was on the outside wall of my parent's bedroom, where my sight was joined by the shuddering snore echoing through the open window like it was trying to wake the dead. As a child, it had been a strangely comforting sound because it meant *he* was asleep. There was only cause for concern when it stopped.

I waited as my eyesight was reduced to binocular vision and thought about a plan. Not many options for a fly, to be fair, but my fear of failure was eased by my excitement at seeing my mum again. Not only that, but I was back to save her, to extend her life by the years she deserved, and somehow convince her that Fatty was right and there is a God.

When the excess images had faded away, I examined my body. Nothing could shock me now. My six legs were thin, black and hairy, and with my angled wings I felt like a fighter jet. I gave them a test flap and shot into next door's fence and prepared to fall, but I was stuck to it. *Fucking hell, this is handy. I'm like Spiderman.*

My wings were harder to operate than when I was a horse, and I did a few laps of the house to loosen up and work on various attack manoeuvres. My reactions were razor-sharp, and I could change direction in mid-air like… well, like a fly. Ready for battle, I took a breath and flew in the window.

The room was hot and musty and I hovered in the middle and stared at my parents in bed. My mother was on her side facing away from Fatty. Her eyes were wide open, one of them black, and I knew it wasn't the snoring keeping her awake. She was used to it and used it like I had – as a reverse alarm clock. When it stopped, you'd better wake up and be ready; until then, get as much sleep as you could. Fatty was asleep on his back with a streak of dried dribble down his cheek, and his exhaling was as loud as his inhaling.

I looked away to avoid the pain in my mother's eyes and indulged in a few moments of real-time nostalgia. Simple things like the scraggy curtains and stained wallpaper triggered childhood memories of cuddling up to Mum in the bed when Fatty was out. Her jewellery box was on the chest of drawers – once filled with family heirlooms that dwindled to nothing over the years from Fatty's pilfering. The belt was in the loops of his trousers. How I wished I could pick it up and rain it down upon his head. How many times would make it even? But I was determined the belt would play no part in what happened today. Not if I could help it.

My only advantage was the power of flight, but Fatty was grossly overweight and not the mildest tempered of chaps, so I figured a constant air raid by a vengeful fly might topple him into cardiac arrest. But I had to beware, being so small, and needed an escape route in case the spray came out.

The snoring died to a splutter and cough. The alarm clock was about to go off.

'Woman,' barked Fatty.

My mum rose from the bed and put her dressing gown on and I followed her through the door, broken at seeing her so sad. Yet that was the only memory I really had of her. I gave her privacy in the bathroom and waited on the kitchen ceiling of the place I'd reluctantly called home for most of my life. There were no warm feelings, only memories I'd give my wings not to have had.

Mum entered to make breakfast. Well, Fatty's breakfast, and I watched a familiar scene unfold in a hopeless daze. My mother doing as she was told. Tenacious, yet without an ounce of pride, and I cursed Nobby and Lucy that I couldn't even give her a hug. Instead, I had to sit and watch as she moved methodically between her tasks. Bacon in the pan, eggs at the ready, kettle on, plate out, cutlery down, the paper opened on the racing section and placed on the table. That fucking table. How many times had I cowered under it in self-loathing because I wasn't big enough to defend her?

She was thin and tired and not just from a lack of sleep. I yearned to land on her shoulder and whisper 'I love you' in her ear, but I knew I'd end up with a face full of spray, and that would not be a good start to the day. I felt helpless enough without being killed by the person I was here to save, and realised this could be an ongoing problem. For neither my mother nor my father – nor indeed myself – was shy with the spray.

My hypnotic gaze was diverted to a rising noise coming down the hall. I didn't worry it might be Fatty as Mum and I left the house trouble-free on that day. Plus, I knew what it was. It was one of those fat, buzzing flies that ruin everyone's peace and quiet, and the last thing I needed was for some noisy idiot to upset Mum and make her reach for the spray. It did a couple of laps, eyeing the beads of sweat on her forehead. *Not on my watch, you don't*, I thought as I dive-bombed the intruder and landed a telling head-butt on its side. Buzz winced and wobbled around in circles until Mum lost it enough to open the window. Unfortunately, she closed it again after the intruder escaped.

I sat back on the ceiling and thought about how I'd feel at seeing myself. The fifteen-year-old waif who saw more of his father's belt than his friends. Friends whose lunches I sometimes stole to stop passing out from hunger. How would I feel about what I got reminded of today? Was there any point in feeling sorry for seeing something I'd already experienced? The trauma my younger self had suffered had been and gone. It couldn't be changed, not now. But my future could be.

Mum placed the food on the table and sat down. Then leaned forward and spat in the egg. She straightened and fiddled on her lap before she leaned forward again and spat in the beans. When she had finished this ritual, she left some cash on the table, grabbed my lunchbox from the fridge and walked through the hall. I braced myself. This was the day everything went from bad to worse, and to see the tired and desperate eyes on my young self, knowing by the end of the day my life could be as good as over, would be hard.

Mum entered the kitchen again and my younger self followed. Shoes on, bag over shoulder, ready to go. She slipped on her shoes, grabbed her coat and they were out the door. I so wanted to follow, if only to hear Mum's voice. I certainly didn't want to be in this house. But I had a bone to pick.

*

KEPT IN THE DARK

The keys were in the place no one knew about. The place where she kept private things. Money her husband couldn't drink or gamble away. Sentimental things he would sell or throw out in a heartbeat – her mother's jewellery, photographs, letters. She put the keys in her pocket and left some cash on the table. Then, just like every other day, she went through to the hall to knock on her son's door.

Also like every other day, she worried about her son as well as the job. Not that he wouldn't get up for school. He'd be dressed and waiting; he knew the drill as well as she did, as they'd devised it together. She cooked her husband's breakfast while he sat in his room and waited for the knock, then it was out the door quick smart. No, it was worry about his health, his schoolwork, his future. Her life was already screwed, even at the age of forty, or so she'd convinced herself, but he was so young with so much potential.

She struggled to make normal conversation as they walked to the bus stop and knew he wasn't fooled. He would usually ask her what was wrong, but today he kept silent, as though he knew she needed time to think. His bus arrived first and she kissed him goodbye – riddled with fear at what she had to do, and guilt about why she was doing it.

An appointment with the doctor had been booked for two o'clock. She didn't need it, it was an excuse to finish work early; she knew the surgery would be busy with a backlog of patients and she'd tell the receptionist she couldn't wait. She could have just *told* work she had an appointment, but felt she had to cover every detail to keep herself focused. There was no room for talking herself out of it, or even postponing. Succeed or fail, live or die, today was the day.

Twenty-Five

I heard Fatty rise and fumble with his clothes. The bedroom door slammed and his first point of call was the bathroom, for his morning routine of coughing his guts into the sink, having a piss, then straight to breakfast. No chance of him wandering into the shower.

He entered the kitchen and I was dying to attack, but I had to wait for an escape route first. The window was closed, but the sun was out and not long before he'd open it. I moved to the wall and thought about the mission. *Nobby wants me to stop myself from killing Fatty. But Nobby can get fucked. I need to stop Fatty from killing Mum. And the best way to do that is to kill Fatty first.*

But I had another reason to punish him, for I was convinced it was him who had stitched me up for the robbery. Mum sure told the police I was home at the time, but wasn't alive to confirm her story afterwards, and I thought Fatty had planned the whole thing just to get rid of me. I could never work out how he did it though. How he managed to get inside the school in the first place without being seen. Never mind know where the money was kept. *And if I find the woman he got to make the call, she's going to get what he's going to get.*

Fatty began to devour his breakfast at the table and I had no problem with that. *Bit peckish myself. Mum always did make a good fry-up.* He organised half a rasher and a scoop of beans on his fork and moved it towards that abyss he called a mouth. I floated down and grabbed as much spit-free egg as I could carry, then shat on his fork as I flew away. He saw me and snorted as he stuffed the fork in his gob. *That's it, my pretty, munch it down.*

Back on the cupboard, I tried to figure out how I was supposed to eat. I couldn't chew. Whatever I put in my mouth stayed there. I stared at Fatty enjoying his and shivered. It was no surprise that seeing him eat seemed familiar as I'd spent my childhood watching him put on weight, but a shiver went through me and I threw up over the stolen scraps. Then I smiled as they dissolved into liquid. *Ah, yes. Flies have to puke on their food before they eat it.* I saw it on some David Attenborough show. Fatty was fascinated by them and made sarcastic remarks at Attenborough's expense. But I thought I'd skip breakfast. It wouldn't have surprised me if Mum had been trying to poison him.

I went down to vomit on his fork as I didn't want him to eat anymore. *He can have a few soiled mouthfuls to make his guts a bit dickie, then I need him uncomfortable and restless. The less he has to eat, the more drunk he's going to get. No last meal for this dead man sitting.*

I landed on his knuckle and tugged the scummy hairs that looked like they wanted to die as he reloaded his fork, but he only managed to ignore me for a few seconds before his hand flicked up. His fork slipped through his sausage fingers and slid under the table, and I reckoned the neighbours heard him groan as he bent down to retrieve it, but it was too much for his lack of flexibility and he decided it was easier to replace it from the drawer. He sat back down and reloaded. *Nice bit of scran, hey, Fatty? That's it, stick a few beans on there. Bit more ketchup? Why not? Let's go nuts.* He had another attempt as I worked his ear, but the fork entered his mouth before he flicked his head. This was going to take too long. I needed to change tactics.

I sat on the beans and gave him a wave, but either he didn't see me or didn't care, so I rose to pound his nostril walls. He slapped himself with his free hand and a few beans fell on the floor. Not bad, but I needed to do better. The thing was, it could've been a waste of time; it wouldn't have surprised me if the filthy pig had got on his hands and knees and eaten off the floor.

I took five on the wall and gaped in disgust as he licked his fingers clean of the scraps and whatever else had the misfortune to be stuck to them. I imagined the bacteria on his tongue were only too happy to swap places with their external counterparts.

But I still had no escape route should Fatty get the spray out and needed the window open. I slammed into the glass. *Are you kidding me? I hardly felt it.* SLAM. Still no reaction. SLAM. SLAM. SLAM. SLAM. But it seemed not even a petulant fly was going to drag Fatty away from his breakfast.

I circled his head a few times, then landed on his plate. Nothing. I returned to the window. SLAM. SLAM. SLAM.

This time he was up, and I prayed it was to open the window and not the cupboard for the spray. Bingo. Now the party could start. I could've unleashed an all-out attack right away, but as I figured the best way to orchestrate his demise was to raise his blood pressure to the point of heart failure, I figured I should let him stuff his already clogged arteries with as much cholesterol as he could.

He took his last mouthful with a wash of coffee and dragged the form guide over. I took the opportunity to head back into his ear, making him spray what was left in his mouth over the table. A stream of semi-coherent obscenities filled the air and I caught something about a dirty, stupid, fucking fly. I guessed he meant me. *Dirty? Of course, I'm a fly. But stupid? Oh no, my fat friend. Not on your Nelly.*

He stood and flicked the worst of the coffee off the table and onto the floor as I attacked his other ear, making him spin like a sumo wrestler doing ballet.

'Jesus Christ,' he cursed. 'Why don't you just fuck off? The window's wide open.'

Sorry, fatso, but I think I'll hang around. And as for asking for Jesus' help – good luck with that. I think you'll find he's on my side with this one. At least he's supposed to be.

He grabbed the spray from the cupboard and scanned the room, but couldn't see me behind a jar of flour on the shelf and I knew he wouldn't use the spray until he knew where I was. One of the few humorous memories I had was of him coughing his guts up breathing in that stuff.

Sensing victory, he sat back down and began to indulge in his sloppy interpretation of the form guide. One thing that never changed was his rotten luck on the horses. It blighted my childhood. Many a bruise was the result of his gambling losses. But one man's misfortune is another man's fortune – isn't that what they say? I used to think that was bullshit because his misfortune was always mine too. But now, the fortune I would gain by his misfortune, along with the satisfaction of causing it, would be something to savour.

I did a few laps to let him know I was still there, but he was so involved in choosing what donkeys to lose his money on all he managed was a shake of his head, which made the wet patches under his arms spread. *What you need, mate, is a bit of exercise.* I whizzed to the table and we stared at each other, and I knew he was going to make a move, but his reflexes weren't that sharp, as expected, and I had time to scratch myself and be halfway to the ceiling before his hand slammed down.

He gave up and squeezed his fat arse out of the chair and put his shoes on, then tucked his paper under his arm and headed for the door. I flew out the window and zoomed over the roof. The sky was clear and there were a few birds out, which made me nervous. Most of them weren't a threat. *But them sparrows? Gotta watch them sparrows.* I used to stare out my bedroom window as a kid and watch them pluck flies out of the air. I had nothing else to do, no games to play, and if I left my room I'd get a hiding and so would Mum. I was on the side of the birds back then, but one wrong move now and they could send me to Hell.

I caught up with Fatty and gave his ear a rattle, refusing the puddle of putrid sweat in his jungle of a lughole even though I was parched. His hand arrived when I was long gone and he nicked his lobe with his wedding ring. I didn't know what that metal band was worth, especially after it'd been wrapped around his finger for the last fifteen years or so, but I'd seen him at the sink with soap, grease, baby lotion, the fucking lot, trying to get the thing off his fat finger so he could flog it.

A trickle of blood ran down his lobe and he tended to it as I changed ears, but sustaining an attack while laughing was tricky and he nearly caught me. But that scenario was not an option. Failure due to a swipe from Fatty, before he'd even had a drink, talk about embarrassing. I held fire and kept my distance all the way to the bookies.

Twenty-Six

From the ceiling, I looked down at the other plethora of drunken losers ready to part ways with their cash through irrational hope as Fatty slapped a wad of slips on the shelf and got to work. He lost on his first race, then put his faith in Martingale's Law and doubled on the next. It served him well, along with the next two races. Only little each-way bets, but enough to keep him interested. The door and windows were closed so it looked like I'd be in there for a bit. It also looked like I had nothing else to do but attack the deadbeats who had me trapped.

Arms filled the air within seconds and I was confident no one had a can of spray in their pocket as I dive-bombed the punters at will. I didn't really want to, but I was a fly. It was what we did. I retreated to the light to catch my breath for round two as a man entered, and I looked at his face long enough to know that round two wasn't going to happen just yet.

Like Moses and the Red Sea, the newcomer's fellow punters parted to create a path to the far corner of the room. Unlike Moses' followers, they stayed put and held their noses. No one looked at the man. No one ever did. The crowd gave him the space his stench deserved as he found a stool, but he didn't place a bet or react to any results – he just sat and stared at Fatty. Fatty didn't stare back, but I got the impression he knew he was being stared at.

Jock, or 'Jock McPlop' as I used to call him, was the local hobo who used to preach the word of Nobby on the side of the street. He had haunted me ever since I could remember. Mum told me to ignore him, and Fatty ordered me to stay well clear of him, but by the time I was about eight I'd begun to taunt him. I didn't know what his real name was, but guessed it probably wasn't Jock. In hindsight, it's distressing that some kids, and even adults, view less functional members of society as if they've always been that way, and were always meant to be that way. I'd like to say I wasn't one of them, and, given my own helpless situation, that I empathised with him, but that would be a lie. I was a constant source of torment to him whenever our paths crossed. But if we'd left each other alone on this day the first time round, both of us would've lived longer than we did.

I could've bombarded him there and then and hoped he chose differently, so there only ended up being one death later that day. But he didn't look at the form guide, as he knew his horse, and I took an educated guess it was going to turn his money into more money. Money that played a significant, yet inconvenient, part in my future.

After a couple of minutes, Jock slipped off his stool and made a bee-line for Fatty. Like everyone else, Fatty smelt him before he saw him and turned away in disgust.

KEPT IN THE DARK

Jock handed him a piece of paper and I nipped over: *callous sally 3.15 kempton park 50/1 to win* was scribbled in barely legible handwriting. Fatty raised his eyebrows and Jock took a wrap of notes from his pocket and handed it over.

That's right, Fatty won this day, I remember, Callous Sally. And it looks like it was a tip from Jock, with Jock's money.

Jock then headed for the door and again the crowd parted, unable to breathe until he was outside.

The door swung closed behind him and I wasn't sure what to do. I hadn't expected Jock to walk in, to be honest, but it made sense as I did wonder where he'd got the money from; I didn't think he'd acquired it by risking precious booze money on a rank outsider. I had to get out of that sad place anyway. If I missed Fatty leave, I knew where he'd be for his obligatory afternoon skinful.

I followed Jock to the crossroads, where he stopped – perhaps thinking about a bit of preaching before lunchtime – and I hung a good distance from his face. Not because I was scared of a swipe, but because of the wretched stench that emanated from him. His dark sunken eyes gave me the shivers and I swore he was staring back. Then he turned and headed towards the park. I held fire; being around trees might not be safe. Nobby did a good job giving birds camouflage amongst the leaves, not to mention the invisible cobwebs strewn all over the place. I felt compelled to follow, though, but stayed high, out of harm's way.

*

Jock entered a small clearing in the middle of the bushes, which was his home when the weather was warm and dry. Like a summer retreat. But he was rarely there during the day and it was where I'd seek solitude when Mum was out and Fatty was passed out. To nurse my wounds, have a good cry and plot my revenge. Which, strangely enough, never included me being a fly.

The time spent in there was the closest I ever came to praying. Looking back, you'd think Nobby would've used the opportunity to give me a nudge, but I got nothing. Not even a messenger pigeon crapping on my head. One thing I did get, though, when I was about eight, was a visit from Jock one sunny afternoon to sleep off his lunchtime drink. It was the first time I'd encountered him directly, and was the catalyst for a feud that lasted until the day we both died.

I'd got off the bus from school and seen Fatty through the pub window. His glass was full and he didn't look drunk enough to get thrown out yet. Mum was at work and I thought I'd chill in Jock's house for a while. But ten minutes in, my solace was broken by the rustle, groan and thud of him taking an unorthodox route through the bushes and falling flat on his face next to me. His eyes stayed open as he landed and I made a hasty exit through the intended gap. What wasn't intended, however, was for me to leave my school bag behind.

I didn't realise until Mum asked me to do my homework before *he* got home. I told her I'd left it in the park. My lying to her would be another nail in her coffin. She lied to me sometimes, but I always knew why. I didn't know how I knew, but I could always read her. Not her exact thoughts – not even Nobby could do that – but her eyes gave me an insight into how she felt. And when she said things like she 'wasn't hungry' so I could eat more, I always saw through it. Whether it was a gift from God or a child's intuition, I didn't know, but I always humoured her, understanding it was to protect me. She didn't need to send me back for my bag. I was out the door before she had the chance.

I ran through the bushes expecting to find Jock still on the ground. Which he was. What I didn't expect was for him to have regained enough consciousness to stand and relieve himself over my bag before falling back down. It was soaked through and I had no desire to salvage anything, but this didn't turn out to be a problem. Mum gave the school some excuse and Fatty didn't even know the bag was missing, for he never took a blind bit of interest in his boy's schoolwork. But that wasn't the issue. Of all the places Jock could've gone, including his pants, which wasn't unusual, he chose a kid's school bag, and from that moment on he was on my hit list.

I had nothing to gain by seeing what he was up to now. Finding out what homeless people did with their private time other than drinking and pissing themselves didn't really do it for me, and I'd be reacquainting myself with him later anyway; and given the hideout probably contained every fly-eating creature known to man, I thought it wiser instead to go check on Fatty.

*

The town looked different from high up and reminded me of when I was a kid, dreaming I could fly, as far away as possible. Now I could fly, I had to stay there, which was ironic. But at least my younger self would be able to flee the nest when I was ready, with Mum alive and Fatty dead.

He was still in there, bless him. Callous Sally was in action. Jock's tip. But she was a couple of lengths short down the home straight and not going to make it. *But it won – at least it did the first time. Fatty and Jock were flush. What's changed?* I skated along the window to see the torture on his face. He had needed this one bad. *Oh, how I'd love to go in there and make things worse, but he'll be out soon enough.*

Poor old Sally trotted home in second place and Fatty threw his screwed-up slip at the cashier, then headed out the door with his tail between his legs. I followed him to the pub, confused about what I'd changed to make a horse lose from miles away.

Twenty-Seven

The Horse and Hound, or the 'Haunted House' as it was known by locals, was Fatty's drinking hole, and his only one, given that he was barred from every other pub in town. Its nickname came with rumours that it was in fact haunted, but it was widely believed to be from the ghost-like drinkers that came and went through its doors.

Fatty was on his favourite stool at the bar, but the barman didn't look too lively, and as Fatty wouldn't be going anywhere for a while, I cruised through to the games area. It'd changed since I was last there. Well, before since I was last there. No, since I was last there. Fuck off.

A couple of lads were enjoying a game of pool and a lunchtime pint. *Well, well. If it isn't Simon Tunnell and Jason Sutton.* My old foes. Bullies, if you will. They were often the bane of the few moments of freedom I had from Fatty, and if they weren't there, my time would be ruined worrying they'd turn up. *And it looks like they've fooled the barman into thinking they're eighteen, but I know different. Let's see if I can get them barred.*

Tunnell lined up his shot and I entered his ear, causing him to miscue, and me and Sutton folded up. I let Sutton play without distraction, but he wasted his two-shot advantage and Tunnell was back at the table. Without delay, I was back in his ear and his head flicked up, making his cue whack the table light as the black ball rolled prematurely into the pocket. He cursed the bastard fly, then clocked Sutton. Seemed they had a few quid on it. Not a bad punch but Sutton stayed on his feet. Tunnell followed up with a haymaker, but missed and fell into him, taking both of them to ground. The effing and blinding filtered through to the bar and a man rushed in. *Wait. It's Fatty! This is gold.* I went for him, top speed. I wasn't having him ruin my fun.

The hilariousness of seeing him run for the first time ever made it hard to fly straight, and I missed his nostril and bounced off his cheek as he reached the two idiots. Tunnell was on his knees pounding the crap out of Sutton and there was blood everywhere. As Fatty bent to intervene I bolted in and out of his nose, causing him to smack his head on the corner of the pool table before landing on the feuding couple. This was too much. I hovered over the trio and examined my work. There was blood on Fatty's head and I tried to see how bad the cut was as he rolled over and struggled to his feet. Just a little nick, but the drama must've put a little strain on his ticker. The barman made a lethargic entrance to drag the two guys apart as I flew in Tunnell's ear to remind him who'd started it before following Fatty back to the bar.

*

KEPT IN THE DARK

The usual sombre nature of the watering hole had taken on a new feel. The barman was in a heated dispute with Tunnell, while the punters propping up the bar took advantage of his preoccupation by reaching over to top up their ales. Stolen fair and square. Two cops entered and one took his cuffs out while the other radioed for an ambulance on his way to tend to the semi-conscious Sutton. *Wow, Jimmy, you really nailed this one.* Fatty remained on his stool and sipped his scotch as the other punters followed the crowd through to the games area with morbid curiosity. Then the door opened. It was Jock. His face was strained as he walked over and sat on a stool at the far end of the bar, which at least suggested he was aware of his hygiene problem.

Fatty glared at him, as always. It was the only thing me and Fatty had in common, our dislike of Jock. Although mine was more of a love-to-hate thing, whereas Fatty's was pure hatred. Jock read Fatty's body language and kept his mouth shut. He didn't even order a drink when the barman returned to his duties. I landed on his head and ruffled the three hairs on his barren crown. *I don't want you in here, Jock. Not today.* He shook his head and slapped himself.

'Fock ye,' he said under his breath.

I was on the ceiling when the barman came out to collect the empties from the tables and clean the ashtrays, and as soon as he was out of sight, Jock slipped off his stool and walked behind the bar. He grabbed a tumbler from the shelf and had a cautious look around as Fatty downed his drink.

'Large scotch,' Fatty said. It was an order, not a request.

Jock took Fatty's empty glass and hooked it under the optic. Double splash. He did the same with his own glass, then put a five-pound note in the till and returned to his stool.

I assumed that because Jock had been drinking there his whole life there'd been an agreement of sorts. Where if he stayed clear of the other customers and kept his mouth shut, then a blind eye would be turned when he served himself. But a fiver without change had me confused. This was 1985. Nobody was paying a fiver for two large scotches. And it wasn't like he was flush. His horse had just lost.

Fatty took a sip of his fresh drink and leant back on his stool to make sure the barman was still out of earshot.

'What are you doing here?' he said.

'Aye, ye dinnae mind me bein' here when Ah'm fillin' up ye glass,' replied Jock.

'The race,' said Fatty.

'Noo more races. Yer nearly there. Just dee it.' There was a tired desperation in Jock's voice, but Fatty didn't respond. 'He's noo wee bairn anymore,' Jock continued. 'Ye cannae leave withoot me, Ah cannae goo on. Just dee it.'

Fatty smirked and I had no idea what they were talking about. But this conversation sounded familiar.

'You'll go when I say you go,' said Fatty.

Go where? Just do what? Are they planning to leave? Together? And a wee bairn? Was that me?

'Yer nearly there,' Jock said again. 'Just dee it. We had a deal.'

KEPT IN THE DARK

'You didn't go to the track. You're not keeping your end.'

'Ah been keepin' my end f'years. Just dee it.'

'One more race. For my family,' said Fatty.

I nearly dropped from the ceiling.

'Dinnae gimme that shite. Ye been bashin' ye famly since ye had'em. Ye coulda done this another way.'

Jock necked his drink and got up for another, then sat down again as the barman reappeared with each of his fingers and thumbs clamped on a glass.

The conversation stopped when the barman was back where he belonged, and I conceded that what had been discussed was beyond my comprehension. So I attacked Fatty until he mumbled something to the barman about spray. No such luck, for Fatty, that was. Why should the barman worry about the fly? I wasn't attacking him.

Fatty growled, grunted and waved his hands as I made a general nuisance of myself around his head until he got lucky and caught me with his palm.

I dropped to the bar with a dazed head and crumpled wings. *Fuck. If he sees me it's all over.* I closed my eyes, and prayed that when I opened them I'd be looking at Fatty, not Lucy.

*

It was the first time I'd ever been happy to see the fat bastard's face. I kept still as he swilled the last of his scotch, which was easy considering I was pretty much paralysed. He must've thought I was dead for he could obviously see me, and I was glad when he went for a piss so I could crawl to the end of the bar without risking a fatal blow.

The damage wasn't as bad as I'd thought. My head was throbbing and my legs were weak, but my wings were unfolding back into shape and my mind was clear. But I was in no fit state to go anywhere, never mind fly home and engage in battle. All I could do was sit and wait. In another pub, I would've been fearful of the bar being wiped, but there was no danger of that here; the bar hadn't been wiped for God knows how long. This was still a setback, though. Precious time was being wasted and I had no idea how long I'd be incapacitated.

I looked over at Jock and wondered what his story was. Everyone gave him a wide berth except me, and he gave everyone a wide berth except Fatty. The one person who treated him worse than I did. *Just dee it.* Just do what? It was impossible to tell how old he was – maybe seventy, maybe a hundred. His face was hidden by a thick grey beard, except for a few patches where his follicles couldn't be bothered to grow anymore. The skin on his bald head had the texture of paper-thin bark, and his sunken eyes looked like they'd seen things they wished they hadn't. Their loneliness and desperation gave me a shiver and I had a moment of empathy mixed with guilt about how I used to treat him. His ancient clothes were frayed and threadbare with stains that just would not wash out. He had a hump on his back that forced him to wear a jacket two sizes too big. I used to call him the 'Hunchback of Jocktredame', or the 'Booze Camel', pretending it was where he kept his alcohol. In hindsight, I guessed I partly taunted him in rebellion against Fatty's demands that I keep well clear of him. But as I looked at him from across the bar, I saw someone a lot like me. Stuck in a life that hadn't served him well. Someone who wanted to die and rest in peace.

*

I always wondered how a fly could receive a backhander from a human and drop dead, then be flying around ten minutes later. Result for me, though. I was nearly as good as new. But a couple of things were nagging me: Callous Sally's loss, and the conversation Fatty and Jock had had. It seemed Jock was supposed to go to the races, and that he didn't meant their horse lost. But I hadn't interfered with Jock, short of exchanging a stare. How could staring at a fly have changed his mind?

Fatty returned and ignored Jock as he headed for the door and I followed, knowing I'd at least changed *his* timeline. The first time he'd stayed in the pub all afternoon, but this time he was heading for home. Not that it ever felt like home. Home was where you felt safe and wanted to be. For me it was a place of fear, a place to avoid if I could help it. But we couldn't help it, me and Mum, we had to be there to cope with the endless demands and punches.

*

The fresh warm air perked me up and I was ready for the big push. It was 2.20 p.m., and I had until 4 p.m. before my younger self walked past the pub. Then I had an hour to stop myself from being arrested. Would that save Mum? I didn't know. But even if it did, I couldn't risk Fatty being around to try again tomorrow.

He entered the off-licence to buy his afternoon refreshments and I steamed ahead to get to the house first. I didn't know why. Maybe I needed to follow my intuition.

ROBIN MURPHY

*

Then I knew why. Mum was in the kitchen, agitated. There was a bag on the table I'd never seen before, a large holdall. It was open, but I couldn't see what was inside from where I was in the garden. She was staring out the window as I stared in, and then she walked out the back door. I couldn't imagine why. She knew better than to relax in the garden, even when *he* wasn't home.

She didn't relax. Instead, she picked up my football and blatantly threw it over the fence into next-door's garden. This was weird. She didn't even throw it in frustration. And that she headed straight back inside meant she'd come out to do that and only that. I followed her in and sat on the ceiling as she checked her watch before removing a large jar of flour from the shelf. It had no lid, and a handful of fluffy white powder fell onto her shoulders as she fumbled it. She put the jar on the sideboard below and brushed herself down, then pulled a wooden chopping board from the rack and leaned it on the shelf against the wall. This strange behaviour became stranger when she pulled two pillows from the holdall and stuffed them back to back in front of the chopping board before giving them a firm pad to keep them in place. I'd never seen them before either, but they were quite ripped. No use for sleeping on. Especially on a shelf. She had a habitual glance down the hall as if to check Fatty wasn't there. He wasn't, but he soon would be.

As if she knew, she upped her pace and pulled out several cans of cheap soda from the holdall along with a short length of rope, then grabbed the freezer door handle with both hands. It was the same freezer we'd had since before I was born as far as I knew, and it'd been jammed for years, needing a fair tug to open it. Fatty had bought it primarily for his beer, as the freezer compartment in the fridge wasn't big enough, and he could open it with a flick of his wrist. If there wasn't any room for his beer, he'd take whatever was in the way and throw it towards the bin for someone else to pick up.

Mum secured one foot on the fridge below and yanked the freezer handle until the door flew open, then filled it with the soda like her life depended on it. When it was full, she reached for the rope and tied it to the handle.

Whatever she was doing, it was clear she'd done it before, more than once. But it was going to turn nasty if she was there when Fatty arrived. Apart from decorating the kitchen with torn pillows and overfilling the freezer, leaving no room for his beer, she should've been at work, earning his beer money. She of course expected Fatty to be out all day, as he was the first time this happened. But she couldn't leave it like this, even if he wasn't about to walk in. He'd walk in some time.

A key rattled in the front door, but Mum didn't hear it and carried on with what seemed to be the losing of her mind. Within a split-second, I was in the hall.

It was easy to halt him in his tracks. He had a bottle in a brown paper bag in one hand and an open can of beer in the other. Not ideal defence against a frenzied fly attack. He wouldn't drop the open can for obvious reasons, and dropping the bottle could've been worse – he was well over six feet, which made a long drop from his hand to the floor. The best he could do was to shake his head, winking and blinking, as I alternated between his eyes. He couldn't move forward because he couldn't see where he was going, and his back wouldn't tolerate the stress if he bent to free his hands. But Fatty had another trick up his sleeve, or should I say in his mouth; suddenly, tilting his head back, he blew a generous stream of beer into the air. I hadn't expected him to be so creative and was unprepared for the wash of lager that slammed me into the ceiling. I couldn't see anything after that, but I heard Fatty plod towards the kitchen.

Twenty-Eight

Susan saw that the money she'd left was gone – not that she'd expected it to be there – which meant he'd be in the pub until 6 p.m., when he knew dinner would be ready.

She took a holdall from the cupboard under the sink and placed it on the table. It was already filled with the items she would need for the robbery – her disguise, a roll of sticky tape, a small hammer, a screwdriver and, of course, the keys. Her watch read 2.25 p.m., which meant she had a few minutes to give her homemade contraption a final test run. But there was one other thing to do first, which was to throw her son's football over the fence.

She got the idea when she opened the freezer a few months back. She hated that freezer. It was older than she was and it took her body weight to open it, the seal having gained strength over the years. But on that day, she realised a way to put her hatred of it to good use.

One shelf was packed too tight and the rim of a beer can was caught on the lip of the door, and when she heaved it open, the can shot over her head and crashed against the wall behind her, and she realised if her husband had opened the door it would've hit him in the neck. She let the fantasy play out like any other daydream until the can became a knife. A big knife. Spring-loaded from the back of the freezer. He'd fall and bleed to death, surely, and she would surely be arrested. She'd need an alibi, and a good one. Someone whose word would be trusted without question. She would get her son arrested and accompany him to the police station. The trap would be set before the police arrived. They would see her husband alive and well, and she'd insist they escorted her back indoors on her return. To find her husband dead. The perfect crime. Now she had to make sure the police had a reason to turn up.

But leaving through the front door became a no-no when she heard footsteps in the hall. She knew it wasn't her son, he was at school, and no one leaves school early. But people do leave the pub early. The footsteps stopped and she heard an irritated grunt, and imagined her husband staring at her with X-ray vision through the wall. Why else would he have stopped and grunted? She didn't have time to care. She cleared away her props, stuffed the pillows back in her holdall and slipped out the backdoor.

*

I stank of booze, but it could've been worse. Especially as there was no commotion from the kitchen. I flapped to clear my wings, then I was down the hall.

Mum had gone, and so had the holdall and the pillows. The freezer was closed, the rope was no longer attached to the door handle and the jar of flour was back on the shelf in front of the chopping board, but he would never have noticed that. The only other sign she'd been there was a light scattering of flour on the floor. Fatty didn't clock that it hadn't been there when he'd left this morning and stamped his whisky on top of the freezer. He threw the paper bag towards the bin and emptied his can down his throat, before grabbing two more from the fridge and giving the freezer door a pull.

Packets of vegetables spilled onto the floor and he growled as he stuffed a can inside, but wasn't interested in picking up the food and shoved it with the side of his foot so he could close the fridge door. He didn't care much for vegetables; as long as the meat was good and his beer was cold, what anyone else wanted was neither here nor there.

He headed through the backdoor with the other can. *It's a nice day. Why not?* I would've followed, but an unfriendly noise was rising down the hall that would've seen me cross the room.

The buzz fly entered. It was the one I'd done earlier. Its damaged wing buzzed irregularly as it headed for Fatty and circled his head, but Fatty never liked flies and grabbed the spray from the table. Then Buzz turned for me. It closed in with its tree-trunk legs, but I was in no mood to square up to this unit, and two inches away from it I shot sideways. Fatty was still by the door, spray in hand, watching me and Buzz zoom around, then he squeezed his fat finger on the button and the air filled with evil molecules like footballs of acid. I retreated high in the far corner, but Buzz was in a better position and disappeared down the hall. I needed to think fast. *When the air clears it's gonna be back.* Fatty went outside and I could only guess what the time was. I didn't need to play hide-and-seek right now. My only advantage was that dumb idiot couldn't move a muscle without being heard in the next room.

The air began to clear which meant I needed to be outside with Fatty. There were still a few acid balls in the air, and as I crossed the room I smashed into one. It burned my eyes and wings and my breathing was strained as I lost height. I needed water. *The bathroom door is down the hall on the left*, I thought as I banged and thumped into the wall. Left. Just keep left. *This is insane. How can I fail at such an early stage? And it wasn't even me that triggered Fatty to unload. If I survive this, I'm going to put that buzz cunt through Hell on Earth.*

I fell through the door and collapsed in the shower tray. I needed a puddle, but it had been a few hours since Mum had had a shower and there was little moisture. I was fading fast, ready to call it a day and prepare for the fires of Hell. A blurry shape came at me. *Looks like it found me. Come on then, you fucker. Finish me off.* I closed my eyes and waited for the pounding, then… WHOOSH!

The droplet engulfed me and I scrambled as it washed me towards the drain. But amidst this panic, there was relief as the water cleansed me of the spray. My wings were heavy, but the pain had eased, and my eyes, although still blurred, felt less like they had pins in them. The worst of the water went before me and I stopped short of the hole. I was okay, but the showerhead was ready to drop another bomb. *Thanks, but one is fine.*

*

I rested on the hall doorframe as the sun pierced through the window and cut a band of light across the kitchen. The remnants of spray still glistened and I wasn't going to make the same mistake twice, so I waited. But not for long. Fatty entered and tossed his empty beer can towards the bin. The last suds splashed over the wall as he took the fresh one from the freezer and replaced it with another from the fridge. Then a misfiring Buzz entered behind me. Fatty also heard him and gave the kitchen another spray, and as the evil stuff shot up, I dived down and clung to the underside of his beer can. As soon as I landed I knew I was in trouble. Fatty liked his beer cold, see, very cold, hence the freezer routine, and my legs were rooted to the condensation as we passed through the door.

He sat in his garden chair and I heard the crack and fizz of the can being opened as I tried to wriggle free. I went up with his arm as he had a taster, and on the way down I prayed he kept the can in his hand. *If he puts it down, I'm either squashed or trapped.*

I breathed easy as he put his wrist on the armrest with me and the can hanging over the edge. That wretched deckchair. It was back in one piece, but I remembered the day it collapsed. One hell of a funny sight, but boy did I get it. It was instigated by the two brawling idiots from the pub – Tunnell and Sutton. Fatty was semi-conscious in the garden and in no mood to be woken by a couple of annoying kids who wanted to do to me what he would do later. I was in my room wishing they would fuck off.

Punch and Judy were aware of Fatty and his mood swings as I never pretended my home life was happy – when he was in the mood he swung his fists – and they knew he could do their dirty work for them. So the derogatory remarks about his unfortunate weight problem rained over the fence and into his subconscious, and soon enough he began to stir. Then he thought he was awake enough to rise and shut the mouths of whoever was disturbing his afternoon beauty sleep with cruel insults. He got halfway up and – nope, not good enough – the chair collapsed like a bad move in Jenga. Needless to say, Tunnell and Sutton were in hysterics and trotted off knowing their work was done. I had an involuntary chuckle but knew what was coming. He picked up a piece of broken chair and made me tell the hospital I fell off my bike. I didn't even have a bike.

*

The warm air soon loosened my legs and I was back dangling in front of Fatty. He always ended up in the garden on a hot day – fuck knows why – maybe he liked forcing his sweat glands to put in an extra shift, making his red face even redder. And, of course, those damn annoying flies. Then there were those little extras, like the stench of next-door's dog's eggs, a smell so bad it used to be an issue between the neighbours as to what they fed it. It wasn't Pedigree Chum that was for sure. But that was to a human. To a fly, it was like the menu from the finest restaurant in town.

He looked like he was about to nod off, which meant he'd wake grumpy and sunburnt and take it out on me and Mum. I needed him awake and drinking, so I jabbed his forehead until he reached for the spray he'd brought out with him. I wasn't sure why he thought it would be much use outside, but he seemed to enjoy pressing the button. A mild breeze blew it back into his face and he coughed as he launched the can into the long grass. I hoped it stayed there.

KEPT IN THE DARK

It was 2.45 p.m., going by Fatty's watch. One hour and fifteen minutes to go. *How do I keep him awake? Where's Yappy? I hope they haven't taken the little runt out for a walk.* I flew over the fence and through the open backdoor, and there on the kitchen floor was the friendly neighbourhood pet having an afternoon nap, so I flew in his ear. His reactions were faster than Fatty's, but he didn't have arms so could only use his mouth, and he was never going to catch me with that. His yap echoed through the house as I continued my assault, and then the roar of Mad Beryl entered the room.

'Jesus Christ. What the hell are you barking at?' she moaned as she dragged Yappy out the door. 'Can't I get a bit of peace in the afternoon?'

I followed Yappy outside and resumed my attack. *Come on, Rex, give us everything you've got.* Piercing barks filled the air and I knew what was coming next.

'For fuck's sake,' came the cry from over the fence.

I made Yappy bark for another twenty seconds or so, then flew back over. Fatty was on his way inside, so I zoomed in the window and landed on the ceiling. More suds stained the wall as he did his target practice at the bin on his way to empty his swollen bladder so he could fill it up again. The heavy monotonous sound of him pissing into the middle of the toilet bowl filled the air, and was soon joined by a blast of noisy wings from my left. Buzz was on the edge of Fatty's chair and had no idea what was about to happen. *Come back in here, will you? Stop me from doing what needs to be done?* It was facing away and its wing was still damaged, so I hoped to take it out without too much trouble.

I crawled up the chair leg and reached the seat where Fatty rested his fat arse. There was a puddle of spray in the crater his cheeks had made, and against my insect instincts, I scooped my wing through it. It burnt like hell as I crept over to Buzz and flicked it in its eyes, making it spasm and vibrate over the edge. I jumped down and stuck a leg in its eye until it stopped moving, then hopped in the sink to rinse my wing with any moisture I could find.

Fatty didn't bother to wash his hands. Well, it was a waste of valuable drinking time, wasn't it? He did his fridge-freezer beer routine, then we headed for the living room, where he slumped on the couch and picked up the remote. Time was pressing, and he was too relaxed for someone who needed to have a heart attack before the hour was out.

I thought back to the last time we were in this room together. There was one missing, but he wouldn't turn up for another thirteen years. Which, coincidentally, was the day I last arrived back in my hometown. Which, uncoincidentally, was the day Fatty was released from prison. Which, coincidently or not, was the day all three of us died.

I'd gone straight to the house. Not that I wanted to, I'd vowed never to set foot in there again, but I had unfinished business. It hadn't been lived in since that day. The day that death had rained down in the kitchen. The day that had started my countdown to when Fatty was released from prison and back in the house. Where death would rain down again, only this time on him.

It was his house, bought and paid for. How he paid for it I would never know. I never saw him do a day's work, ever. Needless to say, he bought a bungalow so he wouldn't have to climb stairs. The weed-covered path hadn't felt footsteps in the thirteen years since the last police officer left the scene of the crime, and I retrieved my key from under the hedge.

The living room was dark and a sheet of dust covered my shoes as I pulled the curtains, but the window was thick with grime and took a shove to open it. The room was how I remembered it. A couch and a TV. That was it. The bedrooms were also how I remembered them. A bed and a chest of drawers in Fatty's, and a mattress and a cardboard box for a table in mine. I closed the doors. Neither of us would be sleeping there again.

The kitchen blinds were closed, but light streamed through the damaged slats and lit up the flies as they zipped across the rays. I flicked the light switch – nothing – so I yanked the blinds and looked up at the empty fitting, and involuntarily recalled how, on that fatal day, Jock had leapt like a ballet dancer and smashed the bulb with his head.

Filthy cobwebs covered every corner like brown candyfloss. Everything was quiet except the flies. Just like it had been in the time between Mum's last breath and the police turning up. I didn't look at the floor. I knew she was no longer there, but I didn't look. There was only one person I'd come back to see – until I walked into town and saw Jock, and the state he was in, and the money he had. I heard his Scottish growl before I saw him, standing in the same place he always stood, preaching the same Word of God he always preached, and I'd spent every day of the last thirteen years wondering how I'd feel if I saw him again. Incredibly, he was waving a wad of notes in the air. Not so incredibly, he was drunk out of his mind.

He ranted about Heaven and how wonderful it was, and how only those who believed would be worthy. He warned about the evils of money, and how God punished those who coveted wealth as he sporadically stooped to pick up stray notes that fell from his over-filled pockets. And he wasn't in sync with the accepted social graces of the time as he used the notes as a microphone to spout the Good Word using expletives like punctuation. I did feel sorry for Jock, but he had stopped me from killing Fatty as soon as Fatty had killed Mum. When he could've saved Mum instead. Then he had disappeared. But now he was back, and I could kill two birds with one stone.

All I'd ever known of Jock was that everyone avoided him. Myself included, unless I was bored or angry. And I thought no one would ever know him, not even the doctors and nurses at the hospital, for he would surely die alone and on the streets. And if he didn't manage to spend every penny of that money on himself, on booze, and then hoped it killed him, the remainder of his windfall would fall into who knew whose hands. No, it was better off in my pocket than his. He'd had his chance at life and blown it. He'd also played a part in blowing my life – not that I'd had much of one anyway.

I sat in the cafe that had sprung up while I'd been away and ordered a pot of tea. The pub was opposite, which was potentially Fatty's first port of call, and don't think I didn't want to go in there and get hammered and deal with tomorrow if and when it came. But I saw an illusion of redemption, a way to ease my conscience through what I thought was justice and compassion, which it was. Nobby didn't think so, but what the fuck did he know about justice and compassion?

Jock continued to spit out his damning account of mankind and I hoped he'd become empty of alcohol before I became full of tea. His eyes caught me through the window and he did a double take – holding my stare as I held his – then he stuffed his cash deep in his pockets, screwed the lid back on his bottle and staggered away across the road. I gulped my tea and followed.

When I arrived at his wildlife house he was crouched in ambush behind a tree. Bits of him stuck out as he swayed and I saw a raised bottle in his hand. Not exactly SAS material. I had time to brush the branches from my face before I disarmed him.

I'd never mugged anyone before, but he was weak and gave no resistance as I ignored the stale piss and BO burning the insides of my nose and went through his pockets, half expecting to pull out a dead rat or a handful of fleas. I left his bottle where it was and was soon counting his money. There were ninety-nine fifty-pound notes. One short of five grand. He called me the Devil as I dragged him to his feet, but it meant nothing to me. Except that I wasn't the Devil, and sincerely hoped that Jock never met him.

There was no protest as I frogmarched him across the park and through the back alleys to the house. Partly because I'd stuffed the money back in his crusted pockets and lied that he could keep it, and partly because I'd calmed him with my answer to his question. Which was 'Are you going to kill your father?' My answer was also a lie, but it knocked me for six that he asked it. I lied about the money because my pockets weren't big enough, and I lied about the killing because the poor fella's legs wobbled when he asked. He didn't even plead with a couple of old ladies who said 'hello' as they passed. Perhaps he heard their muffled comments on his hygiene.

I thought to offer him a shower, but didn't want to watch a scene from *Psycho* unfold if Fatty caught him. Instead, I plonked him on Fatty's couch while I grabbed a knife from the kitchen, and when I returned, he was swigging from his bottle as he fingered a fistful of cash.

I stood behind him, with one eye out the window and one eye on the back of his head as he smacked his lips and rustled his money. Counting it, I thought. Wetting his fingers so he could flip through the crumpled notes, I assumed. The irritating sounds were frequently joined by a slurp and swallow of his precious whisky. A celebratory nip every time he counted a hundred, I guessed. It wasn't until Fatty appeared at the garden gate, being my cue to skip behind the door, that I saw Jock from the front and realised the only notes he had left to rustle were two fifties.

His pockets were flat against his frail body and the couch cushions were sewn to the rest of the upholstery. No gap to tuck anything. I looked at the floor around him – nothing. His face hung like his beard was trying to jump off it and his eyes were glazed over.

'Where's the money?' I said.

He forced a smile and pointed to his belly, then tucked a note in his mouth and swallowed it whole with a mouthful of scotch.

KEPT IN THE DARK

Fatty took his time, probably had to de-rust his key as I had done, but as soon as I heard him fumble it in the lock I gripped the knife behind me. *He'll burst in and attack Jock, and I'll jump out and attack Fatty. Job done. I'll make sure Jock's prints are on the knife then disappear and he'll be left with the body to explain to the police. If he survives. And if he can't convince them he's not the killer, he'll no doubt go to prison.* Which seemed unfair, but I concluded he'd be better off in the big house than living in the bushes. At least he'd stay sober and get three square meals a day. *Although he'll need to shit out that money before he feels hungry again.*

What I hadn't planned for was Fatty being pleased to see Jock, and for Jock to resume the conversation they'd had in the pub earlier that day.

'Come oan, just dee it,' he said.

Fatty smirked. 'Where's the money?'

Again, Jock pointed to his belly. 'Five grand. It's proabably started te digest, so ye might wannae dig it oot quick.'

He closed his mouth and puffed his cheeks like he wanted to throw up but was determined not to, then tipped his head back and spread his arms wide. The relief and anticipation on his face made him look fifty years younger and I shivered. Then his face regained the fifty years when I stepped into view with the knife.

Fatty spun around, and amazingly seemed more pleased to see me than he had been to see Jock. I guessed he hadn't seen the knife and opened his arms as if for a hug. The relief and anticipation on his face was akin to that of Jock, but I didn't honour his request for a cuddle. Instead, I plunged the knife into his chest.

Jock leapt off the couch with a screech and tried to bundle me to the floor, but he was almost weightless and I ignored his frantic pleas to spare Fatty's life as I flung him off. Fatty fell to his knees and flopped backwards, then showed his lack of first-aid training by ripping his shirt open and pulling the knife out. Thick red gunge gushed over his chest and blood trickled from the corner of his mouth as he smiled.

Jock scrambled over and slotted the knife back into Fatty's wound, reducing the flow to a staggered plop like a faulty drinking fountain as he wept in Fatty's ear.

'Ye cannae leave. Please dee it. It's noo too late,' he said.

Fatty's face turned evermore white as he gurgled and pulled the knife back out, rejuvenating the spurt. He jabbed it at Jock, but was too weak to reach and it slipped through his fingers as he closed his eyes.

The relief Jock had shown a few moments prior had gone and he shook like he was about to spontaneously combust. Then he pounced on me like a lion on an antelope and we collapsed to the floor. His rage had given him a burst of strength. Despite his scrawny frame and his belly being full of fifty-pound notes, I struggled to contain him as I edged towards the knife. I had no intention of killing Jock, but whether I liked it or not, I was now in a fight to the death.

I pinned him to the ground and suggested he surrender, but he didn't hear me over his howls and hollers and for him there was no surrender. I clasped his jaw and drove the knife sideways into his throat. Two bodies for the

KEPT IN THE DARK

police, and no one would buy it that they had killed each other. I had to disappear.

The slurp as Jock pulled the knife from his neck didn't register and I reacted too late. His arm passed the point of no return and my breath dropped to fits and starts as I stared at the upright handle on my chest. I didn't pull it out. You get stabbed, you leave it there to stem the flow. I could feel the blade inside me, but shock overrode the pain and I couldn't move.

I wanted to see Fatty die for a final moment of satisfaction, but I was half-blind and he wasn't visible. Jock went next. His shoulder rubbed against mine as he trembled and shuffled away to take his last breath as I waited to take mine.

The next thing I knew I was in limbo, waiting for Nobby and Lucy to make up their minds as to where I was supposed to go before I started this ludicrous chase through time. Strangely enough, it happened only yesterday, although a few days had since passed, but now it was all thirteen years in the future. At least it would be if I didn't get back to the pub in time.

Twenty-Nine

Ideally, she would've liked to have done it after dark, but that was not possible given the time frame. She had to be done and dusted and home by five. Her strategy for getting in unseen, at least as herself, included dressing like one of the cleaners, but her budget only stretched to charity shops and even then she had to humiliate herself by haggling. She shuffled her disguise into shape in a public toilet, then braved a gap in her paranoia and began the short walk across the street to the school gates.

The side door she had observed her real-life alter ego enter on her reconnaissance provided ample cover once she'd run the gauntlet across the playground, and she pulled her gloves on and fumbled the keys like she'd never opened a door in her life. She convinced herself a hundred people were watching the thief break into the school as the key slid into the lock, then held her breath as she turned it and pushed. There was no alarm. This was good, and as she'd predicted, but it meant the cleaners were inside. She'd picked the cleaner her son disliked the most to impersonate – Mrs Seal – although her schedule had to be learnt the hard way, by watching her turn up every day for two weeks to be sure she was consistent.

The windowless corridor was dark, and she hoped it stayed dark. Her disguise might fool strangers from a distance, but the cleaners knew each other, and knew that none of them walked around stuffed with pillows to make them look fat. Her footsteps echoed as she edged along the wall like a cat burglar and she expected them to be heard at the local police station, never mind around the corner.

The growing roar of a distant vacuum cleaner helped dampen them until she reached a classroom with its door open and lights on. A cleaner was inside. It was Mrs Seal. Her big mouth had got her son into trouble more than once; the spiteful witch had even had him beaten up by older kids. She bent to do under a desk, and Susan hoped the vacuum hose would slip and suck out her nastiness as she hurried past.

Outside the office, she turned on the torch and used the second stolen key. And once inside, she locked the door and leaned against it. Her heartbeat hurt her chest and her head felt like it was being squashed, and all for the sake of the few pounds that were in the petty cash box. Yet it was so much more important than that.

She'd seen where the secretary kept the box during meetings to discuss her son's behaviour and knew they were easy to break into, so she balanced the torch on the desk and wrenched the box open with the hammer and screwdriver. It crashed to the floor and she froze. Surely someone had heard it. She pushed her ear to the door and aimed her eye out the window – nothing. She didn't count the money, but it looked about two hundred pounds. She tucked it in the bag and slipped out of the room, leaving the door unlocked, and began her journey back.

The classroom was dark and the corridor was quiet, but the witch could still be nearby. She wasn't in the clear yet, and her footsteps again increased her paranoia as she cursed herself for forgetting a simple thing like soft footwear. Then the click of her heels was joined by the squeak of trolley wheels from around the corner. The classroom door was locked and there was no time to make it back to the office. There was nothing to do except wait to be seen.

The nose of the trolley appeared and stopped and the sound of spray took over, which gave her a bit of time, but there was still nothing she could do. She would be heard if she took one small step. The trolley squeaked forward again and the blood drained from her head, making her dizzy for real this time. Then the trolley swung around and disappeared the way it had come, and she waited for her heart to restart before using the noisy wheels to dampen her footsteps until they faded away.

She crept back through the side door and took the masking tape from her bag, then taped up the window and drove her elbow through the glass. Relieved she had the focus to smash it from the outside to make it look like someone had broken in, not out. Now she had to make the call.

Thirty

Jock was still in the pub and soon to leave, where he'd fall into my younger self if I didn't interfere. That's what screwed me the most. Had I not walked past when I did, the familiar chase wouldn't have ensued, the initial result being two hundred dabs in my back pocket. But it wasn't there for long.

So the experience that needed to be erased from my younger self's future was what happened after he fell into me. My head hit the side of the bus I'd been on that was now waiting at the lights, and the back of my hand took the weight when I hit the ground, resulting in grazed knuckles the police would later conveniently attribute to me having punched a window. Jock turned with the apparent intention of apologising, and then saw it was me and his demeanour soured. Until he realised I was hurt. Then he smiled.

I couldn't remember what I shouted exactly. Probably something like *Ooch the noo, you sweaty wanker*. But I did recall him replying *Next time Ah'll push ye under a bus that's movin', ye wee shite*. There were two streets before we would part ways to our relative homes, and it was disturbing that he had a safer home life than I did, for he lived alone even if it was without a roof, which in my book was guaranteed safety. I stalked him with a sore hand and a headache that were to be eased through laughter.

An apple core from a lunchbox was always a handy missile. They're easy to grip and when they land they explode. I wiped the blood from my hand over it and launched it, and if I may blow my own trumpet, to hit him square on his crown from forty-odd feet was none too shabby. Fragments of apple splattered sideways and brown dribble ran down his neck, and with my superior speed, agility and desire to antagonise, I sped towards him as he closed in. This wasn't the first time we'd done this. I would turn in the alleyway, then slow down to keep him interested. Sometimes he'd carry on, sometimes not. That day he gave up when he crashed into the fence and staggered off, not realising he'd dropped his wallet. Naturally, I stopped.

Now if it had been a stranger other than Jock and they weren't chasing me, I would've let them know; I'm not an arsehole. But find me a fifteen-year-old boy who wouldn't have done the same in that situation. Jock would've only drank it the next day anyway, so it made more sense to be in my pocket than his. I might've had a chance if I'd kept his wallet as well. But hey, I didn't.

*

As much as I wanted to, I couldn't risk waiting to see my younger self, as it would've given me less than a minute to stop Jock leaving when he did, so I nipped through the window as he swirled the last of his firewater and waited for his arm to move to his mouth before I landed on his nose. I couldn't look at his eyes, I just couldn't, but I had no choice but to smell him as his drink barely touched his lips before it flew from the glass and passed his ear.

Will he go for another? I thought. What did he have going on that was more important than drinking right now? Either way, the extra seconds should've disturbed time enough for my younger self to pass. He looked into his glass and I looked out the window. As I recalled, I had my obligatory look in to see if Fatty was there.

Jock put his glass on the bar, but the barman didn't ask if he wanted another. I assumed it was because he either wanted him to go, or was happy to let him serve himself. I backed away from the smell and stuck to the window, waiting for a skinny school boy to walk past and arrive home without Jock's cash. Only then could I be sure I'd made a significant difference to my future.

The bus blocked the sun as it stopped at the traffic lights outside, which meant I'd just gotten off around the corner and would appear any second. Jock's eye followed the barman as he restocked the fridge. *Have another.* I thought. *If you want to keep your money, have another.* He glanced at the clock on the wall and slid off his stool as a young Jimmy Linton appeared, sauntering along with his bag over his shoulder, praying Fatty was still in the pub. He was the first time, but I had seen to that.

For the rest of this story, I shall primarily refer to my younger self as Jimmy, to save any confusion.

Jock swayed between the tables as seated customers recoiled at his odour, and his exaggerated movements caught Jimmy's eye outside. I couldn't help but smile as

Jimmy offered an offensive hand gesture and mouthed what looked like 'Scottish twat' before walking on.

Jock saw him and lengthened his stride, and I followed him out and expected to see Jimmy on the corner, armed with an apple and a wisecrack. We looked both ways – nothing – so we headed left to the crossroads, then left around the corner, and I saw the apple core soar from behind a parked car long before it splattered on his head. Not quite the forty feet that time, but a hit was a hit. Jock's face turned so red I'm sure I could smell the juice running down his cheeks being cooked. We hightailed after Jimmy, but as funny as this was, it wasn't good. The detour to the bookies was a must today.

Finding out how much Fatty had lost was always a fair way to gauge his mood when he got home. Gareth the cashier barely had to say the number; his sympathetic look would be enough for me to expect a hard time. But this day he would serve as an alibi, to show I was there at the said time of the robbery, which apparently was happening right now. That, along with no money about me and no cut hand, should save the day, at least for Jimmy. Mum, on the other hand, would have to be saved separately.

I watched Jimmy turn into the alleyway and slack the pace, which allowed me to catch up before Jock appeared. He stopped and leant against the fence to cough his guts up.

'Leave me alone, ye wee devil-child,' he said with phlegm shooting from his mouth.

His words echoed down the alleyway and I waited for him to resume the chase. But he had a change of heart and turned back, with his wallet safe in his pocket.

KEPT IN THE DARK

Good. Now, Jimmy, take your foot off the pedal and calm down. You've had your fun, so go to the bookies and then home. Mum needs you.

Jimmy entered the betting shop with Jock nowhere to be seen and I felt I'd done what I needed to. But something was on my mind, apart from the obvious; there had been something about Jock that I couldn't put my finger on, but I needed to follow my intuition again and hung a right towards the park. The sun was high and I stayed away from the shadows.

*

I heard the crack and split of a fresh bottle being opened as I passed through the bushes and found him leaning against a tree. The one he'd hid behind when I mugged him. It was smaller. This time he had nobody to ambush and poured half the whisky down his throat as though his mouth was a kitchen sink, then tossed the lid over his shoulder and slid down the trunk. I dived in the wildflowers to take the sting out of his natural musk and scanned the air for anything that might eat flies. When I felt safe, I floated towards him.

Three feet from his face I felt sick and pulled away to a smell-free zone. Sunbeams shot between the leaves and splayed shadows across the ground as he stared at his bottle, and I felt another wave of guilt about the hard times I'd given him all those years ago. To look at him then, after what I'd since learned about the meaning of life, or lack thereof, with the sadness in his eyes, and think that if he didn't die believing in God his afterlife would be even worse, made me hate Nobby even more. For if all that ever existed had lived lives of joy, free from sin and suffering, and it was only Jock who had been hard done by, Nobby still had a lot to answer for.

I knew I should've gone back to the house, but something wasn't right about Jock. That face. Those eyes. I had seen them a thousand times as a kid, yet when I saw him that morning there was an element of surprise, like I didn't expect him to be there, even though I knew he would be.

He jutted out from the trunk among the sun and shadows that distorted everything else in my view, with his head tipped back and his eyes wide open. Wide awake, yet longing for rest. I looked at the ground around him and realised what was wrong with him. He didn't cast a shadow.

Gabe. You silly bastard.

I stared at the man who should've spent the last thousand-plus years living it up in Heaven and thought about what this meant. I looked at his hump. *I guess Nobby went with wings that only lasted long enough for his angel to complete his mission. The same with his invisibility, it seems. Everyone ignores him, but they can see, hear and smell him. And Fatty knows him.*

I floated closer. He still stank, but ironically it was the safest place to be, given that not even things that would eat me dared venture into his vicinity. And now that the stench was understandable, it was easier to stomach. Besides, I needed to talk to the silly old fool.

I hovered about his shoulder and shouted – nothing. I didn't recall him having supersonic hearing, but if he ever did, it was gone. His bottle was by his side, on its side, with the raised neck keeping an afternoon tipple inside. But he didn't know I wanted him to finish it.

KEPT IN THE DARK

I thought back to our encounters in my childhood and how I had tormented him. I didn't think it was wise to tell him that the horrible kid was me, at least not yet. But I did have good reason to warn him about the kid, for it was me who would kill Gabe in thirteen years' time, and it was him who would kill me. But whether I could get him to hear me, let alone convince him I used to be a horse, I had no idea.

He picked up the bottle, and when the last drop fell into his mouth and before he cast it aside, I flew in. The fumes made me light headed and I found the driest spot to land.

'JOCK,' I shouted. Then remembered who I was talking to. 'GABE, IT'S ME, JIMMY THE HORSE.'

He held the bottle in front of his face and I wondered if he'd remember me. It had only been a day for me, but over a thousand years for him. He had one eye closed, but I didn't think he could've seen me even if I was still a horse. I shouted his name again and he opened his mouth to speak, then stopped and stared at the label. There was an outline of a stag on it. He smiled and swayed from side to side, probably with double vision in the one eye that was open.

'Ah'm on ma way,' he said.

He thought the stag was talking to him and tried to stand.

I shouted again. 'GABE, I'M JIMMY THE HORSE. IF YOU CAN HEAR ME, SAY MY NAME.'

An echo of slurred mumbles filled the bottle and his arm wobbled as he struggled to his feet.

'Would ye be a talkin' fockin fly there?' he growled in his weird Scottish brogue.

'GABE, DO YOU REMEMBER ME? I'M JIMMY, THE TALKING HORSE.'

His expression turned from one of confusion to one of recollection, then he dropped to the seat of his pants in fits. The bottle slipped through his fingers and I flew out to hover three feet from his face. He attempted a word, which sounded like it began with a *J,* but he didn't finish the *i* before he folded up in hysterics.

I hopped back in. *If he picks it up again and I'm not in it, he'll think he's hallucinating.* I clung near the open end in case he thought he was humiliating himself and launched it against a tree. Then I'd have to wait for him to finish another bottle before dialogue could be resumed, and I didn't want him to drink anymore, not today.

He tried again to say what I hoped was my name, but he still couldn't get to the *m* without folding up. Time was slipping and his wheezy giggles were an obstacle, so I flew out and held my breath as I did a little dance on his nose. He stopped laughing and looked at me with both eyes. If he didn't have double vision before, he did now.

'Jimmy the talkin' fockin hoss.' I thought that was what he said, anyway.

I shouted 'Yes', then remembered he couldn't hear me outside the bottle. I cruised back in and moved further down as an eyebrow covered the bottle neck. His eyelashes stroked the rim as a tired eye peered in and I was vulnerable. If he felt scared or threatened, he could stick his thumb in and trap me. I shifted closer.

'Say something,' he said, suspicious.

'GABE, IT'S ME. JIMMY THE TALKING HORSE.'

'Ye dinnae look like noo hoss te me,' he said with a giggle, knocking me around as he tried to steady his arm. 'Wee Jimmy the hoss fly.' He pulled his head back. 'Where are ye?'

.I sat on the rim and waved my front legs. His mouth curled from ear to ear to reveal brown teeth that were worn to the root.

'Get te fock. Is it really ye?' he said.

I slipped down as he brought the open end to his ear, but I didn't look in. I feared his ear wax was radioactive.

'HI, GABE. IT'S BEEN A LONG TIME, BUT IT SEEMS LIKE ONLY YESTERDAY.'

He looked back in. 'What the fock are ye deein here? If yer after the sol, yer gannae have a hard time dressed like that. What happened te ye hoss?'

'DON'T ASK,' I said. 'NOBBY'S STICHED ME UP AGAIN. BUT NEVER MIND ME, WHAT THE FUCK ARE YOU DOING HERE? DON'T TELL ME YOU'VE BEEN ALIVE SINCE WE LAST MET.'

'Dee ye think Ah have an open ticket te Heaven and back whenever it takes ma fancy? Of course, Ah been here.'

'BUT WHAT HAPPENED?'

'After ye left, the prophet went mad. He got the revelation mixed up and waged war on anyone who dinnae believe him.'

'HOW DO YOU KNOW HE GOT IT MIXED UP IF YOU CAN'T REMEMBER WHAT YOU TOLD HIM?'

'Aye, Ah cannae remember what Ah telt him, but Ah knoo what Ah dinnae telt him.'

'WHICH WAS?'

'Te goo aroond killin' anyone who dinnae believe him. Why would Ah have telt him that when Ah knoo they would all goo te Hell? Some people joined him, and at least pretended te believe him, and he telt'em te slay the unbelievers wherever they foond'em. It became a bloodbath. People was bein' crucified. Some had their hands and feet cut off. The lucky ones got thrown in jail and tormented aboot how it would get worse when they died.

'Ah kept tellin' him it wisnae what Ah had said, and that he needed to help me find the sol, but he was havin' none ay it. All he wanted te dee was cast terror inte anyone who dinnae believe him. Ah gave up soon after. Ah couldnae bear te stand by and watch all the killin'.'

'WHERE DID YOU GO?'

'Ah just flew as far awee as poassible. Ah had te keep stoapin f'ra rest and a drink, but was soon in a place where the prophet's people hadnae reached. Everyone was still a Christian, so Ah stayed f'ra while and hoped it might be there.'

'HOPED WHAT MIGHT BE THERE?' I said, wondering what the fuck he was going on about.

'Noaby's sol, Ah keep tellin' ya. Searchin' the world for someone who dinnae want te be foond was yeasless, so Ah stayed where there was plenty te drink and hoped it would show up.'

'AND DID IT?'

KEPT IN THE DARK

'Noo. But it wasnae long before the prophet's men turned up lookin' f'trouble. He wasnae wi'em, but that they had reached this far meant it had te be stoaped. Ah hung aroond te find oot what they were sayin' in the hope that he had come te his senses.'

'AND HAD HE?'

'Jesus, noo, the message had got worse. They gave everybody one chance te convert te the prophet's word, and if they didnae take it they were slaughtered on the spoat. It dinnae take long f'anyone sober te fall inte line. Then they moved across the lands te wage war on anyone they foond. Ah needed te put a stoap te it, so Ah flew back te find the prophet again, then Ah killed him. Pushed him o'er the edge o'a moontin. Ah thought that would dee it, but by the time the word of his death had spread it was tee late.

'Ah flew the seas after, but there was so much water Ah thought the Lord had brought the floods at last. Ah stoapped whenever Ah saw land for a wee drink, but most places Ah couldnae get one for love nor money. Ah ended up in Scwotlan aboot two hundred years ago. There was plenty te drink there. Why are ye back anyway?'

He was leaning forward with his legs akimbo and his arms across his thighs, bottle clutched in hand. His dropped his head to his chest and looked as close to a zombie as one could get. The poor bastard couldn't even drink himself to death.

'HOW DID YOU END UP HERE, IN MY HOME TOWN?' I said. 'HOW DID YOU KNOW I LIVED HERE? I DON'T REMEMBER TELLING YOU.'

'Neither dee Ah, so dinnae flatter yersel,' he said, perking up. 'Dee Ah look like Ah keep a fockin diary? Ah'm not here for ye. Why the fock would Ah be?'

'BUT HOW COME YOU'RE STILL ALIVE?'

'Cos Ah cannae fockin die. Ah'm an angel. Ah have te stay till the mission is complete.'

'BUT YOU COMPLETED THE REVELATION. YOUR MISSION WAS OVER.'

'That wasnae *my* mission.'

'WHAT DO YOU MEAN?'

'Just fock off and leave me alone, will ye, Jimmy.'

He slumped on his side and I had a moment of sympathy like I'd never experienced before. He'd been alive for more years and lived through more centuries than anyone who had ever walked God's green Earth. Thrown into a winless battle by Nobby, Lord of the Idiots. Too old to live and too scared to die. But I didn't have time to pester him about why he was here. I needed him back at the house.

'GABE, I NEED YOU TO COME WITH ME. I NEED TO SAVE MY MUM.'

'And what ma would that be?' he said with a chuckle. 'The hoss or the fly?'

'GABE, THIS IS SERIOUS. YOU NEED TO COME WITH ME. IT WAS YOU THAT TOLD ME TO COME BACK HERE.'

His mouth screwed up and his hand shook as I made a swift exit.

I think he aimed for the tree, but his hand-to-eye coordination wasn't good and the bottle crashed through the bushes. It didn't smash, but it was too far away for him to hear me.

'Fock ye, Jimmy, ye cont,' he said. 'Ah cannae fockin die and Ah cannae fockin live. The last thin' Ah need is ye tellin' me what te dee.'

He fumbled a fresh bottle from his jacket, but even though I was sure it wouldn't take him long to give me another microphone to work from, I didn't want him to drink it. He was three sheets to the wind as it was, and if he was going to help me take down Fatty, I needed him more sober than Fatty. It was already a close call.

He brought the bottle to his mouth as I headed to his eye, and he took four or five gulps as I tugged on his eyelashes. He didn't bat an eyelid. Literally. I backed off as he let out a breath of fresh scotch, combined with the stale residue of whatever he'd thrown down his neck for the last thousand years or more, and plunged to his lap, half-pissed. He looked down and showed me his teeth again.

'Wee Jimmy, Ah'd forgotten about ye. Are ye still here?'

That he could remember me as a horse from many hundreds of years ago, yet forget about me as a fly from a few seconds ago, was incomprehensible, but part of why I liked the guy so much. I couldn't talk to him, though, or even ask him to retrieve the empty from the bushes, and was scared he'd take another swig and forget about me again. My legs were wobbly and my vision was blurred, but my wings lifted me away. Maybe they could smell him too and were having none of it.

I darted back and forth a foot from his face and waited for him to remember that he couldn't hear me unless I was in an empty bottle. He did, but instead of digging the empty from the bushes, he emptied his current effort down his throat like it was lolly water. Since I'd been there, he'd drunk two large bottles of neat scotch, in around ten minutes. If that wasn't power drinking, I didn't know what was.

He held out the bottle and I hopped in, but he was a bit shaky.

'PUT THE BOTTLE DOWN,' I said, waving my front legs up and down.

He lowered it with a wobble and laid it on the ground, then rolled on his side and shuffled his ear up to the open end. He belched, and I thanked the Good Lord for not making man breathe out of his ear. I couldn't see Gabe's face, but I felt he had something to say.

'Wee Jimmy,' he said, calm and lucid.

I didn't reply. His tone worried me.

'Wee Jimmy,' he said again with more authority.

'YES, GABE. I'M STILL HERE.'

He turned his head and a watery, bloodshot eye appeared, elongated over the curved glass.

'Wee Jimmy, please tell me yer a genie in that bottle that's come te give me just one wish.'

A ball of water grew in his eye, and I thought that not only was he about to cry, but that he'd been crying forever. I couldn't blame him. He was a believer who got dragged out of Heaven and sent to do what Nobby couldn't, and to cut a long story short, he'd been alive forever. He couldn't sleep, he couldn't live, he couldn't die, and he stank. And so said the Good Lord above. I felt like going in for a hug myself. The poor bastard.

KEPT IN THE DARK

Unfortunately, I was also a poor bastard and I couldn't help him. But there was a way he could help me.

'GABE, I NEED YOU TO COME WITH ME. I NEED YOUR HELP.'

His skeleton fingers grasped the bottle as he groaned to his feet, then he held it short of his lips and took a deep breath.

'Ohhh… wee Jimmy the horse-fly, come dance with me…' he sang with a stagger as he attempted a dance move.

I escaped as he tripped and fell, then flew back in as he rolled over and sat up.

'Ah need the sol te get back te Heaven, Jimmy,' he wailed. 'But the dark sol is gannae kill it, and Ah'll be alive forever. Please, tell me Noaby's sent ye back te help me.'

He's lost it. The poor old sap.

'BUT THAT STILL DOESN'T EXPLAIN WHY YOU'RE HERE.'

'F'fock's ake, Jimmy. For the sol.'

He's crackers. I can't listen to any more of his nonsense about souls. I need to get back to the house.

Thirty-One

Gabe being here had me rattled, even more than the sparrows above me in the park. *I must've told him where I lived. Has he been looking for me? He's known me since I was a kid and only ever tormented me, and I only ever tormented him. But I can't see him finding any souls here. Maybe Fatty's told him he can find the soul and is fleecing Gabe until he catches on. That's why Gabe gave Fatty money in the bookies and bought him a large scotch in the pub. But there's more chance of Fatty finding a soul in himself, than finding one for Gabe to get back to Heaven.*

Fatty was unmissable through the front window. Sprawled over the couch with a can on the go. It always struck me as strange whenever I walked past a house close to the path and its occupants were sitting with the curtains open so everyone could see in. Although with Fatty it made sense as he was happy to stare back, and if anyone held their stare for more than a second, he would see it as an invasion of his privacy and storm out to challenge them to a punching competition.

KEPT IN THE DARK

I flew in the kitchen window and down the hall to find him dozing. One of his eyes wasn't quite closed. *I wonder if I can prise it open a little.*

There was a minor tremor as I landed astride the saggy curtains north and south of the hole in his head and steadied myself. *Yeah, I reckon I can gain enough purchase on his lids and lashes to make him realise it's a fly's arse he's looking at.* I pushed my legs apart and a hand flopped up to brush me away, but he was a bit weary and used the wrong one. His can slipped through his fingers and emptied itself over his lap. Both eyes pinged open, but he was more interested in his spilt beer as I flew away.

He didn't have a bad result, as it happened. He was nearly out anyway. It still looked like he'd pissed himself, but it could've been worse, or funnier, whichever way you looked at it. With a heave and a ho, he hauled his hefty frame to his feet and headed through the door. I guessed to get a refill rather than change his pants.

I tapped his forehead along the hall, but the drink had numbed his sense of touch and he didn't flinch, which wasn't something I'd anticipated. *If he doesn't react to me, I may as well get drunk too and forget the whole thing. Or maybe I should go for a more sensitive area.* I zoomed ahead and sat on top of the freezer. It was a fair bet both eyes would be wide open when he saw another fresh beer staring at him.

He opened the door and I steamed into his right one.

'Gabe wants his soul,' I shouted as I backed away.

He slammed both eyes shut. 'Arrgh! What the fuck?'

I landed on the ceiling and caught a ghostly figure through the window. It was Mum. It may sound harsh calling her ghostly, but the way she stood at the gate with her holdall over her shoulder gave me the shivers.

Fatty slumped on a chair and dug his chubby knuckle in his eye socket. I didn't know whether to make his situation worse or to try and workout what Mum was doing, especially since she carried on past the house. *Where's she going? She never has anywhere else to go once she's in the potential eye line of Fatty. She's supposed to come straight home today. The same as before.*

I flew outside and saw her enter the phone box across the street, and I was on the window beside her before she'd finished dialling. *Who's she calling that's more important than going home?*

'Hello,' she said. 'Yes, I'd like to report an incident…'

*

Susan felt calm as she made her way home. Not because she was overconfident or didn't care about potential consequences – losing her son would be unbearable – but she just didn't have anything left. And she wouldn't *really* lose him; there would be visiting hours. But getting caught was not on the menu. Why should it be? Sure, there would be an investigation into the man stabbed to death in his kitchen, but using the police as her alibi was as good as it got. And if everything backfired, no one else would be in trouble.

Her son could not be there, that was clear from the start. She had no idea how the night would play out and didn't want him caught in the crossfire. Plus, she knew he'd be glad his father was dead and proud of his mother for doing it, and thought it might show when questioned by police. But getting him out of the house was easier said than done, because her husband decided who left the house and when. The only time they left the house of their own accord, except for school or work, was after a beating. Susan had thought about this carefully – a fresh black eye on her boy on the night his father was killed, with him being forced to lie about where he got it from, could be disastrous. But there was no alternative. No plan B. He had to go. This was what she was going to do. She might fail, but failure wouldn't necessarily mean no freedom for her. She could end up dead. That would be freedom. But for her son, it would be out of the frying pan and into the fire.

She covered every possible scenario as she walked home and lost anything that might place her at the scene – the coat, the pillows, the masking tape, the hammer, the screwdriver, the keys – all dropped in various waste bins along the street. She left the gloves in the bag as she would need them at home, then she counted the money – two hundred and fifteen pounds in tens and fives. She would have to get change for the phone call.

*

Her husband's raised voice made her stop at the gate. He was still home, even though she'd left enough money for him to stay in the pub all day, which meant he'd lost it on the horses, which meant he'd be in a worse temper than usual. Would that require a change in her plan? Not necessarily. If she could keep out of his way. The police would still turn up and he wouldn't interfere when they questioned his son, and he hopefully wouldn't open the freezer until they had gone.

She crossed the road to the phone box and took a slip of paper from her purse, then took a deep breath and dialled.

'Hello. Yes, I'd like to report an incident,' she said in an awkward false voice. 'I have just seen a boy climbing through a smashed window at the school. He ran off and nearly knocked me over. I think it was that boy Jimmy Linton... yes, I'm Judith Seal. One of the cleaners at the school...'

*

I could not do anything, say anything, or think anything. I was numb. She hung up and walked away and I stayed stuck to the window. The numbness was there for a reason, but it was no good to me where I was, and I ignored the pain and confusion thrashing inside me and forced my senses back into gear. But I couldn't look at her as I overtook her and flew back in the kitchen window, to see Fatty at the table, still rubbing his eye. I hovered for one second, then let him have it.

Tears blurred my own vision as I bobbed and weaved through his frantic arms, looking for a way to his eyes. He stood and opened the cupboard for the spray that wasn't there, then grabbed his form guide to up his defence. His eyes closed, so I turned my attention to his ears.

'Get the fuck out, you little bastard,' he yelled as he slapped his face with the paper.

The front door opened and Mum rushed through the hall. I retreated to the wall, but I still couldn't look at her as she dumped the holdall on the table and pulled out a six-pack of beer.

'Woman, where's the boy?' Fatty said.

KEPT IN THE DARK

'He's gone to help Margaret in her garden to earn some pocket money.'

What, another lie? What is she doing to me? My own mother. After all I've been through to make it here to save her.

Fatty slammed his fist on the table and demanded food, then grabbed a beer and headed back down the hall, no doubt relieved I was on a break. I stayed put, relieved about nothing. Mum stuffed the holdall in the cupboard under the sink and removed the chopping board from the shelf. But my desire to hug her had gone, for the first time ever, and if dying truly meant dying I would've killed myself. But that was never going to happen. At least not yet.

I braved a look as she fiddled at the table, broken yet alert. She always looked broken, but that day there was a certain look in her eye, a look beyond fear or apprehension, a look of anticipation, maybe even a look of hope. But most importantly, there was a look of defiance, and I realised the lie about me working at Margaret's had been made up on the spot, because she'd expected me to be home, as I was the first time. So what was she playing at? Fatty couldn't have put her up to this. She wouldn't have stitched me up for him even under the threat of violence. *But she did it. I just heard her. And the police are on their way to arrest me.*

I thought maybe I'd misread the signs and she was having a breakdown, which included irrational behaviour such as throwing balls over fences. But as heartbreaking as that would be, it would've explained a few things. The first time at the police station, she had something on her mind more important than her son being detained by the law. I also remembered her unusual silence when we left the house that morning. It meant nothing at the time, but I never forgot it. And now I had a second crack at finding out.

*

Her husband's voice was raised when she entered the garden. 'Get the fuck out, you little bastard.'

She waited for her son to obey his father's command. He would surely appear in two seconds. But he didn't, so she rushed in the front door convinced her son was being beaten. Instead, she found her husband attacking his own head with a newspaper. She stopped. Half terrified he'd gone mad, and half amused at him looking so foolish.

'Woman, where's the boy?' he said when he'd composed himself.

'He's gone to help Margaret in her garden to earn some pocket money,' she said.

She didn't know how long that lie would last. She assumed her son would either be at home or out on the order of his father. And if his father didn't know where his son was, it was something else to worry about. Neither she nor her son stayed out without his permission, which was why she said he was earning money to soften the blow. If a few extra pounds were coming in, they would be his.

Her immediate concern was the money in her skirt. He was more agitated than usual, which often meant he wanted more than food, and she feared his verbal aggression could turn into sexual violence in a heartbeat.

He banged his fist on the table. 'Food,' he said before he grabbed a drink and stomped back down the hall.

KEPT IN THE DARK

Susan did what she needed to do while she went through the possibilities of her son's whereabouts. He wasn't held back at school or they would've called, and he knew better than to play with his friends straight after. That didn't leave many options. Was he hurt? Whatever the reason, her plan for them to be out of the house was contingent on him being there first. A mother and father alibi wouldn't necessarily be waterproof, so she intended for the neighbours to see him. They wouldn't like being disturbed by the boy next door asking for his ball back, but they'd know he came straight home from school.

But she'd already made the call and the police would arrive soon, and if her son wasn't there, he'd have to find another alibi by himself, and she'd have to find another plan. Then a key slid in the front door.

*

Jimmy appeared down the hall with a mischievous smirk. I didn't know why, he certainly didn't have any part in this, and he didn't have Gabe's cash. Mum had the nerve to kiss him like she did the first time, like she did every time, but I'd surely done enough to stop him being arrested, or at least charged. His defence should've been in the bag, with Gareth as his neutral alibi, clean hands and empty pockets. I watched him head to his room before Fatty called him in for a slap, and I was tempted to follow, but Mum was consuming my thoughts, even though it was hard to look at her. But I had to look.

I always changed my school clothes straight away to stop blood ruining them, and if the sun was out, I'd put on my red T-shirt and pretend it was a Liverpool top, then go out the back and let my imagination take me far away.

Usually to Anfield or Wembley, but anywhere other than home would do. The first time, I had stayed in my room and imagined me and Mum spending the money behind Fatty's back as I counted and recounted my windfall. All two hundred quid of it. It was the most money I'd ever seen, never mind had, and I didn't remember being guilty one bit. I did now, regardless of it being Gabe's, but he could've seriously hurt or even killed me had the bus not been there to block me from the road. I didn't expect him to kiss my hand better, but to just walk away with no more than a smirk was always going to get my back up. And it wasn't like he'd earned the money, or even earned the stake money.

Mum glanced back and forth from the window to the hall as she peeled potatoes over the sink and I wondered where Jimmy was. I was always back out in one minute. There was fuck all else to do in my room. I didn't have a TV and I always rubbed one out in the bathroom.

*

The potatoes were on the stove with a sprinkle of salt, while an egg sat on the side waiting to be cracked. *She makes mash tonight, I remember.* Not that she or Jimmy were ever going to eat it. A slab of marinated steak was on a plate and the beans were in the saucepan ready for heating. She opened the cupboard under the sink and pulled out a pair of plastic gloves from the holdall and squeezed them on, then went back in for a large knife which I'd never seen before. She rested the knife on top of the freezer while she placed the soda cans on the table. Then she yanked the freezer door open. The knife vibrated over the edge and clattered on the floor and her trembling hand picked it up and put it on the table. Then she pushed Fatty's cans to the back of the freezer and stocked the soda in front.

She's really lost it. Does she not know what he'll do?

But when she rammed the knife between two cans with the blade pointing outwards, I realised she knew exactly what he'd do. Two fingers held the tip in place and she pulled away as the suction on the door seal slurped. I didn't need to be a rocket scientist to work out what happened next.

Things had turned very strange. I thought back thirteen years to when she died, later that day. We arrived back from the police station and Fatty was in the kitchen, with a beer from the fridge instead of the freezer (there was no condensation on the can). He smirked as we entered with the policeman and I thought it was because of his win on the gee-gees, but I remembered that Mum looked like she'd seen a ghost.

When the policeman left, he gave me the look to go to my room. I didn't want to blatantly disobey him so I walked away and opened my door. Then closed it again and stood in the hall. There were shouts and demands, then a scream from Mum, and I rushed back in to see her slumped on the floor, eyes closed, motionless. A knife was stuck in her face. Blood pumped over her cheeks as I tried to wake her, then she let out a harrowing sigh. No breath followed. Fatty stood across the room with his arms out as if on an invisible cross.

I didn't consider risks or consequences as I drew the knife from Mum's face and rushed him. He never flinched, until Jock appeared from nowhere and leapt across the kitchen, clipping the light and smashing the bulb before landing between us. The knife barely grazed his shoulder, but it was enough to throw my aim and all three of us collapsed on the floor. I was first up, but Fatty had the knife, so I ran out to call an ambulance and hid around the corner.

When the ambulance arrived, Fatty was at the table, sobbing like a baby with a toothache. Jock had disappeared, and I never saw either of them again for thirteen years. I assumed Fatty had stabbed Mum himself, but it seemed she had planned to kill *him*. And if she succeeded this time and got away with it, my mission could be achieved without me having to do much except watch him die. But it hadn't worked the first time; the trap was still set when we returned, and he made Mum fall victim to it. *Did he know? Does he know now? Is that why he's on the scotch? To stay away from the freezer?*

She left the potatoes to simmer and stuck the steak in the pan. I headed out the window to wait for the police.

Thirty-Two

With one eye up the street and one eye on Fatty through the front window, I thought about Gabe, and wished I'd had more time to quiz him about why he was here. I figured I must've told him where I lived. Given what I drank that day I could've told him anything. But how was he not dead and in Heaven if he'd completed his mission? Okay, it wasn't exactly verbatim from what Nobby had told him, but Nobby wasn't to know that and he would've wanted to know how he got on anyway. Gabe may have lost his mind, but he knew something he hadn't told me. Or had he told me something I didn't understand?

I thought again about the conversation in the pub when Gabe had poured his own drink. *Just dee it... we had a deal.* Had Fatty told him he'd located the lost soul and Gabe had fallen for it, and Fatty was stalling for more money? The fat horrible bastard. Was that why the conversation had stopped when the barman returned? Did Fatty not want anyone to know he knew Gabe outside of the pub, and hear him talk of missing souls to get back to Heaven?

I found it ironic that Gabe had lost his invisibility, yet everyone still ignored him, except me and Fatty of course. He was never going to lure anyone into any kind of social circle, and his attitude when he preached would never make anyone believe in Nobby – not even believers are drawn to those sorts of guys. He would stand on the traffic light island in the middle of the road, isolated from pedestrians. I used to think it was so no one could punch him, then I thought it was him being aware of his odour and showing a bit of consideration. Like when he sat in the corner of the pub by himself.

Fatty told me in no uncertain terms to stay well clear of him, but I never asked why. Then when I returned, I feared it was so I wouldn't tell him that Fatty wasn't qualified to seek out and catch missing souls, Nobby's or anyone else's, and that he must've been doing a number on Gabe for years. I remembered on occasion Fatty coming home with more than a few bob, claiming he'd won it on the horses, but seeing as Fatty never won on the horses, I assumed they were down payments on his little private investigation venture. No wonder Gabe was down and out.

I was being a bit harsh in saying Fatty never won on the horses. Callous Sally had won the first time, which was why it was a mystery it didn't win this time. What had changed? In the pub, Fatty had been upset that Gabe didn't go to the races, and I assumed a different scenario had played out on that first occasion when Callous Sally had won. I didn't know how much Fatty won, but he had been singing a drunken song about Callous Sally when he got home. *Did Gabe go to the track the first time and somehow fix the race? Did his stench somehow affect the horses or the jockeys? But it's miles away and he can't fly.*

A car turned into the street. It was the police. I looked at Fatty through the window, too busy poking his food to notice it park in his line of fire, and too lazy to look up as the officer approached the gate, but I wanted to be at the door to hear every word said. I floated along the top of the hedge and settled where I could see Mum through the window. She saw the policeman, but pretended she didn't, and waited for the knock before going to the door.

'How can I help you, officer?' she said in an unconvincing tone of surprise.

'Hello, Mrs Linton,' said the policeman. 'I'm sorry to trouble you, but I wondered if James was home.'

'My son? What's this all about?'

'I would like to have a few words with him if possible.'

'Could you please tell me what this is about?' she said.

'There has been a break-in at the school, and James was seen running from the scene.'

'That's impossible,' she said, overacting. 'He came straight home from school and has been here ever since.'

'Well, I'd still like a word if he's home?'

Yes, he's home. And that he was still in his room made me nervous. I bolted over the policeman's head, passed Mum's shoulder and squeezed under my door. Jimmy was sitting on the edge of his mattress, still in his school uniform, with a stupid grin on his face and a wad of notes in his hand. *Where the fuck did he get that from?*

The knock on the door startled me even though I knew it was coming and I was on the ceiling in a flash.

'Jimmy,' called Mum.

Jimmy jumped up and stuffed the money under the mattress. *Not a good move, Jimmy, mate. That's where I put it the first time, he's gonna find it.* Mum opened the door with the policeman standing behind her.

'The policeman wants to talk to you, Jimmy. Is it okay if we come in?'

Jimmy nodded.

Mum turned to the policeman. 'Do you mind if we talk to him in here? His father's not feeling well.'

'Of course, mam.'

She closed the door and I sat back where I'd hidden the cash. The notes crunched and I waited for the copper to pounce and search the bed. The first time he'd searched me first, then flipped the mattress like he was on a Colombian drug bust. The notes flapped around as if in a séance and we all stood in silence waiting for them to settle. As I was sitting down this time, I hoped the slight change would make him take a different path in his search. But he was still going to end up at the bed, and there was nothing I could do about it. Or was there?

'What time did you leave school today, Jimmy?' said the policeman.

'Normal time. Why?' he replied.

I was on the cop's lip before his next question. He blew a little raspberry as I hopped up and tickled his nostril walls before working his ears until he didn't know which one to protect. Jimmy and Mum shared a guilty smile as the panicked arms of the law waved ferociously as I tried to guide him away from the bed like a sheepdog. Then I caught Jimmy slipping the money out and passing it to Mum. *The policeman won't search her. She's not a thief.* I returned to the ceiling to let the officer carry on with his investigation and hopefully be on his way without further questions.

What happened between Jimmy and Mum was very significant. If she had wanted to stitch him up she would've given the money straight to the policeman, so he could use it to wave away the persistent fly before putting it in a bag marked 'EVIDENCE'. *But she still made that call. That's why the police are here.*

'Would you mind if I asked you to stand up and empty your pockets for me, Jimmy?' said the policeman, still red-faced from his ordeal.

Jimmy did as he said. There was no chance of the cop mistaking Jimmy's money as being stolen; I never had more than a few pounds in my pocket at any one time, so I was willing to bet the notes Mum had tucked in her skirt on there being squat for the cop to find. Jimmy flopped his front pockets out and sure enough they were empty, then he turned to show his back pockets were flat against his arse. There was no need to wonder why my father wasn't there making sure his son was treated fairly. He wasn't particularly fond of the law – past misunderstandings had dampened any further cooperation between them. The policeman could've been working Jimmy over with his truncheon, and as long as he kept his screams to a minimum, Fatty would've barely flinched. The policeman looked around the room and stopped at the bed.

'Could you stand aside, please, Jimmy?' he said.

Jimmy moved next to Mum, who put her arm around him with a squeeze as the policeman slipped his hand under the mattress, and I nearly dropped from the ceiling as he lifted it. The first time, my magazine flopped open on a page that left nothing to the imagination, but the worst of my embarrassment was spared by the horror of the money spilling everywhere. Now I expected Jimmy's face to go bright red, especially as he was in Mum's arms. But lady luck shone on him and the magazine stayed stuck to the underside of the mattress, out of sight.

'If you're going to arrest my son, I demand I come with you,' said Mum.

Odd thing to say, seeing as he'd never mentioned a word about arresting him. I was under the impression he was about to apologise and bid them a good day.

But why did she make that call if it wasn't to get me arrested? She wants me out of the house and wants to come with me. But why? So she has an alibi when Fatty opens the freezer? That makes sense.

The policeman glanced around the room, but there wasn't much else to search. No cupboards or drawers. Just a cardboard box for a bedside table and a small pile of soiled clothes on the floor, which were the total sum of my possessions, short of my ball in next-door's garden. Hardly a room fit for a chosen one. He screwed his face up as he lifted the pile of clothes with his foot, by this stage hoping he didn't find anything, I shouldn't wonder.

He turned to Mum. 'I don't think I need to take up any more of your time at this stage, mam. I apologise for any inconvenience or embarrassment,' he said, knowing full well he was the embarrassed one.

Jimmy sat back on the bed as me and the policeman followed Mum to the front door. She was clearly shell-shocked he was leaving without them, and I felt her wheels turning on how to get him to take them away, but not even I could come up with anything. She would have to face the evening head-on.

*

Even though I'd now changed my history, it didn't mean I'd saved the day. Fatty was in the living room, waiting to kill or be killed. Mum closed the door and closed her eyes as the failure hit home. Not that she had any success stories to compare with. Her idea of success was to go to bed with a full stomach and no reopened wounds she had to be careful not to lie on. But I feared this was a failure she had counted on being a success. One that was integral to the overall plan which appeared to be the killing of Fatty. Talking of which, now the police had left, it was a wonder he wasn't rolling down the hall swinging his fists. I floated towards the living room and resisted the urge to check on Jimmy. His privacy was more important than Fatty's.

Fatty was at the window, staring at the policeman on his radio – who was probably giving the station a debrief that didn't include the fly attack. His plate was upside down on the carpet next to a puddle of baked beans, and mashed potato was splattered over the wall. His half-eaten steak lay below. The police car pulled away as me and Fatty headed down the hall, and I hoped Mum had hidden the cash somewhere good. *But where the fuck did I get it from? I certainly didn't get it working at Margaret's.*

I didn't have time to speculate as Fatty grabbed Mum's hair and dragged her back down the hall. She screamed, but before she was out of breath I was up his nostril, spinning like a waltzer car. He rubbed his nose with one hand as he slammed her head into the thermostat on the wall with the other, and there was a click and a shudder as the boiler started for the first time since spring. Then he was all arms in the air and his elbow scuffed me. No damage done, only embarrassment, and I withdrew to float above his head, not knowing what to do. I could've continued my counterattack, but that would've made him more aggressive and the inevitable even worse. He grabbed Mum's hair again and cuffed her face with the back of his hand, which brought Jimmy to his door.

'Get back in there,' said Fatty.

Jimmy said nothing. I never did in those situations; there was nothing I could say that wouldn't earn me a slap. Saying nothing would often earn me one, mind, but I would stand there anyway. Fatty forced Mum into the living room with her hair wrapped around his fist and shoved her face into the mash on the wall. I sat on the doorframe so I could see everyone.

'Eat it,' he said. 'You made it, you eat it.'

He pushed her face so hard she couldn't have eaten it if she wanted to, but she knew she'd better try or he'd have seen it as disobeying an order. The tip of her tongue touched the potato and I could take no more. I shot to his face and sliced my wing across his eyeball. Mum fell to the floor as he blinked away the irritation and put his foot on her head.

'Eat it,' he said, rolling her face towards the steak.

She ignored the grime and dust and ripped a piece of meat off with her teeth. *It could be the only thing she gets to eat tonight.* I head-butted his ear to at least let her finish her mouthful, but he had a bee in his bonnet and shook his head. *Nope, not good enough. You're gonna have to do better than that, fatso.* Mum winced as he tightened his grip, so I tightened my strategy. He blinked and squealed as I punched his eyes with my legs, then noticed something Fatty hadn't sticking out of Mum's skirt. It was a piece of paper, but it didn't look like cash. I pulled away and went down.

It was a betting slip, and I could just make out the horse in Fatty's remedial handwriting – Callous Sally. And it said it had been paid. *But it lost. At least it did this time. This is getting weird.* There was no money visible, but Fatty's winning betting slip was sticking out of Mum's skirt, and if he saw it there was going to be merry hell.

I thought back to the bookies to make sure I hadn't misread what had happened. Gabe had walked in and spoken to no one but Fatty. He never placed a bet, but gave Fatty the tip and some money, then left. I didn't see Fatty place the bet, but he was sure pissed the horse lost.

Why didn't Gabe go to the track? And how did he fix it the first time? I should've asked him.

Fatty yanked Mum off the floor with a piece of meat hanging from her mouth and I was in his eye again, which I instantly regretted as he slammed her head into the wall. She dropped back to the floor as he let off a tirade of slurred insults which I wasn't sure were meant for me or Mum, then he stopped. Jimmy was at the door with the deadpan look I always used to distract him. The betting slip was about to fall out of Mum's skirt and any action I took would've made matters worse.

Fatty took a break to sip from his can as Jimmy tended to Mum, but it would only be a few seconds before he'd be adequately refreshed, and the slip needed to be removed from the scene immediately. I didn't see what Jimmy did with it, which was nice. I always was swift with my fingers.

'Can she have a lie down, now?' said Jimmy.

Weird hearing my voice, but I prayed Fatty said yes.

'No,' he replied. 'Get back to your room.'

Jimmy clung to Mum and resumed his poker face. This wasn't unusual behaviour from me. I would often physically cling to Mum when Fatty had his fists out, hoping to soak up some of the punches. I couldn't turn off my pain receptors like Jesus, but I could dampen them and stay within the pain barrier longer. Maybe it was simply the law of diminishing returns, but it was necessitated by my instinct to protect my mother, and that would never diminish. In life or death.

Fatty finished his beer and dropped the can at Jimmy's feet. I knew what he wanted Jimmy to do, and usually I would do it, but not today, I thought. Because the look in my young eye told me I wasn't moving. It seemed Fatty had also seen the look in my young eye, otherwise he'd have taken my petulance as an affront to his authority and broken off a piece of furniture to beat us with.

'So you think you're big enough now, do you?' he said.

The room stopped and I didn't have to wait for an answer, because I knew what it was, and it wouldn't have changed just because I'd stopped myself from being arrested. It was no, I didn't think I was anywhere big enough. *But tonight, I might have to be.*

'You hungry, boy?' said Fatty. 'You sticking close to your mother in the hope of being fed?'

KEPT IN THE DARK

Don't you dare, you fat bastard. Mum had taken the lion's share of the meat, but the beans were on the floor and the potato was still stuck to the wall, which wasn't a surprise considering her mash was lump-less to the point of faultless. She put egg in it, you see, the secret ingredient to any good mash.

Jimmy didn't answer, and it was surreal not knowing how he was going to react. But it wasn't Jimmy's reaction I was worried about. Fatty took a step, and to my surprise Jimmy offered up his fists. This was a first. Never in the fifteen years I'd been under his control had I ever thought, outside of daydreaming, about challenging him.

Fatty smiled, almost with relief, and this moment of pride brought a tear to my fly eye. A moment of growth and honour that was only a few minutes away had I not been arrested the first time. And I never knew. *Was I about to come of age? Or think I was?*

Mum had moved into the recovery position. Conscious, but silent. This was unusual, as she would normally always be on her feet to protect me, but she knew my stance was also unusual and stayed put. This was an unusual night for all of us. The early evening temperature had dropped and I felt more lethargic by the second and didn't have the strength to do anything to anyone. I also didn't have the mental strength to watch a scene unfold that would become another memory to try and lose.

I wobbled back through the hall in a daze, fighting the instinct to fly out the window. The light was fading, which was when the big things appeared to feast on the little fuckers that bugged the shit out of everyone during the day. Nobby had that one covered. Make the vulnerable ones live by day and the monsters live by night, then no one would get hurt. But I did know that regular flies *did* tend to sleep outside, a bit like Gabe, under leaves and such places where they felt safe. They also tended to sleep alone, which made me wonder why I could see a bunch of fly arses huddled together like penguins in the Antarctic behind the jar of flour on the shelf. They clearly hadn't seen what was happening behind them, but maybe that was because I had a better set of optics than them. Although a pair of human arms with fists would've served me better than the six skinny legs the size of Fatty's eyelashes I'd been granted to work with. I'd been granted wings again, though, let's not forget, which I assumed were so I could watch everything fail from a safe height.

I slid down the wall as a stream of warm air rose over me like a kick up the arse, and I stayed as close to the radiator as I could without singeing my wings, thankful for the silver lining to Mum's head hitting the thermostat.

With my senses refreshed, I slunk to the windowsill behind the taps and checked on the proceedings above. I hadn't been seen. And neither had the spider, who couldn't believe its luck as it spun fresh lines to trap the dozing flies in, and I wished I could've given it a hand.

The roar from the living room that had been continuous since I'd left was strangely comforting, because it meant that Mum and Jimmy were still alive. Then Fatty gave a defensive groan and I wondered if Jimmy had thrown his first punch. I belted down the hall.

*

Mum was still on the floor, nursing a fat lip, and Jimmy was slumped against the wall with a bloody nose, eyes wide open, and a disturbing demeanour. I didn't know whether it was from fear, or because this was the night I came of age.

Fatty stood proud in the middle. Self-satisfied at once again exercising his dominance over his defenceless family. Then he turned his head and I laughed out loud. His hair was smudged with clumps of mash, and I looked down to see a skid mark in the beans on the carpet. He must've taken a slip and tumbled into the wall and wiped the mash clean with his head. Which gave me an idea. Mum and Jimmy would have to survive for another minute or so. I shot back down the hall.

*

The mash bowl was on the draining board with sticky white crumbs scattered around it, and I stomped around to coat my legs before taking off, keeping in eclipse with the dark wall as I hovered near a fresh spindle of fine silk. I gave old Percy the Spider a wink but he wasn't interested at this stage; he'd done this before and was waiting for me to fuck myself. But I didn't try and land straightaway; the last thing I needed was to intentionality fly into a fresh spider web dressed in potato trousers, in the hope they worked as a barrier against the glue that Nobby designed to make sure flies had just as hard a time as everything else he'd created. I dabbed the web with a leg. The edge of the mash stayed stuck but it was easy to pull my leg free. *Pick the bones out of that one with your eight legs, cunt.*

It was a shame, really. I wished I could've watched Percy complete his intricate trap then wait for the panic that ensued. But even if I did have the time I didn't think Percy would've, as I saw a movement in the huddle of flies as I dismantled part of the web with my food shoes. A bit counterintuitive, but I needed help from as many of these bastards as I could rescue. I snuck through the web and over to the stirring flies that were being hoodwinked by their biggest foe, and shoulder-charged the nearest one. He bumped into his mate in front, and like dominoes the rest woke. I was halfway across the kitchen before any of them were airborne.

I turned to see half of them struggling in the web, alerting Percy to his first catch of the day, while the lucky ones chased me into the living room. I wasn't worried. *They won't be firing on all four cylinders yet. They'll need food first.*

I zoomed over Fatty's potato crown and sat on the wall as the mini swarm entered and forced his head into a frenzy of flicks and shakes. The air filled with mash and flies and I wished I had a camera. Jimmy and Mum crawled through the door, and I felt no need to assist the hungry and grouchy buzz boys in keeping Fatty distracted. They looked just fine to me.

The three of us entered the kitchen and Jimmy wiped the blood from his nose before Mum grabbed him for an extended hug. Far too long for my liking. I felt the need for bonding, but they had to make a swift exit or prepare for war. The flies were only going to be on Fatty's case until he rid his grotesque head of the potato, then he'd bound in to resume battle.

'Go and sit in your room,' whispered Mum.

Jimmy shook his head and clung harder. Then he pulled away with a look that meant business. 'I'm staying here,' he said.

KEPT IN THE DARK

Quite a common thing for me to say. I could never sit in my room when Fatty gave Mum a hiding, but I usually had a crackle of fear in my voice. That night, I spoke with an attitude of defiance. The apparent turning point I'd been so close to before. I had nothing to lose by fighting back. He'd have beaten the hell out of me anyway, so I might as well have tried to get a satisfactory punch on his nose while I was at it. It wasn't going to knock him out, more's the pity, but he'd have known that from then on my punches would only get harder. But this was from the point of view of Jimmy on the ground. From the ceiling, I didn't think it would be as straightforward as getting a hiding before bed to fight another day. Mum knew this too. Her plan had failed and she had to up her game.

'Where did you get the money from?' she said.

'Gareth at the betting shop. Dad put a bet on earlier and thought it lost, so he threw away the ticket, but someone called Stewart had an inquiry and it won. Gareth said he wouldn't say anything if I didn't.'

Good old Gareth. He must've found the slip on the floor. Fatty will be heartbroken when he finds out.

'Is the money safe?' said Jimmy.

She nodded as he handed her the betting slip. 'You left this in your skirt,' he said.

She folded it up and hugged the table, like some kind of ritual, then straightened up again as footsteps thumped down the hall. Jimmy stayed in front of her with his arms folded. She placed her hands on his shoulders as Fatty walked in. He no longer had the same hairstyle he'd had ever since I remembered. It was now pointing due north, greased together with potato and dead flies.

I may have changed the future, but I still had to stop history repeating itself. But how? I couldn't overpower him, and if he was about to do what I was sure he was about to do, then my mission was about to crash down around me.

Fatty's fists were at the ready and so were Jimmy's. I knew he'd make short work of him and Mum if I didn't intervene. His eye was my favourite thing to attack, being the most sensitive part of him, and they say the eyes were the windows to the soul. *Maybe Gabe's soul is hidden in there.*

It was strange. I'd been antagonizing Fatty virtually non-stop since he'd got up that morning, yet he was still surprised when I attacked him. Fuck knows what sound he made this time as I head-butted his eyeball and bounced to safety without using my wings. *Fucking hell. Even his eyes are fat.* He stuck the back of a hand over his eye and I waited for Jimmy to take advantage of his vulnerability. If he was going to fight, then he had to fight. It wasn't like Fatty could call it unfair if he was hampered by a fly. But Jimmy stayed in front of Mum. A fair tactic, as approaching him one at a time would've been fruitless.

Fatty rubbed his eye and began to unbuckle his belt as Jimmy stood with his fists in the air, but Mum hauled him back and he didn't resist. Then Fatty had no choice but to leave his belt alone and wave me away as I swooped down and pounded every inch of his face. I urged Jimmy to use this opportunity to get a clear shot in, but Fatty grabbed his scruff and launched him into the table. He kicked him as he fell, then drew his leg back for another shot as Mum shouldered him in the back, causing him to trip over Jimmy and crash into the table. Three of the legs collapsed and the table gave way, leaving Fatty sprawled among the splintered wood, motionless, his eyes staring without focus. Jimmy stood up and I hoped he laid the boot in, but he had other ideas and took a knife from the draw. It wasn't as large as the knife Mum had jammed in the freezer, but it was big enough to penetrate Fatty's blubber.

'You fat bastard,' Jimmy screamed as he ran towards him.

No. No. No. If Jimmy kills Fatty, he'll go inside. I need to kill him.

I darted within twelve inches of Jimmy's face and we both stopped dead. The whole world seemed to stop too. He still had the knife raised, but we were definitely having a moment. Mum pulled Jimmy's arm down and tried to take the knife, but his white knuckles said he wasn't going to let go.

Fatty tried to hoist himself up by the tabletop, held at an angle by the one leg still attached, but his loose belt buckle caught the edge and he thumped back down. The remaining leg squeaked as it loosened and toppled, and a tin box slid out from a makeshift shelf on the underside of the tabletop and smacked him on the head. It hit the floor with a crash and an assortment of collectables spilled out, including a bundle of cash. The betting slip wasn't there, though. It never made it to the floor, having become stuck to his head.

It must've been Mum's little hiding place. Neat. Fatty was forever searching the house when he thought Mum had a few quid tucked away. Who would think to look at the underside of the kitchen table? But it wasn't hidden now. It was three inches from Fatty's big round head, which had another trickle of blood running down it.

Jimmy and Mum fell over each other to get the money and I was compelled to assist, especially as he'd seen the knife and thought Jimmy was moving in for the kill. But he didn't put his hands up in defence or even plead, he just stood and smirked, and the fork he'd dropped at breakfast was stuck in his backside. I steamed into his right eye and scratched his lens with my legs, but the bastard closed his baggy lid right over me as I wriggled for my life. *I'm inside Fatty. Inside him. Can there be a worse place to be?*

It opened and I was out, but I was hurt. I was flying in spirals and hoped either Jimmy or Mum grabbed the cash as he swiped at me. Then he screamed as his arms disappeared, and I found the safety zone to see his hands replace the foot Jimmy was drawing back. *Straight in the knackers. Nice touch, Jimmy, mate. I owe you one.* Mum had commandeered the cash, but the slip was still stuck to his head, and everyone knew it was there but him. *Mum's mash. Is there anything it can't do?*

I made it to the windowsill, but Fatty's eye had shaken me. My vision was hazy and I only had one working wing. I couldn't fly or fight. I rubbed my eyes, but all I saw were the fuzzy outlines of Jimmy and Mum in the corner, and the fuzzy outline of a fat man crippled in the middle of the room as he waited for his testicles to cool down. He regained his voice and let off a stream of insults you wouldn't say to a dog, never mind your wife and son, which raised my temperature, which was good, but only for keeping me alert. I tried to take off, but my wing was killing me. I needed some kind of anaesthetic.

Fatty's temperature had also risen, it seemed, and he refreshed his blood-alcohol level with a generous swig of whisky, but he was a busy man and didn't have time to screw the lid back on before he slammed it down near the sink. A splash plopped onto the sideboard. *I'll have to neck some and hope it dulls the pain.* Fortunately, my legs were okay, if a bit stiff, and I walked along the sill and hopped down. The dollop rose before me like a golden dome and I could almost smell the hangover in it.

Maybe if I get the chance at Fatty again later and dare go back in his eye, I can employ the old mash potato trick with a scotch twist. Could sting a tad.

I would never usually drink neat whisky, vile stuff by itself. Add a splash of water and an ice cube and I'd drink with you till the cows came home. *But tonight, I'm going neat. Not exactly Gabe-style, and not at his prices. Five quid for two doubles? Why would he do that? Serving himself while the barman was otherwise occupied? And buying Fatty one on demand? I should have asked him.* I closed my eyes and skulled until I wanted to barf.

Nope. Still fucked. And soon my legs would be too. I moved away while I could still walk and took cover behind the taps. The room was spinning and my wing throbbed. *What can I do, though? Walk over and kick him in the nuts too? I can't see and I'm pissed.* All I could do was sit and listen.

'Go on, drink some more, you coward,' said Mum as Fatty had another go at the whisky.

I didn't see Fatty as a coward. He never backed down from anything. Not from a confrontation, an argument or a fistfight.

'Nobody tells me what to do, least of all you,' he said as he pulled the fork from his fat arse and flung it among the splinters on the floor. 'You do as I fucking tell you.'

He turned to Jimmy.

'And as for you,' he said, 'are you going to use that knife or play with it? And where's the money?'

Shit. He saw it.

'What money?' Jimmy said, no doubt praying Fatty wasn't a hundred percent sure what he saw.

'Don't lie. I know you were working at that bitch Margaret's after school today. How much did she pay you?'

Please, don't answer.

'She's going to pay him at the weekend,' said Mum.

'Yes,' Jimmy said, not knowing what the hell she was talking about. 'And if you touch us again, I'll kill you.'

I included me in that *I'll*. Jimmy didn't know I was there, but our eyes had met, and that I'd made him stop when he'd charged Fatty with the knife, before he'd saved my skin by giving him a nudge in the nads, made me wonder with desperate hope whether Jimmy included me as well.

There was silence. I couldn't make out the knife in Jimmy's hand, but I knew it was there, and I wondered why Fatty hadn't confronted the threat. Any other day he would've belted me to within an inch of my life if I so much as handed him a warm beer, and as I'd offered resistance for the first time, which consisted going at him with a knife, followed by a kick in the bollocks and a death threat, I wondered why he wasn't spreading us all over the house like butter. Maybe he was waiting for Jimmy to drop his guard, but I didn't buy that. He'd been waiting my whole life for me to think I was big enough, and me being tooled up wouldn't have put him off. He'd have relished the challenge.

So what was the holdup? Don't get me wrong, I was grateful, obviously, and this layoff gave me time to rest and think. But Fatty was also thinking, which was strange as he never thought about anything, just acted, and I knew he hadn't thrown his last punch. Especially if he saw what was on his head.

Flies aren't supposed to drink whisky. Why hadn't Attenborough mentioned that? I couldn't have drunk more than a couple of atoms' worth and was about to die of alcohol poisoning. My front legs folded, my others followed and I flipped on my back, vibrating like a dying fly. Then I puked, and that it splashed off the tap and onto my wings was a godsend. That good old Scottish pride might have been no good for a fly's insides, but sprinkle it over a fucked wing and it was like fairy dust. I flipped over for a vertical take-off but veered straight into the tap. *Yeah, you know what? The whisky may have numbed the pain, but my wing still ain't flyable.* I took a closer look and saw a chunk missing from the edge, and what was left was torn right through to my body, and I realised that neither me nor Gabe were going to be flying again anytime soon. The injuries I'd picked up at the Haunted House were fairly superficial, but I couldn't see a torn wing sewing itself back together. I needed a miracle, and wasn't going to hold my breath for one of those, not in that house.

Fatty was still in the middle of the room, swearing at something which wasn't necessarily Jimmy or Mum, who were huddled in the far corner, no doubt praying he didn't brush the last of the mash from his hair as they offered desperate words of appeasement.

I was still on the window sill, incapacitated, and wondered if Fatty was also incapacitated in some way, or had he just thought what I'd just thought? To wit, if he killed us, his party would be over. No more slaves and no more freedom. And his little gig with Gabe would be on hold until he got out of prison, just like it had been before. That was if he got out this time. Double murder of wife and child? At fifty-plus years old? He'd die in prison, and Gabe would have to find someone else to find his soul. *Just dee it.* The words recurred. *Just do what?* I thought. I should've asked him. Put him straight on who Fatty was.

I still couldn't see much beyond a couple of feet and wondered if Percy was still beavering away up top, preparing the unfortunate ones that never made it for consumption. I put on more mash shoes and crawled up the wall to examine the fine silk that Nobby stuffed Percy's pockets with. *It sure is thin and sticky. And just what the doctor ordered.* Whether he saw me leap off the shelf as he shot a fresh line I neither knew nor cared, but I needed to time it right as it was a long way down and I didn't want to make my injuries worse. I grabbed the line above Percy's head and ripped it free, then swung like Tarzan back up to the shelf as Percy fell helplessly to the ground.

KEPT IN THE DARK

This is ridiculous. I know I've got six legs, but winding this stuff into a figure-eight around my wing is a nightmare. I guessed I shouldn't have been surprised, as it was designed to fuck up flies, but even if I had fingers I'd need the dexterity of a harpist to fashion it into a bandage. Fatty groaned, and I turned and squinted to see Jimmy still had the knife, but Fatty was preoccupied and I needed to get back amongst it. The bandage would have to do. It looked a mess, but I didn't think it would fall off. I test-flapped and rose in a straight line. *Thank you, very much. Now, where's Fatty?*

I couldn't make sense of his body language through my glazed eyes. *Maybe he's found his little hat and is trying to read his own scribble. It can't be long before Mum's mash starts to itch.* The blood from the head wound he'd sustained at the pub had leaked through his hair and soaked clean into the grime on his collar, and Jimmy and Mum were still in the corner but not holding each other. They needed their hands free for the next round. But when was that going to be?

What is Fatty's problem? I moved closer, alert for those bear paws, and saw his right eye wink as though it were having a seizure. *Oh, I am sorry, fatso. Did I leave a part of me behind when you nearly ripped me apart like Lucy in the sky did? Well, it's no good to me now. I got Percival to sort me out with a squeeze of his superglue, works a fucking treat. If you get my wing out before you die, you can feed it to next-door's dog for all I care.*

Going head first into his good eye like before would be dangerous. Joe Bloggs the fly might not have learned from his mistakes, but I did, and I approached Fatty's blind spot, carrying the longest, sharpest splinter I could fly with. Then, like a medieval knight, I swooped around and drove it into his pupil. There was a pop as his lens deflated like a thin pastry crust and I felt a pang of satisfying sadism as I backed away. His scream shook the foundations of the house and I was surprised the windows didn't shatter. Yet not a squeak of sympathy came from either me, Jimmy or Mum. Instead, we acted in unison and scarpered out the backdoor to save our eardrums.

I sat on Mum's shoulder and the three of us huddled in the garden while we waited for him to stop complaining. We couldn't run away, the betting slip was still stuck to his head, which was only a fingernail's breadth from his fingernail, and he knew the feel of a betting slip like a mole knows the feel of a worm.

The air filled with wails and howls as he blindly tumbled over table legs and crashed into cupboards, but the neighbours wouldn't care; they'd just turn the TV up. I never even went round to ask for my ball back, should it sail over the fence via a badly timed overhead kick or Mum having a breakdown of her senses. I always ran the gauntlet over the fence, because knocking on the door would result in getting a punctured ball back.

His voice finally ran out of steam and he dropped to his knees, which was Mum's cue to go back in. I hopped onto Jimmy's shoulder and we stayed in the garden and watched through the window as she knelt with fake concern and mumbled something sympathetic about his eye as she patted his head to remove the slip. He didn't respond and instead tried to curl into the foetal position, but he'd put on a bit of weight since he was a foetus and bringing his knees to his chest was a trying task for him.

KEPT IN THE DARK

I wondered what Mum had planned now she'd removed the slip. She could've killed him right then, he was at her mercy, but she wouldn't have done it in front of me. Not a hope.

But will I do it in front of her? I did go for him with a knife. Would I have stabbed him if I hadn't intervened?

Mum returned with the slip screwed up in her hand.

'What shall we do?' Jimmy said.

'I want you to go to Margaret's. I'll come and get you soon.'

'No way,' he replied.

I was glad he said what I was thinking, because I knew what she had planned if he complied and hoped he stuck to his guns.

'Why don't we both go to Margaret's?' I said.

Now that's a better idea. Leave him to me.

We went inside to see Fatty still down and not an immediate threat, but if they stayed she'd have to call an ambulance, otherwise they'd have had to put up with his wails all night. If they went round to Margaret's for a cup of tea and a chat, by the time they'd returned Fatty would've either opened the freezer and met his fate, or found his own way to hospital. And he'd have his work cut out convincing anyone that a fly had attacked him with a splinter.

Mum took the knife from Jimmy's hand and dropped it in the sink with a clunk, then stuffed the cash and the betting slip in her coat pocket and they were out the door.

I, however, hadn't finished with Fatty yet. Oh, no. I was behind the taps with my new lance at the ready, waiting for Jimmy and Mum to move out of earshot so they didn't have to endure Fatty's screams again.

Thirty-Three

I now had the upper hand on Fatty as a fly and a human for the first time. He was half-blind and in pain and it was a moment to savour. My eyesight was back to 90 percent and my bandaged wing was no more than a little sore.

As soon as Jimmy and Mum disappeared through the gate I landed on his cheek and balanced my lance, but he had other things to worry about than the fly that had made a bad day worse. His hand was cupped over his splintered eye and he'd managed to blink my wing out of the other. It was open and dark and bloodshot and reminded me of the fires of Hell. Quite fitting, really. I thought about what he'd been doing to Gabe and wanted to make him suffer even more. Ironically, Gabe wasn't there to stop me this time, but I couldn't work out why he'd been so keen to save him last time.

No one had heard the conversation in the pub because no one else was there. The barman never served or spoke to Gabe. Neither did anyone in the bookies. Neither did anyone in the street. When he preached, passers-by would stare in his direction, confused. I thought it was confusion at his incoherent ramblings. The two old ladies who said hello to everyone never even glanced at him. Mum never spoke of him, and whenever I encountered him in my youth I was always alone. No one mentioned him. Ever. When he walked through the pub he was careful not to touch anyone. And he didn't cast a shadow.

Gabe's still invisible. To everyone except me and Fatty.
I puked again, but not from the whisky. *Ah need the sol te get back te Heaven,* he had told me. *Just dee it,* he had begged Fatty. I thought about my childhood, the first one; Gabe was very much there and it was before I'd died and gone back to meet him. I *couldn't* have told him where I lived. But he was there. *He's noo wee bairn anymore... Just dee it.* He wanted Fatty to kill me. That was why he was so keen on saving him that day. Fatty had told him I had the soul and he wanted Fatty to kill me for it.

Had Gabe been trying to kill me too? *Next time Ah'll push ye under a bus that's movin, y'wee shite.*

*

I didn't have time to worry about being eaten. As the crow flies was my only option, and I ignored the cool air zapping my energy as I pelted over the trees and through the gap in the bushes, praying Gabe was still there.

He was, though he'd been shopping since I'd left. A half-full bottle was clasped in his hand and a fresh empty lay next to him. He was sitting up with his eyes closed, probably daydreaming about being dead. I hopped in the empty and called his name.

One eye half opened as he turned towards the bottle. 'Wee Jimmy, Ah'd forgotten aboot –'

'SHUT THE FUCK UP AND LISTEN.'

Both eyes pinged open and he pulled his head back.

'GABE, I CAN SEE YOU.'

'Ah see ye too, wee Jimmy,' he said. 'It's good te have ye back.'

'NO, GABE. YOU'RE STILL INVISIBLE.'

'Of course, Ah am.'

'BUT I CAN SEE YOU.'

'That's cos yer a wee fly that's been sent by Noaby.'

'NO, I COULD SEE YOU WHEN I WAS ALIVE.'

He didn't know that I kill him and Fatty, and that he kills me, in thirteen years' time. Although I had every intention of stopping two of the deaths this time around.

'Ah never even knew ye when ye was alive,' he said.

'GABE, THE KID THAT TORMENTS YOU IS MY YOUNGER SELF. THAT'S WHY I'VE COME BACK. WELL, NOT FOR YOU, BUT TO SAVE MY MUM. YOU WERE THERE WHEN SHE DIED. YOU STOPPED ME FROM KILLING FATTY.'

'Ah dinnae remember that,' he said, shaking his head.

'THAT'S BECAUSE IT HASN'T HAPPENED YET. I'M HERE TO STOP IT.'

He picked up the bottle and furrowed his moustache-like eyebrows as he peered through the glass.

'Yer the little shite?' he said, quiet but stern.

'GABE, I DIDN'T KNOW IT WAS YOU. I HADN'T EVEN MET YOU YET.'

Until then I'd been convinced his ramblings were the result of many lifetimes wandering the world, drinking and wishing for it to end, yet knowing it never would, unless he did what he was here to do. Whatever that was.

He trained his eyes on me like a scientist through a microscope. 'Dee ye think Ah'm a fool?' He put the bottle down and struggled to his feet with his fists up, just like in the desert. 'Ah knoo the difference between a good sol and a bad sol. Ye father's been raisin' ye te be a killer.'

'STOP. I'M NOT GOING TO KILL YOU,' I said, then realised the sickening irony.

His cheeks rose to stop a tear as he sank to his knees.

'GABE, I'M SORRY. I WAS JUST A KID. I DIDN'T KNOW WHO YOU WERE.'

'Oh, Jimmy,' he said, trying to steady his bottom lip. 'Ye really dinnae knoo who ye are, dee ye?'

'I DO. THE KID IS ME–'

'Ah knoo who ye are,' he cut in. 'It's ye that dinnae knoo.'

'DON'T KNOW WHAT? I'VE COME BACK TO KILL FATTY, MY FATHER, AND SAVE MY MUM.'

I stared at his eyes, but this time there was no shiver. The mystery of why I had them before had been solved.

'Are ye tellin' me that Noaby sent ye back te kill ye father?' he said.

The answer to that, of course, was no. Quite the opposite. And he hadn't even sent me back to save my mum – that was my mission. Okay, he had sanctioned it, but he didn't care about my mum any more than he cared about anyone else who didn't believe. But I didn't want to give Gabe too much information at this stage. I still couldn't get over the coincidence of him being here and somehow in cahoots with Fatty.

'NO,' I said. 'NOBBY WANTS ME TO *SAVE* FATTY, BUT I'M NOT GOING TO. I'M HERE FOR MY MUM ONLY.'

'Oh, Jimmy, ye poor wretched fool,' he said, shaking his head. 'Ye really dinnae knoo why ye been sent back here, dee ye?'

'TO SAVE MY MUM AND REDEEM MYSELF. IT WAS YOUR FUCKING IDEA.'

'Redeem yersel fe what?'

'MY SINS.'

'Get te fock. Noaby dinnae care aboot sins anymore than he cares aboot ye wee ma. He only cares whether ye believe. Ye knoo that as well as me.'

He had a point, but I still didn't know where he was going with this.

'SO WHAT DO YOU KNOW THAT I DON'T?'

'Tell me what sins Noaby's upset aboot.'

I felt I should tread carefully, yet I didn't know why. I could've told him anything about the future and he wouldn't have known any different. Especially as he'd forgotten it was him who'd told me to come back here. I decided to be honest.

'I KILLED MY FATHER, REMEMBER.'

The veins in his face drained downwards like mercury in a thermometer that had been put in a freezer. A tear followed one of them and he began to blub. I thought back to that day in the kitchen when Gabe had been so keen to save Fatty, then to thirteen years later in the living room when he'd wept as Fatty lay dying. What kind of hold did Fatty have over him?

He threw his head back and howled like an injured wolf with his hands together in prayer. 'Oh, Jimmy,' he cried. 'Please, tell me ye dinnae. Please.'

'NO, I DON'T KILL HIM FOR ANOTHER THIRTEEN YEARS.'

'Ye mean he's still alive now?'

'YES, BUT WHY–'

His veins refilled themselves. 'Ye dee that te me again and Ah'll rip yer fockin wings off and send ye te Hell.'

'WHY, GABE? WHY DON'T YOU WANT FATTY TO DIE?'

'Cause Ah need the sol te get back te Heaven.'

'DON'T BE STUPID, GABE. FATTY'S BEEN LYING TO YOU. HE CAN'T FIND THE SOUL.'

He gave me the same incredulous glare I'd given him all afternoon. 'What ye talkin' aboot,' he said. 'He already has it. Ah can see it.'

'WHAT HAS FATTY TOLD YOU? THAT I HAVE THE SOUL?'

'Ye? Noaby's sol? Ye wish.'

I didn't know how much of what he was trying to tell me was based on reality, and how much was a delusion his handful of brain cells had conjured up, but I knew that somewhere in his head was information that I didn't want to know. I didn't reply, and wished I'd stayed at the house.

'Ye and ye famly are riddled wi'sols, Jimmy,' he said. 'Dark ones, Noaby ones and wee little Jimmy ones.'

He rolled over with the now annoying laugh I'd found so appealing in the desert, but this wasn't funny anymore. I needed him to come clean.

'WHAT'S GOING ON, GABE? TELL ME.'

KEPT IN THE DARK

He sat up. The laughter had gone and his eyes drooped. 'Ye are with a dark sol, Jimmy. Ye belong te Lucy. So fock off and leave me alone.'

He fell to his side and closed his eyes.

'NO, GABE, I NEED TO KNOW. WHY DOES FATTY WANT TO KILL ME? WHO AM I?'

He reopened his eyes and looked at me as though I were the one who was nuts.

'Did ye just say what Ah think ye did?' he said, raising his eyebrows to form more creases on his head.

'FATTY, MY FATHER. DOES HE WANT TO KILL ME?'

'Have ye loast yer fockin mind there, wee Jimmy? Why would he want te kill *ye*, unless he's loast *his* fockin mind?'

'GABE, YOU'RE FREAKING ME OUT. PLEASE TELL ME WHAT THE FUCK IS GOING ON.'

He shuffled his scrawny arse around to make himself as comfortable as the lumpy grass would let him, then looked behind as if to make sure no one was listening. He lowered his voice to a whisper.

'The firstbon o'Noaby's sol comes with a dark sol,' he said. 'And if it kills its father, Noaby's sol will be destroyed.'

'SO WHAT'S THAT GOT TO DO WITH ME AND FATTY?'

'Ye are the only ones that can see me. Have ye noo been lisnin te a word Ah said?'

I was starting to put two and two together. I prayed I came up with five.

'SO I NEED TO DIE TO SAVE THE SOUL?'

'Noobody wants te save Noaby's wretched sol. We want te destroy it.'

'WHY? WHO HAS IT?'

I immediately wished I'd never asked and didn't want him to spell it out. I cut back in before he had the chance.'

'BUT YOUR MISSION? YOU WERE SUPPOSED TO GIVE MO A MESSAGE AND YOU DID.'

'Aye, my mission was te give Mo a message, but that didnae mean Ah could then just fly back te Heaven. The only way Ah can get back is te be killed by Noaby's sol, and the only way Noaby's sol can get back is te be killed by the dark sol.'

'WHO IS IT?'

'Ye father has Noaby's sol, Jimmy. And if he dies, Ah'll be alive forever.'

So Fatty has Nobby's soul. Does he now? I think Gabe's got himself a little confused.

'WHY WOULD FATTY HAVE NOBBY'S SOUL?' I said.

'Cos he got sent back doon.'

'FATTY? GOT SENT BACK DOWN WHERE?'

'Fe fock's sake, Jimmy, and Ah thought Ah was the stupid one. There's noo shuttle bus te Heaven and back fe us chosen ones. Once yer here, yer stay here till ye die. And there's only one way for the sol te die.'

I didn't reply. I felt sick and tried to stop my mind from wandering back three days, to two thousand years ago, but I couldn't. I was well aware of the only way the soul could die and had watched it happen, and watched Jesus disappear, to either Heaven or Hell, or so I assumed. And since then there'd been no reports of another blood sacrifice. But there'd be one in the living room in thirteen years' time.

'WHAT'S THE DEAL WITH ITS FIRSTBORN?' I said, not wanting to know.

'As soon as Lucy's fruit was eaten, the dark sol became alive,' he said, 'and would live in the firstbon o'Noaby's sol, and if the first-bon kills its father, Noaby's sol will be destroyed. Ye father's been raisin' ye te kill him, Jimmy. So the sol will be destroyed and he can goo te Heaven. Withoot the sol, Noaby cannae drag anyone else oot te dee his dirty work fe him.'

I dropped to the glass and fought the disturbing fuzz that festered in my stomach, but the penny was working its way down whether I liked it or not. I only hoped Gabe gave me time to process this information before he fucked my head up even more. I thought back to when I first met Nobby. *You are with a dark soul*, he had said. I thought back to when I first met Lucy. *You are of a dark soul*, he had said. I thought it was because I was a murderer, but I think they thought I knew, then realised I didn't.

'Ah hate te break it te ye like this, wee Jimmy. But Noaby dinnae send ye here te save yersel, he sent ye te save his precious sol. Ye are the firstbon, wee Jimmy. The dark sol. Ye belong te Lucy.'

My mind was spinning in the bottle. *I'm Lucy's dark soul. The firstborn of Nobby's soul. My father. Fatty. Jesus!? He was abusing me because he wanted me to hate him and kill him. And I did.* Then something else hit me.

'If I have the dark soul, what would happen if I died believing in Nobby?'

'If ye died believin', yer'd goo straight te Heaven. Noaby would knoo aboot it but wouldnae care, as long as it hadnae killed its father. The dark sol cannae dee any harm in Heaven. He'd see it as a victory.'

'BUT WHERE DO YOU FIT INTO ALL THIS, GABE? HOW WILL THE SOUL HELP YOU GET BACK TO HEAVEN?'

'The sol is the only thin' that can kill me, Ah already told ye. That's why Ah had te find it. Ah think Noaby made me like this so Ah would find Jesus and get him te carry on spreadin' the message or die tryin'. But if wee Jimmy kills Jesus before he kills me, then it's all over. He'll goo te Heaven, Noaby will lose his sol, and Ah'll be wanderin' aroond till the end ay time.'

I thought about that day in the living room. Gabe eating the money. I guessed he wanted Fatty to cut him open for it. Probably the cleverest idea he ever came up with. Then there was the smile on Fatty's face when I stabbed him. I had destroyed Nobby's soul and he was off to Heaven. That's why Nobby dragged me away from Lucy's clutches. He knew I had a dark soul. Then when he interrogated me and realised I didn't know I had it, he kept quiet. Cheeky bastard. And that's why he was so keen to find out whom I'd killed. I wasn't stupid enough to think Nobby had had my interests at heart on my first three missions. It was always about him, and I didn't blame him for using me to try and restart the clock, but it wasn't because he wanted me to redeem myself – it was because I'd destroyed his special soul. Lucy also seemed surprised I had a dark soul after he'd stripped me of my body. Then he realised I didn't know I had it, and also kept quiet.

KEPT IN THE DARK

I had to assume the freezer trap was still set, but was reluctant to tell Gabe that Fatty was in danger. I was on his side here, but there were a few things that still didn't fit.

'WHY DOESN'T FATTY HAVE ANY POWERS?' I said. 'AND WHY DID HE WAIT SO LONG TO HAVE A CHILD?'

'Noaby took his poowers away when he sent him back doon, which must've included his impotency. Ah guess Noaby overlooked that one. Jesus thought that if he fathered a child, Noaby would send him te Hell. But Ah telt him his firstbon would have the dark sol, and that if it killed him, Noaby's sol would be destroyed and he would goo te Heaven. That's why he had ye, and that's why he's been bashing ye. He wants ye te kill him.'

And he won't be disappointed.

'WHY ARE YOU PAYING FOR YOUR DRINKS?'

'Cos Ah just wannae feel normal. Ah dinnae wannae be stealin' and robbin'.'

'BUT WHERE DO YOU GET THE MONEY FROM?'

'Ah take it from the bookies. They rob folk day in day oot.'

I'm not sure that's the best way to do it, but marks for effort.

'WHY DIDN'T YOU GO TO THE RACES TODAY? I HEARD FATTY COMPLAINING.'

'Ah dinnae knoo. Ah was gannae, but something telt me not te. Ah cannae explain.'

'HOW DO YOU FIX THE RESULTS?'

'Ah goo te the track and put the hosses off. Me and ye father had a deal, but Ah dinnae want him te win too much or he might start enjoyin' life. Ah was only deein it till ye was big enough te kill him, then he was supposed te kill me first, but he hasnae, and yer not getting any younger, and Ah'm afraid yel kill him first.'

'IF ONLY THE SOULS CAN KILL YOU, WHAT HAPPENS IF MY YOUNGER SELF KILLS YOU?'

'Yer a wee dark sol, Jimmy. Ah'll goo straight te Hell for failing Noaby. Either that, or he'll send me back here. Ah could kill ye, but then ye father would be alive forever and would never kill me oot o'spite.'

My plan for him to help me kill Fatty had just washed away like the scotch down his throat.

'WHAT DO YOU WANT ME TO DO?' I said.

'Wee Jimmy, le'me tell ye somethin',' he said as he glugged the rest of his drink and patted his jacket for another.

'GABE, PLEASE.'

He looked down and picked the bottle up. 'Wee Jimmy, Ah'd forgotten aboot ye. Are ye still here?'

'GABE, YOU WERE GOING TO TELL ME SOMETHING.'

He grinned and I was worried he'd decline back into hysterics. This needed to hurry along before we had to start all over again.

'Wee Jimmy, Ah remember what Ah was gannae tell ye,' he said, having a light-bulb moment.

'WHAT?'

'We're both focked,' he said. 'And ye got noo chance.'

'WHY?'

'Ah hate te break it te ye, Jimmy, but yer a wee fockin fly. Ain't noo fly gannae save or kill anyone.'

KEPT IN THE DARK

He stared at the bottle, holding it with a steady hand that belied what I'd seen him drink, and I wanted to say something before he needed another, but I only stared back. I'd skipped through the ages via Nobby's magic wand, but poor Gabe had been drinking his way through the centuries, invisible to all except two, unable to die except at the hands of one, and instilled with a fear it would go on forever.

He flopped on his side and put his hands under his head for a pillow. 'Ah'm soo tired, Jimmy,' he said. 'But Ah cannae even slep.'

I thought about Fatty at the house. Was he still nursing his eye? Had he opened the freezer? Was he on the floor with a knife in his neck, bleeding to death? If Gabe was telling the truth, he needed to know.

'GABE,' I said, ready to escape should he take the news badly.

He opened one eye and stared at the label. I shouted again and he cracked a smile as his other eye opened.

'Ye talkin te me there,' he said.

'YES, GABE. YOU NEED TO LISTEN TO ME.'

'Dinnae worry, Ah hear ye lood and clear,' he said. 'Ah'm on ma way.'

That would've been encouraging had I told him what he needed to do, but he thought the stag was talking to him again and tried to scoop himself up. I had another holler of his name and he dropped back down. *He definitely heard something.* I shouted again and he brought the open end of the bottle to his eye.

'Wee Jimmy, are ye still here? Ah'd forgotten aboot ye.'

'GABE, WE NEED TO GET BACK TO THE HOUSE. FATTY'S ABOUT TO DIE.'

He sprung upright, sober as a judge. 'Jimmy, if yev killed him Ah'm gonna rip yer–'

'NO, HE'S STILL ALIVE. BUT MUM'S SET A TRAP TO KILL HIM. COME WITH ME IF YOU WANT TO DIE.'

He chuckled. 'Ye wee ma's been tryin' te kill him fe years.'

'WHAT?'

'Ah've been watchin' ye hoose since ye was bon. She's tried poisonin' him a few times, but she's noo gannae dee it like that. He needs te bleed te death.'

'GABE, SHE'S SET A TRAP WITH A KNIFE. IF IT WORKS, HE *WILL* BLEED TO DEATH.'

He leapt to his feet, but I couldn't wait for him to walk to the house in a staggered line. I was gone.

Thirty-Four

I'd been running off adrenalin since I left the house, but the temperature hit me as I stayed low across the park. The night was closing in and this was bat territory, and bat feeding time. I gave the trees a wide birth, which made my route longer and me colder.

I approached the house and needed the radiator badly, but I knew I'd have to wait a little longer when I saw a lump on top of the garden hedge. I closed in and realised it was Gabe. He was face down, but he'd had the brains to leave the bottle by his ear. I flew in.

'GABE,' I said.

He turned over and smiled. 'Wee Jimmy, ye flew off withoot me.'

'HOW THE FUCK DID YOU GET HERE?'

'Ah flew.'

'BUT YOU DON'T HAVE ANY WINGS.'

'Aye, and ye dinnae have any vocal chords but ye can still talk. The wings are just fe steerin' and landin'. We're both deed and we can both fly. Just like the auld times.'

'BUT WHY ARE YOU HIDING IN THE HEDGE? NO ONE CAN SEE YOU.'

'Ah'm noo hidin'. This is where Ah landed.'

'WAIT HERE. I'LL GO AND CHECK INSIDE.'

*

I scanned the kitchen as the radiator pumped life-saving warmth into my senses, but the freezer was closed and there was no knife in Fatty's head. He was at the window, with one hand on the edge of the sink and the other over his eye. There was dried blood on his face and neck neck, but not much. More than you'd expect from a splinter cut on a finger, but he was a long way from bleeding to death. Gabe wasn't done yet. I nipped back outside.

*

Susan tried to make sense of her failure as they hurried away. She hadn't bothered with a plan B. What could've ever gone wrong? Apart from everything. Him coming home early. Her son not being arrested. More violence. More humiliation. She was supposed to kill him, not injure him, and it wasn't even her doing. A strange force had entered the kitchen and poked him in the eye.

Then her memory poked her in the brain. She'd left the trap set up, and no one was in the house except him. He was only injured at the moment and it was clear no one had attacked him, but if he opened the freezer – there was no one to find him except her, or her son, and there was a clear sign of a struggle, and she no longer had an alibi. Tears and panic welled up. She had to go back.

Her son would never agree to go to Margaret's on his own and she couldn't tell him why he should, and he'd never let her go back to the house alone anyway, so they both turned and soldiered back.

*

Gabe was still on top of the hedge, or perhaps more in it than on it. He didn't have the grace to hop and hover like a garden bird, so he'd tried to wrestle himself over the edge and worked his way further down. The bottle had worked its way down with him so I swerved through the twigs and hopped in.

'NO NEED TO PANIC. HE'S HURT BUT NOT DYING,' I said.

'That's good te knoo,' he replied. 'Let's goo and get a drink.'

'BUT THE FREEZER'S STILL CLOSED.'

'Ah dinnae mean from ye freezer, the pub's just doon the road.'

'NO, GABE. I MEAN THE FREEZER DOOR IS CLOSED. MUM SET A TRAP IN THERE. IF HE OPENS IT, HE'LL BE STABBED.'

He wriggled and slipped further down as I backed out, and I wished I could give him a hand.

'Ah'm gannae have te fly oot,' he said. 'Fock knoos where Ah'll land, mind.'

I moved sideways to give him room and heard footsteps. Jimmy and Mum were a hundred feet away, with Mum half a yard in front and walking with purpose. She couldn't see Gabe, but Jimmy sure could, and I didn't want him asking Mum why the strange man was stuck in our hedge. My only hope was that Mum was between Jimmy and the hedge when Gabe came into view. I hopped back in the bottle.

'GABE, STAY WHERE YOU ARE AND DON'T MOVE. ME AND MUM ARE BACK.'

He tried to curl up as twigs pierced his frayed clothes, but I doubted he felt pain. At least his liver didn't.

Jimmy and Mum were twenty feet from the gate with him on the wrong side of her, nearest the road. I needed him to be on the inside when they turned right through the gate. I closed in.

With ten feet to go, I landed on Jimmy's nose and we both stopped dead. We locked eyes and stood rigid like a couple of statues.

Mum carried on a step, then stopped too. 'Are you okay, Jimmy?' she said. 'You can wait here if you like.'

Jimmy shook his head which encouraged me to lift away, but our eyes were still locked as I guided him to walk on the inside before we turned. There was little chance he'd see Gabe from there, as long as he didn't move. I was an inch taller than Mum, but couldn't see over the top of her head. It was when we straightened up down the garden path I needed to worry about. We needed to be level, and stay level. Then Gabe moved the empty up to his eye. Whether he was searching for me or double-checking its contents I didn't know, but it meant I had to do something I didn't want to.

I swooped in and jabbed Jimmy's left eye, making him shriek and wave me away, then I jabbed his right. Another shriek and Mum stopped and turned with another word of comfort. Gabe was now adjacent, but there was nothing to see for Mum, and Jimmy was too busy dabbing his eyes to notice the human shape inside the hedge. We passed the danger zone and I escorted them to the front door. As

KEPT IN THE DARK

soon as they had entered, I turned back to let Gabe know the coast was clear. He was gone.

I rose and scanned the air – nothing. I swooped to the back garden – nothing. Except Yappy taking a nap under the tree next door. There was only one place Gabe would be and I wasn't going to kid myself I could stop him. *He'll be back when he's back.*

Chapter Thirty-Five

I perched on the jar of flour and watched Percy cocoon my fat foes below. My legs were re-coated in mash in case I needed to re-dress my wing, and Mum's purse was on the far end of the shelf. But I didn't think she was back for that, as she had taken the money with her.

Fatty had found himself a chair amongst the debris. He was near the corner, facing away, with his left hand cupped over his injured eye, and his right hand down by his side. But something wasn't right. He was still wailing, but different from before. It sounded forced. If he was bluffing for sympathy, he was in the wrong kitchen.

There was a fresh line of blood on his fingers and more smudged into his neck, but he was a long way from bleeding to death. This was good all round. Fatty was in pain, it brought Gabe more time, and, most importantly, Jimmy and Mum were safe. The tabletop was propped against the back door – a possible exit blocked – which meant he was mobile enough to plan ahead. It wasn't beyond removal but wouldn't be done quickly.

KEPT IN THE DARK

Jimmy and Mum were standing in the doorway and I didn't know if Fatty knew they were inside yet. It was doubtful he heard them over his wails. The freezer was still closed and still no sign of the knife. Mum glanced around, no doubt looking for the same thing, but she didn't tell me to go to my room this time, which was good, because it meant she wasn't about to kill him. It was also good because I feared Fatty was waiting for Jimmy to leave before he acted. Neither Jimmy nor Mum approached him, as they'd also picked up on his crocodile tears and were holding a buffer zone.

I looked at the loops of his trousers. The belt wasn't there, so I moved across the room to check his right hand. The end of his belt was wrapped around his fist with the buckle resting on the floor next to his bottle, and his good eye was open. I scouted for another splinter.

*

Susan set a pace between normal speed and obvious haste and told her son she'd forgotten her purse, which she had, but there was nothing in it. The cash from the robbery and her husband's winnings were tucked safely in her pocket.

Her husband was still in distress but had moved. He was in a chair, bent forward with a hand over his eye. She looked at the freezer – it was still closed – but she was reluctant to open it as it wasn't possible to disarm it without setting it off. There was no way to open the door slowly. You either yanked it, or it stayed shut. And she didn't want her husband to see the knife fly out and miss him. His good eye was on her blindside, but she knew the difference between his cries of pain and his cries of bluff, and knew the eye was open and alert. She also didn't want the trap going off in front of her son; he was clear from harm where he was, but there was nothing to be gained by him seeing it.

Her purse was on the shelf, on the other side of the room, where her husband's good eye could see. She didn't need it, but she knew that if she didn't run the gauntlet her son would. She tiptoed over the broken wood, and her son followed.

*

I was back on the jar with another lance as Mum headed towards me, and I wished it was to hug me, but she needed her purse for some reason. If only I could've thrown it to her. Jimmy was close behind her. Not because I was a mummy's boy, but to guard her from the inevitable attack, which happened as soon as they passed the point of no return. I was sure Fatty moved as quickly as he could, but in reality it seemed like slow motion.

He rose and swung and the belt buckle met his bottle with a smash, and he watched in horror as the last of his whisky spread across the vinyl floor in amber-coloured zigzags. Then he dropped the belt and picked up the broken bottle with the neck still attached. Four protruding shards pointed at Jimmy and Mum as Fatty backed to the hall door and shoved it closed with his elbow. They were nearer the back door, but seconds they didn't have were needed to drag the tabletop clear. I dipped down and soaked my lance in a river of whisky.

The room was quiet except for Fatty's low growl as his working eye flitted between Jimmy and Mum, deciding whom to attack first. He picked Mum, which was a mistake. He took a step and jabbed at her, but I was already in his airspace and did a loop the loop to gain velocity, sitting astride the splinter like an angry witch. I aimed for his eye and still saw no evidence of Nobby's soul. Not that I expected to – he'd been vigilant in covering his tracks since time began.

I didn't know what happened. Perhaps my wing caught the light and triggered a reflex in Fatty's brain, making his eye snap shut a millimetre from contact, but I needn't have worried. His eyelid had been opening and closing for longer than I'd previously thought and had worn down to an almost translucent wisp. The splinter pierced his skin and I heard the satisfying pop of his other lens as I backed away leaving his lid pinned closed like a club sandwich.

There were no deafening cries this time, which was nice. He just sank to his knees and, dropping the broken bottle, raised his hand to join the other like he was playing peek-a-boo. Jimmy and Mum remained in the corner as he exhaled with a chesty whine – a noise that was drowned out by a crash in the back garden.

*

Susan wasn't happy her son followed her across the kitchen, but she was proud of his courage. She knew her husband was going to strike, but she also knew it wouldn't be done with speed and surprise. He was cumbersome at the best of times. With only one eye, and a hand covering the other, he wouldn't be much of a threat, even with a weapon. She was more worried about what she was going to do when she'd retrieved her purse, as she still had to disarm the freezer.

She and her son jumped at the smashed bottle, but they stepped clear of the swinging belt into the far corner. Her husband grabbed the broken bottle and blocked the exit to the hallway as she glanced at the back door. The tabletop leant against it. She closed her eyes as he jabbed at her, then opened them again when she heard another smash at her feet. The strange force had poked his other eye and she backed against the wall as he dropped to his knees. There were no screams, just a gasp. Then she jumped at the crunching sound in the garden. She looked through the window and rubbed her eyes, unable to believe what she was seeing.

*

I had an open view of the crash site through the window. Part of the adjoining fence next door had folded in on itself, and if I wasn't mistaken, Gabe was wrapped up in it, and he looked quite out of it. He may have been invisible, but the fence he was dragging towards the house wasn't, and he'd have moved faster if Yappy didn't have his growling teeth clamped on the other end.

Jimmy and Mum stood rooted to the spot. Fatty also turned his head towards the noise, but had to use his imagination on this one. My imagination went into overdrive at what Mum must've been thinking as next door's rat dog pushed a busted fence panel across the lawn. Jimmy stood next to her, and, of course, he could see the real cause of the freak show, but didn't know that Mum couldn't.

Fatty wasn't enjoying himself. Both hands were still up and fresh blood chased through the ravines in his arm blubber and swelled to a pouch on his elbow. It dropped and disappeared as soon as it hit the vinyl.

So Gabe was right. Fatty is Jesus. Who'd have thought?

KEPT IN THE DARK

Now I saw Gabe's predicament. When Fatty's last drop of blood fell, he'd disappear and Gabe would be alive forever. *I guess he has been alive forever.* And if it was Jimmy who had drawn his last drop, Fatty would go to Heaven, and Nobby's wretched soul would be destroyed. One out of three wasn't good enough.

I also saw Fatty's predicament. He couldn't kill Jimmy, or at least he didn't want to, because *he'd* be alive forever. He needed Jimmy to kill him. I tried to picture him with a wizard's beard and a cloth sack for a dress, but his change in body shape wouldn't let me. But those eyes. The same eyes I'd stared into three days and two thousand years ago. I couldn't look into them now for obvious reasons, but the shiver would never leave me.

A growl came through the window, but I couldn't tell if it was Yappy, or Gabe, who'd been inching towards the backdoor with an unopened bottle in his hand. He wouldn't use it for a weapon, not while it was full. Mum had also been inching towards the backdoor. The tabletop grated as she dragged it free and grabbed the door handle. She wasn't alone in thinking Fatty was in no state to stop her. He had nothing to think of or worry about except his eyes.

Jimmy's attention was fixed on Gabe outside, causing him to miss Mum's struggle. But from the shelf, I had a clear view of everything and everyone, including Fatty, who was on his knees searching for what remained of the bottle. It was in his vicinity and not long before he'd find it, but I could do nothing. Not much point in attacking his eyes again, and if he'd composed himself enough to carry on without the gift of sight, working his ears and nose wouldn't have created a major distraction.

I checked on Gabe, who'd made it to the backdoor and was fighting off the fence with his legs as though a shark had him. Everyone inside was static, apart from Fatty, who'd found the bottle and was moving his head like a chicken as he jabbed and poked the air. His beltless trousers were beginning to slip down. He had one hand over both eyes and his various wounds still wept, and I was surprised Jimmy and Mum didn't notice his blood disappearing when it hit the floor. But Mum was more concerned about the glass, and Jimmy was more concerned that Gabe was about to open the door.

'Mum, don't open the door. He's coming,' Jimmy said.

She stopped and looked at Fatty, who pointed the two remaining shards where he thought the backdoor was.

Mum let go of the handle just before it turned from the outside and the door flew open with a creak. She got shoved into the shelf and the jar on it shuddered as if in an earthquake as I jumped off to hover in the middle of the room. I looked down at what could've been a photograph. Fatty was dead still, I guessed to work out whether we'd both escaped. Mum was dazed, but with it enough to not move. And the only part of Gabe moving were his eyes as they checked Fatty up and down, for blood loss, no doubt. His unopened bottle was in his hand and Yappy was growling at him from the doorway. Jimmy stood still in the corner, and I wasn't sure what he was thinking. He could've been wondering why Jock had barged in via an unorthodox and destructive route through the garden. *We don't have a bell, but a good rap on the door usually does the trick.*

KEPT IN THE DARK

Or perhaps he was wondering why Mum hadn't reacted to Jock standing next to her.

Whatever, no one except me had noticed the only other thing moving, which was the flour. The jar had toppled on its side and white powder was spilling onto the shelf. Then there was a split and crack as Gabe opened his bottle and Fatty lunged forward and smacked his face on the edge of the door. His trousers dropped to his knees and he staggered back with blood pissing from his nose just as Gabe stepped in and tripped over the tabletop. His legs stopped at the waist as his upper half jacked sideways over the sideboard and his head whacked the shelf. The jar spun and continued to empty itself over the edge of the shelf. But there was nothing I could do. This was going to happen.

Gabe straightened up and swigged his bottle as flour snowed on his head and shoulders to make a fluffy white balaclava. Mum buckled at the knees and clung to the sideboard as she tried to comprehend what her brain was telling her, then screamed and closed her eyes. Which was Fatty's signal and he raised the glass. Jimmy leapt over the mess on the floor and jumped at Fatty's arm. But he was too late.

*

Susan wouldn't have fled without her son, who was facing away, looking out the window, no doubt as confused as she was about why next-door's dog was pushing the fence through the grass. She knew dogs were stronger than they looked, but the fence was heavy and the dog was a Jack Russell. But it was by far the lesser of two evils and the door was now clear of the obstruction. She reached for the handle and nearly fainted when her son gave away her position. It was their only escape.

She let go, then the door flew open and knocked her to the side where she smacked her head on the shelf. Three things happened. First, she disturbed a fly that flew off in a panic. Second, the jar of flour toppled. And third, the room filled with a smell that made her nostrils hurt. She heard the jar fall and didn't care about the fly. All she saw were the sharp shards in her husband's hand, which had stopped like everything else in the room. Then it seemed the strange force had hit the shelf above her head and flour spilled into her peripheral vision. She braved a glance, then screamed as it stopped in midair, above a hovering whisky bottle, then screamed again, more loudly, as her husband's raised hand came down. She closed her eyes as her son rushed over, and hoped he'd make it in time. He didn't.

*

Fatty stood proud, with his arms wide like he was on an invisible cross. Like he was reliving old times as he waited for me to avenge my mother's death. His eyes, nose and neck dripped with blood, but Mum wouldn't have to clean it off the floor.

Gabe also stood proud, in between Mum and Fatty, with two shards of a whisky bottle stuck in his chest and a grin the size of the Amazon estuary. He pulled out the glass and dropped it as dark blood gushed out like a couple of teapots were being poured from inside his chest. It hit the vinyl and disappeared as though the floor was a mirage, then he shook off the flour and brushed down his jacket before turning to Fatty with a smile. Between them, they looked like characters in a horror film with a healthy make-up budget.

Gabe sank to his knees as Mum reached for the invisible man who had just saved her life, while Fatty still had his arms out, waiting for Jimmy to do to him what he thought he'd just done to Mum. Gabe dropped his smile and screwed his face up as the blood slowed and his tears shed. His sobs were low because he was weak and tired, more tired than any man who ever lived, and stronger than any man who ever lived. He would now have his wish, which was to leave this wretched planet that had held him prisoner for thousands of years. Unseen by all, except for an unfortunate father and son he'd had to seek across the world for millennia to get one of them to kill him. If it wasn't so funny, it would be tragic.

*

Susan felt a body against hers and nearly fainted at the smell as she thanked God her husband had missed and fallen into her. She opened her eyes to see the back of a white head an inch from her face. Over its shoulder stood her husband with his arms out, wearing a smile she hadn't seen since their son was born.

The white figure moved away and she gaped at its lack of lower torso and legs. Its arms stopped short of the elbows, and the whisky bottle still floated in the air below. She quivered at its featureless face as it turned, and saw two slots in its chest with nothing but kitchen in them. There was no blood and no sound of despair as the ghost-like figure shook its head and disappeared. She couldn't help but reach out to feel for what had just saved her life, but there was nothing. She ran to her son and held him tighter than she ever had, as though making sure he was real.

*

Gabe was on his back, sobbing with relief as the reality of his imminent death at the hand of Fatty sank in. Fatty, meanwhile, looked impatient. He would've heard Gabe's tears of sublime elation below him, but I guessed he didn't know he was there and thought it was Jimmy on the floor, weeping over Mum's body.

Jimmy clung to a shocked but alive Mum, who was facing away from the bloodied bodies and probably thought it was Fatty crying. Jimmy was looking over Mum's shoulder at the two messengers Nobby had sent to save mankind from Lucy, no doubt wondering why their blood vanished on the vinyl like new snow on a warm road. But it wouldn't be long before Gabe disappeared and Fatty realised Mum wasn't dead, and that Jimmy wasn't going to kill him. Yet.

Yappy, who'd been watching all this with his tongue hanging out, probably as confused as everyone else, got to his feet and wandered back across the garden.

*

If Gabe's life had to flash before his eyes before he died, we were going to be there for a while. What he'd actually done with his time not even God knew, and I doubt Gabe remembered much of it either. But I couldn't help but hope his darting eyes were looking for me, and I couldn't believe I was up on the shelf, while my old friend, drinking buddy and hero of the world died, when I should've been at his side. There was little danger in going down, as Fatty wasn't going to search the garden for the spray anytime soon, and as I lifted off with an unintentional swerve due to my unravelling wing, my own joyous tears at Gabe achieving his wish after so very long blurred my eyes.

Then I stopped. It wasn't voluntary. I shook with everything I had, but I was going nowhere. I could wiggle my legs, but my wings? Forget it. Perce made his way over and I saw his face up close.

Jesus! He's got eight fucking eyes as well as eight legs. I bet Fatty wouldn't mind a couple of them right now.

He salivated like a rabid dog as he stopped next to me and I took one last glance at Gabe on the floor. His breath had slowed, but his eyes still danced around the room, and I shouted 'Goodbye', knowing he couldn't hear me. Or maybe he could, as his stare stopped at me. He felt for his bottle, but I didn't expect him to see my predicament through his tear-filled eyes. I guessed he just wanted to raise a toast.

He filled his mouth, but didn't swallow. Instead, he inhaled through his nose and spat the whisky out like a garden hose. I closed my eyes and mouth and braced myself. Then, for the second time that day, I was saved by a WHOOSH!

I pinged out of the web and slammed into the wall behind. Perce landed next to me, but we were now playing on my terms. He was as stunned as I was and still had to walk a few paces to reach me, but I was there for more important things than dinner, and I could fly. The whisky spurt had taken off my web bandage and I spiralled down to what was left of Gabe. I gazed into his tear-drenched eyes as I landed on his nose, then felt his lips move below me.

'Wee Jimmy,' he said with a gurgle. 'Ah'm glad yer still here. Ah'll never forget aboot ye.'

I so wanted to say something back, but not even Gabe could finish his bottle before it slipped through his fingers and onto his chest. A trickle of whisky fell into his wounds as he closed his eyes and took his last breath, then me and the bottle sank to the floor as he disappeared back up to the stars where he belonged. He showed no resistance, made no sound, emitted no smell. He was dead at last, and as invisible to me as he'd been to everyone else.

I'm gonna miss the crazy old bastard and sure hope to see him again sometime. Until then, he can surely rest in peace and get drunk.

My emotions betrayed me and I lost it, and I was surprised my family couldn't hear my howls. But I needed to pull it together, because although Gabe's death was a happy ending, the other half of the equation was still alive. I stifled my tears and looked up. Fatty had lowered his aching arms to hoist his trousers back up and was tapping the floor with his foot, looking for the body he was sure was in front of him. I twirled up to the sideboard before he could squash me.

Jimmy and mum unlocked from their hug and stared at Fatty's low-energy 'Hokey Cokey'. He put his left foot out, he put his left foot in, his right foot copied the routine, then he turned around. But he was never going to find Gabe with a silly dance. Mum must've thought he was after more broken glass and whispered in Jimmy's ear. I had no idea what she said, but he gave her an incredulous look and nodded.

She crept towards Fatty and stooped to pick up the

dropped fork, the belt, and clear the broken glass. But with Fatty blind, it seemed his other senses picked up the slack and he heard her. He goose-stepped on the spot as Mum held her uncomfortable pose, then he seemed to remember something and stepped back to rummage behind him in the sink and retrieve the knife Mum had dropped in there earlier. She was flat against the cupboard with nowhere to move as Fatty raised it, but this time there was no fluffy angel to save her.

'Now,' she said.

Jimmy's hand was already on the freezer handle, and he stood to one side as he yanked it.

*

Susan wasn't aware of what had just taken place on the floor, or that her son had seen the strange man jump between her and her husband to save her life, or that he had watched the limp body fade away into nothing.

She released him from her hug and stared at the bloodied and frustrated man tapping the floor with his foot, then whispered in her son's ear. He nodded before she crept over and bent down to remove any potential weapons from the floor, but her husband stepped back and grabbed the knife from the sink. She didn't move, even when he raised it. Instead, she spoke to her son.

*

Fatty turned as the knife shot into his chest. He wasted no time in digging it out. Blood pumped down his front with an inconsistent splutter and disappeared into his shirt like his body was one big sponge; then he dropped to the floor and ripped at the wound to hurry along his fourth blood sacrifice in three and a half thousand years. Jimmy and

Mum were back in each other's arms, staring in disbelief as the blood seeped from his body and disappeared.

*

So what happens to you now, Fatty? You will soon be in Heaven or Hell and you don't deserve either.

I wasn't sure what he did deserve, to be honest. I couldn't help but feel a pang of sympathy for the cards he'd been dealt by Nobby, and I'd have had a lot more had he not ruined my life and Mum's. I recalled what Gabe said to Fatty in the pub earlier. *Ye could've done this another way.* Yes, he could've, but he didn't, and I didn't shed any tears of bereavement. Neither did Jimmy or Mum.

There were also no tears of relief from Fatty like Gabe had wept, just a contented grin as he closed his eyes and took a gurgled last breath. And this time, both Jimmy and Mum watched open-mouthed as his fat frame faded away like he was beamed up by Scottie, which saved an extra squeeze of lighter fuel down at the crematorium.

*

So did I kill Fatty or not? It was fair for Fatty to assume I stabbed him, and in a way I did, but I didn't know about the knife in the freezer; all I did was open the door. It was hard to know what the technicalities were. If the trap led to his demise, then it was Mum who set it up. Did that mean she killed him? It was her intention, after all. Not that Fatty was ever to know that. Although I feared that he found out the first time when he made Mum fall prey to her own death trap. But did Nobby's soul get destroyed and was Fatty in Heaven? Or was he sitting in Nobby's office with some explaining to do? I didn't care, to be honest. I was more interested in me and Mum enjoying life

KEPT IN THE DARK

without him.

Both Jimmy's head and Mum's were on a slow turn between the floor and each other. The grubby vinyl was back to being just that, with only whisky footprints among the broken glass to show Fatty had been there, and a near-empty bottle on its side to show Gabe had been there.

'What? Where?' said Mum. Her lips kept moving, but no more words came out.

'They've gone,' Jimmy said.

'They?'

'Dad and the old man.'

'What old man? What was the white head?'

'The old man saved your life. Then he... like Dad.'

Jimmy stepped over to where the two bodies had been and tapped the floor with his foot, then turned back and shrugged his shoulders with a smile. Mum smiled back and they threw their arms around each other. I'd not seen such joy on anyone's face since a few moments before when Gabe lay dying. But these three faces were happy for their life. The kitchen had seen all the death it was going to see for a while. All three of us lost it and our tears joined the spilt whisky on the floor. Soon Jimmy and Mum would muck in together to clean it up, and enjoy doing so, as it would be the last time ever.

'It must've been an angel,' said Mum.

Jimmy's face screwed up, yet his smile remained, and I knew what he was thinking. Which was: why would God make a smelly angel that drinks and chases kids? But I hoped to God he believed her, because then he'd believe in Nobby, and so would Mum, and no one would convince them otherwise now they'd seen an angel save

Mum's life and take the Devil away with him. Me and Mum were Fatty-free at last and now awaited Heaven. And Fatty was either already in Heaven, or having the soul ripped from his body before Nobby threw him to the wolves, where Lucy would have to cancel a few appointments to wade through the blubber to get to his bones. Gabe was in Heaven, where he should've been all along, and Nobby either had his soul or he didn't. And if he didn't, he'd never know. He'd sit up there until the end of time to wait and wonder if his soul was still active or had been destroyed. And neither he nor Lucy would know anything about me.

*

Flies live for about two weeks. Two weeks to follow my young self and Mum around and watch us live free. Free from the tyranny of Nobby's soul. A Nobby that wouldn't know he'd been out-thought, regardless of where Fatty had ended up. That I had a dark soul was neither here nor there. I'd never know, and as long as I died believing, I'd slip through to Heaven to be with Mum forever. Unless I somehow lost my belief. In which case, I guessed I'd just have to go all around the houses again.

THE END

Printed in Great Britain
by Amazon